Stevi Mittman

Praise for the writing of bestselling author

has always been a decorator at heart. When she was little she cut the butterflies from her wallpaper and let them fly off the walls onto her ceiling and across her window shades. She remembers doing an entire bathroom in black-and-white houndstooth patent leather contact paper and putting strips of trim on her cupboards.

The Teddi Bayer murder mysteries have allowed her to combine her love of writing and her passion for decorating, and she couldn't be happier. As a fictional decorator she doles out advice on Teddi's Web site, TipsFromTeddi.com, and receives and responds to e-mails on behalf of Teddi.

Decorating is a third career for the prolific Mittman, who is also a stained-glass artist with work in the Museum of the City of New York and private commissions around the country and, of course, an award-winning author. Watch for another of her Teddi stories in the NEXT summer anthology, coming later this year.

In her spare time (you must be kidding) she also makes jewelry and indulges in gourmet cooking. Visit her at www.stevimittman.com.

For those of you who are putting any TipsFromTeddi.com advice to use, please e-mail her your successes and failures at Teddi@TipsFromTeddi.com, and be sure to visit Teddi's Web site, www.TipsFromTeddi.com, for more murder, mayhem and sage advice on decorating!

STEVI MITTMAN

Why is MURDER
on the MENU,
Anyway?

WHY IS MURDER ON THE MENU, ANYWAY?

copyright © 2007 by Stephanie Mittman

isbn-13:978-0-373-88124-6

isbn-10:   0-373-88124-X

This edition published by arrangement with Harlequin Books S.A.

® and TM are trademarks of the publisher. Trademarks indicated with
® are registered in the United States Patent and Trademark Office, the
Canadian Trade Marks Office and in other countries.

TheNextNovel.com

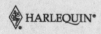

PRINTED IN U.S.A.

Life on Long Island Can Be Murder
by Stevi Mittman

WHO MAKES UP THESE RULES, ANYWAY?

WHAT GOES WITH BLOOD RED, ANYWAY?

HOLIDAY WISHES—
"WHO NEEDS JUNE IN DECEMBER, ANYWAY?"

WHY IS MURDER ON THE MENU, ANYWAY?

This book is dedicated to all the usual suspects:
my wonderful husband, Alan; my terrific agent,
Irene Goodman; my fabulous editor, Tara Gavin;
my oldest and dearest friend, Janet Rose;
and especially to my Ithaca family, Miriam, Isaac,
Glenn and Cathy, who helped me give birth to
Why Is Murder on the Menu, Anyway?, named it and
made me want to write it. Special thanks have to go to
Janet, Miriam and Cathy for their ability to still laugh
on the fourth and fifth reads, and to gently point out any
inconsistencies the plot may have. I love you all.

CHAPTER 1

Design Tip of the Day
"Ambience is everything. Imagine eating foie gras
at a luncheonette counter or a side of coleslaw at
Le Cirque. It's not a matter of food, but one of
atmosphere. Remember that when planning your
dining room design."

—TipsFromTeddi.com

"Now, that's the kind of man you should be looking
for," my mother, the self-appointed keeper of my shelf-
life stamp, says. She points with her fork at a man in the
corner of The Steak-Out Restaurant, a dive I've just been
hired to redecorate. Making this restaurant look four-
star will be hard, but not half as hard as getting through
lunch without strangling the woman across the table
from me. "*He* would make a good husband."

"Oh, you can tell that from across the room?" I ask,
wondering how it is she can forget that when we had
trouble getting rid of my last husband, she shot him.
"Besides being ten minutes away from death if he actually
eats all that steak, he's twenty years too old for me and—

shallow woman that I am—twenty pounds too heavy. Besides, I am *so* not looking for another husband here. I'm looking to design a new image for this place, looking for some sense of ambience, some feeling, something I can build a proposal on for them."

My mother studies the man in the corner, tilting her head, the better to gauge his age, I suppose. I think she's grimacing, but with all the Botox and Restylane injected into that face, it's hard to tell. She takes another bite of her steak salad, chewing slowly so that I don't miss the fact that the steak is a poor cut and tougher than it should be. "You're concentrating on the wrong kind of proposal," she says finally. "Just look at this place, Teddi. It's a dive. There are hardly any other diners. What does *that* tell you about the food?"

"That they cater to a dinner crowd and it's lunch-time," I tell her.

I don't know what I was thinking bringing her here with me. I suppose I thought it would be better than eating alone. There really are days when my common sense goes on vacation. Clearly, this is one of them. I mean, really, did I not resolve just a few months ago that I would not let my mother get to me anymore?

What good are New Year's resolutions, anyway?

Tony, the owner of The Steak-Out, approaches the man's table and my mother studies him while they converse. Eventually he leaves the table in a huff, after which the diner glances up and meets my mother's gaze.

I think she's smiling at him. That or she's got indigestion. They size each other up.

I concentrate on making sketches in my notebook and try to ignore the fact that my mother is flirting. At nearly seventy, she's developed an unhealthy interest in members of the opposite sex to whom she isn't married.

According to my father, who has broken the TMI rule and given me way Too Much Information, she has no interest in sex with him. Better, I suppose, to be clued in on what they aren't doing in the bedroom than have to hear what they might be.

"He's not so old," my mother says, noticing that I have barely touched the Chinese chicken salad she warned me not to get. "He's got about as many years on you as you have on your little cop friend."

She does this to make me crazy. I know it, but it works all the same. "Drew Scoones is not my little 'friend.' He's a detective with whom I—"

"Screwed around," my mother says. I must look shocked, because my mother laughs at me and asks if I think she doesn't know the "lingo."

What I thought she didn't know was that Drew and I actually had tangled in the sheets. And, since it's possible she's just fishing, I sidestep the issue and tell her that Drew is just a couple of years younger than me and that I don't need reminding.

I dig into my salad with renewed vigor, determined to show my mother that Chinese chicken salad in a steak place was not the stupid choice it's proving to be.

After a few more minutes of my picking at the wilted leaves on my plate, the man my mother has me nearly engaged to pays his bill and heads past us toward the back of the restaurant. I watch my mother take in his shoes, his suit and the diamond pinky ring that seems to be cutting off the circulation in his little finger.

"Such nice hands," she says after the man is out of sight. "Manicured." She and I both stare at my hands. I have two popped acrylics that are being held on at weird angles by bandages. My cuticles are ragged and there's blue permanent marker decorating my right hand from carelessly measuring when I did a drawing for a customer.

Twenty minutes later she's disappointed that the man managed to leave the restaurant without our noticing. He will join the list of the ones I let get away. I will hear about him twenty years from now when—according to my mother—my children will be grown and I will still be single, living pathetically alone with several dogs and cats.

After my ex, that sounds good to me.

The waitress tells us that our meal has been taken care of by the management and, after thanking Tony, complimenting him on the wonderful meal and assuring him that once I have redecorated his place people will flock here in droves (I actually use those words and ignore my mother when she looks skyward and shakes her head), my mother and I head for the restroom.

My father—unfortunately not with us today—has the patience of a saint, hard-won from years of living with my mother. She, perhaps as a result, figures he has the patience for both of them and feels justified having none. For her, no rules apply, and a little thing like a picture of a man on the door to a public restroom is certainly no barrier to using the john. In all fairness, it does seem silly to stand and wait for the ladies' room if no one is using the men's.

Still, it's the idea that rules don't apply to her, signs don't apply to her, conventions don't apply to her. She knocks on the door to the men's room. When no one answers, she gestures to me to go in ahead. I tell her that I can certainly wait for the ladies' room to be free and she shrugs and goes in herself.

Not a minute later there is a bloodcurdling scream from behind the men's room door.

"Mom!" I yell. "Are you all right?"

Tony comes running over, the waitress on his heels. Two customers head our way while my mother continues to scream.

I try the door, but it is locked. I yell for her to open it and she fumbles with the knob. When she finally manages to unlock it, she is white behind her two streaks of blush, but she is on her feet and appears shaken but not stirred.

"What happened?" I ask her. So do Tony and the waitress and the few customers who have migrated to the back of the place.

She points toward the bathroom and I go in, thinking it serves her right for using the men's room. But I see nothing amiss.

She gestures toward the stall, and, like any self-respecting and suspicious woman, I poke the door open with one finger, expecting the worst.

What I find is worse than the worst.

The husband my mother picked out for me is sitting on the toilet. His pants are puddled down around his ankles, his hands are hanging at his sides. Pinned to his chest is some sort of Health Department certificate.

Oh, and there is a large, round, bloodless bullet hole between his eyes.

Four Nassau County police officers are securing the area, waiting for the detectives and crime scene personnel to show up. I was hoping one of them would turn out to be Diane, my best friend, Bobbie's, sister, who knows how to handle my mother better than probably anyone except my dad. Anyway, she's not here and the cops are trying, though not very hard, to comfort my mother, who in another era would be considered to be suffering from the vapors. In the twenty-first century, I'd just say she was losing it. That is, if I didn't know her better, know she was milking it for everything it was worth.

My mother loves attention. As it begins to flag, she swoons and claims to feel faint. Despite four No Smoking signs, she insists it's all right for her to light up because, after all, she's in shock. Not to mention that signs, as we know, don't apply to her.

When asked not to smoke, she collapses mournfully

in a chair and lets her head loll to the side, all without mussing her hair.

Eventually, the detectives show up to find the four patrolmen all circled around her, debating whether to administer CPR or smelling salts or simply to call the paramedics. I, however, know just what will snap her to attention.

"Detective Scoones," I say loudly. My mother parts the sea of cops.

"We have to stop meeting like this," he says lightly to me, but I can feel him checking me over with his eyes, making sure I'm all right while pretending not to care.

"What have you got in those pants?" my mother asks him, coming to her feet and staring at his crotch accusingly. "*Bay-dar?* Everywhere we Bayers are, you turn up. You don't expect me to buy that this is a coincidence, I hope."

Drew tells my mother that it's nice to see her, too, and asks if it's his fault that her daughter seems to attract disasters.

Charming to be made to feel like the bearer of a plague.

He asks how I've been.

"Just peachy," I tell him. "I seem to be making a habit of finding dead bodies, my mother is driving me crazy and the catering hall I booked two freakin' years ago for Dana's bat mitzvah has just been shut down by the Board of Health!"

"Glad to see your luck's finally changing," he says,

and he stares at me a minute longer than I sense he wants to before turning his attention to the patrolmen, asking what they've got, whether they've taken any statements, moved anything, all the sort of stuff you see on TV, without any of the drama. That is, if you don't count my mother's threats to faint every few minutes when she senses no one's paying attention to her.

Tony tells his waitstaff to bring everyone espresso, which I decline because I'm wired enough. Drew pulls him aside and a minute later I'm handed a cup of coffee that smells divinely of Kahlúa.

The man knows me well. Too well.

His partner, Harold Nelson, whom I've met once or twice, says he'll interview the kitchen staff and goes off toward the back of the restaurant with a nod of recognition toward me. Hal and I are not the best of friends.

Drew asks Tony if he minds if he takes statements from the patrons first and gets to him and the waitstaff afterward.

"No, no," Tony tells him. "Do the patrons first." Drew glances at me like he wants to know if I've got the double entendre. I try to look bored.

"What it is with you and murder victims?" he asks me when we sit down at a table in the corner.

I search them out so that I can see you again, I almost say, but I'm afraid it will sound desperate instead of sarcastic.

My mother, lighting up and daring him with a look to tell her not to, reminds him that *she* was the one to find the body.

Drew asks what happened *this time*. My mother tells him how the man in the john was "taken" with me, couldn't take his eyes off me and blatantly flirted with both of us. To his credit, Drew doesn't laugh, but his smirk is undeniable to the trained eye. And I've had my eye trained on him for nearly a year now.

"While he was noticing you," he asks me, "did you notice anything about him? Was he waiting for anyone? Watching for anything?"

I tell him that he didn't appear to be waiting or watching. That he made no phone calls, was fairly intent on eating and apparently flirted with my mother. This last bit Drew takes with a grain of salt, which was the way it was intended.

"And he had a short conversation with Tony," I tell him. "I think he might have been unhappy with the food, though he didn't send it back."

Drew asks what makes me think he was dissatisfied, and I tell him that the discussion seemed acrimonious and that Tony appeared distressed. Drew makes a note and says he'll look into it and asks about anyone else in the restaurant. Did I see anyone who didn't seem to belong, anyone who was watching the victim, anyone looking suspicious?

"Besides my mother?" I ask him, and Mom huffs and blows her cigarette smoke in my direction.

I tell him that there were several deliveries, the kitchen staff going in and out the back door to grab a smoke, that sort of thing. He stops me and asks what I was doing checking out the back door of the restaurant.

Proudly—because while he was off forgetting me, dropping in every once in a while to say hi to my son, Jesse, or leave something for one of my daughters, I was getting on with my life—I tell him that I'm decorating the place.

He looks genuinely impressed. "Commercial customers? That's great," he says. Okay, that's what he *ought* to say. What he actually says is "Whatever pays the bills."

"Howard Rosen, the famous restaurant critic, got her the job," my mother says. "You met him—the good-looking, distinguished gentleman with the *real* job, something to be proud of. I guess you've never read his reviews in *Newsday*."

Drew, without missing a beat, tells her that Howard's reviews are on the top of his list, as soon as he learns how to read.

"I only meant—" my mother starts, but both of us assure her that we know just what she meant.

"So," Drew says. "Deliveries?"

I tell him that Tony would know better than I, but that I saw some come in. Fish. Maybe linens. "And there was produce, I guess," I say, recalling seeing a delivery man leave wearing the usual white jacket, this one with a picture of a truck covered with vegetables and fruits all over its side.

"This is the second restaurant job Howard's got her," my mother tells Drew.

"At least she's getting *something* out of the relationship," he says.

"If he were here," my mother says, ignoring the insinuation, "he'd be comforting her instead of interrogating her. He'd be making sure we're both all right after such an ordeal."

"I'm sure he would," Drew agrees, then studies me as if he's measuring my tolerance for shock. Quietly he adds, "But then maybe he doesn't know just what strong stuff your daughter's made of."

It's the closest thing to a tender moment I can expect from Drew Scoones. My mother breaks the spell. "She gets that from me," she says.

Both Drew and I take a minute, probably to pray that's all I inherited from her.

"I'm just trying to save you some time and effort," my mother tells him. "My money's on Howard."

Drew withers her with a look and mutters something that sounds suspiciously like "fool's gold." Then he excuses himself to go back to work.

I catch his sleeve and ask if it's all right for us to leave. He says sure, he knows where we live. I say goodbye to Tony. I assure him that I will have some sketches for him in a few days, all the while hoping that this murder doesn't cancel his redecorating plans. I need the money desperately, the alternative being borrowing from my parents and being strangled by the strings.

My mother is strangely quiet all the way to her house. She doesn't tell me what a loser Drew Scoones is—despite his good looks—and how I was obviously drooling over him. She doesn't ask me where Howard is taking me tonight or warn me not to tell my father about what happened because he will worry about us both and no doubt insist we see our respective psychiatrists.

She fidgets nervously, opening and closing her purse over and over again.

"You okay?" I ask her. After all, she's just found a dead man on the toilet, and tough as she is, that's got to be upsetting.

When she doesn't answer me I pull over to the side of the road.

"Mom?" She refuses to look at me. "You want me to take you to see Dr. Cohen?"

She looks out the window, elegant as ever in yet another ecru knit outfit, hair perfectly coiffed and spritzed within one spray of permanently laquered, and appears confused. It's as if she's just realized we're on Broadway in Woodmere. "Aren't we near Marvin's Jewelers?" she asks, pulling something out of her purse.

"What have you got, Mother?" I ask, prying open her fingers to find the murdered man's pinky ring.

"It was on the sink," she says in answer to my dropped jaw. "I was going to get his name and address and have you return it to him so that he could ask you out. I thought it was a sign that the two of you were meant to be together."

"He's dead, Mom. You understand that, right?" I ask.

"Well, I didn't know that," she shouts at me. "Not at the time."

I ask why she didn't give it to Drew, realize that she

wouldn't give Drew the time in a clock shop and add, "...or to one of the other policemen."

"For heaven's sake," she tells me. "The man is dead, Teddi, and I took his ring. How would that look?"

Before I can tell her it would look just the way it is, she pulls out a cigarette and threatens to light it.

"I mean, really," she says, shaking her head like it's *my* brains that are loose. "What does he need it for now?"

CHAPTER 2

Design Tip of the Day
"A wonderful trick for unifying a room is to use a repeating motif. For example, you could purchase a fleur-de-lis stamp and use it above the chair rail, repeat the pattern with the drapery rod finials, a lamp finial, etc. Keep in mind, though, that too much repetition can lead to monotony."
—TipsFromTeddi.com

My best friend and business partner, Bobbie Lyons, is watching for me out her window and she runs over to greet me in my driveway before I'm out of the car. It's the middle of the afternoon and I happen to know for a fact that she was home all day and has no plans to go out. Despite that, she is wearing silk capris, kitten-heel suede slides and more diamonds than you'll find in the window of Kay Jewelers. "I can't believe it happened to you again!" she says as she slips one of her slides on and off repeatedly.

I tell her, as I already did on the cell the minute I dropped off my mother, that it was horrible, that my mother was impossible, and that she took the man's ring. I don't mention, however, that Drew Scoones was the investigating detective on the case.

"Diane says the guy was shot between the eyes while he was on the can," she tells me and shrugs at her sister's choice of words. "She's pissed because she was investigating a robbery when the call came in so she didn't get to see it. She hates being low man on the police totem pole."

"Well, it wasn't a pretty sight," I assure her. Then I add that it sure would have been nice to see a friendly face there. Bobbie's left eyebrow shoots up and I feel as though I've got one of those electronic banners running across my forehead announcing every thought in my head.

"*He* was there," she says, her short red hair glinting in the sunlight, the new blond streaks blinding me.

I am silent.

"Oh…my…God! He was there!"

"He?" I ask, trying to be oh-so-casual. Unfortunately, her look cuts off this avenue of escape.

"What did he say? Is he still gorgeous? Did your stomach hurt at the sight of him? Are you sorry you didn't get those highlights I told you to get?"

"What are you? Eleven years old?" I ask. Okay, that might be a little harsh, but she is really bugging me. "I just saw another dead body. I really thought that the first one would hold me for this lifetime. So yes, Drew Scoones was there. So yes, he's still good-looking."

This last bit is the understatement of the year. And,

so yes, my stomach did do flip-flops at the sight of him, but I'll never admit it, because it was clear his didn't do flip-flops at the sight of me. Maybe I should have sprung for the highlights after all.

"For all I know, he's married by now."

"He's not." Bobbie says this like she absolutely knows. When I give her the how-can-you-possibly-know-that? look, she smiles and says, "Diane."

I imagine Drew Scoones thinking that I am keeping tabs on him and want to crawl into a hole and die.

"Mom!" Jesse yells out the front door to me, opening it enough to let loose Maggie May, the bichon frise I "inherited" from Elise Meyers, the woman I found murdered last year. (Okay, fine. So I stole the dog. She was dead and her husband, who was trying to kill her before someone else beat him to it, wasn't going to take care of her dog, now was he?) Jesse gestures with his hand that there is someone on the phone.

"It's probably Howard," I tell Bobbie. "He's taking me out to some Iron Chef cook-off thing tonight. Maybe I can beg off."

Bobbie gives me the look. The one that says I'm breaking yet another Long Island rule—canceling an engagement the same day. It seems like, much to Bobbie and my mother's dismay, I will never learn how to get ahead on Long Island. At nearly forty, it's probably too late.

Then she concedes that maybe, under the circumstances, it could be all right.

"Maybe," she says, grabbing Maggie May's collar and

dragging her into the house. "Like if you make up some wild story about seeing some murdered guy on the john...."

"It's Drew," Jesse says breathlessly, and his face is lit up like it's Superman calling. "You should invite him to dinner, Mom," he says, then scrunches up his nose at the thought of my cooking. "Or something, anyway," he adds.

I pretend to be offended by my eleven-year-old's suggestion as I ruffle his hair on my way to the kitchen, where I pick up the portable from the counter and say, "Hello."

"You're gonna love this one," he says, like there hasn't been a three-month lull in our conversations, like I haven't jumped every time the phone rang since the last time he called me, eighty-six days ago. "Your dead guy? He's the one who shut down Sheldon's of Great Neck. Isn't that where you were planning to have Dana's bat mitzvah?"

He knows exactly where her bat mitzvah was supposed to be. He even went with me to look Sheldon's over, to make plans, to pick which room to have the meal in, which one to serve the hors d'oeuvres.

And then he just stopped calling. "What do you mean, 'he was the one who shut it down'?" I ask.

"He's...that is, he *was*, with the Board of Health. He was the food inspector who claimed Sheldon's didn't meet the County's standards. Looks like you are S.O.L. As usual."

"As long as it doesn't make me a suspect," I say. I

mean, been there, done that, and "shit outta luck" beats having to prove I'm innocent—or that my best friend is—again.

Drew just laughs.

"Well, I do have a motive," I concede. "Though you know that I didn't know who he was until this moment. And okay, I had opportunity. I admit I was there in the restaurant when he was killed. But means?"

I think for just a nanosecond and I can't believe what crosses my mind.

"Please don't tell me you've found the gun and it's registered to Rio."

Drew laughs again at the mention of my thank-God-he's-behind-me ex-husband, a man who believed in the principle of survival of the slickest. "I forgot how funny you are," he says.

There's a silence while he waits for me to ask whose fault that is.

I don't.

"So anyway," he says, "I just thought you'd want to know the guy who screwed you is dead."

Ha. The guy who screwed me is on the other end of the phone telling me the guy who screwed me is dead.

"So whatcha been up to?" he asks, just baiting me into asking him why he vanished off the face of my earth.

"Business," I say. "I told you today, I'm doing a lot of commercial properties, restaurants, things like that."

He doesn't say anything, waiting, I suppose, for me to

ask him what he's been doing. Bobbie will give up buying shoes before I ask that.

"Is there anything else?" I ask, as in: is there a reason I'm sitting here holding on to the phone, unable to breathe, wishing that we were still friends? Still more than friends?

"You doing anything tonight?" he asks. I tell him I've got a date, but the cocky bastard sounds like he doesn't believe me.

"Howard is taking me to some charity cook-off," I say.

"Oh," he says. "Howard. That doesn't exactly count as a date."

"He's picking me up, paying for my dinner, taking me to a show, and bringing me home. What part of that isn't a date?" I ask. Bobbie, putting her little crocheted shrug over my shoulders in an attempt to influence what I'm going to wear tonight, gives me a thumbs-up. She seems to think that the right sweater will always win the day.

He tells me, "the part that comes next."

"What comes next is none of your business," I tell him and hang up. I give Bobbie a look that says it's none of hers, either, and head upstairs to get dressed without my fairy godmother to give me her glass slippers, though I think I still have the Manolos she loaned me a few weeks ago.

Howard is simply glowing this evening. It's like he's been lit from within, and he is devastatingly handsome in a beige linen jacket over a chocolate-brown T-shirt that hugs his torso like…Well, I'm not going there, so suffice it to say that Howard is over six feet tall, filled out without any fat, and he has the fastest smile I've ever seen. Nothing lights a face like a smile.

He has told me three times how his friend Nick, the chef at Madison on Park, has been practicing for this evening, how he has made all kinds of entrées and desserts and how Howard has had to try them all. He throws around words like *Provençale* and *forestiere* like I'm supposed to know what he means. He says Nick did a dish with roasted Maine lobster and kabocha squash gnocchi with sautéed black trumpets in sage oil. When I look stricken he assures me that the trumpets are mushrooms and not swans, and shakes his head at me.

"You've no appreciation for good food," he complains as if I'm just being stubborn. He glances at our tickets and gestures with his chin to keep progressing down the aisle of the cavernous high school auditorium where they have set up several kitchens on the stage and placed big TV screens around the room so they can zoom in on the stovetops and prep areas.

What he means is that the other night when he took me out to review a new Italian restaurant for *Newsday*, the Dentice Mare Monte was absolutely wasted on me. As is anything with olives or artichokes or a host of other foods he thinks God invented just to pleasure man.

We get to our row and he grimaces because we are obviously farther back than row B ought to be. He hurries up ahead, sees that there are rows AA to FF before the single alphabet begins, and, with obvious disappoint-

ment, waves me into our row in front of him. Excusing
ourselves, we clamber over people who refuse to stand up
to let us get to our seats—and who then have the nerve
to glare at us when we stumble over their purses and toes.
I remind Howard as we navigate the various obstacles
that the *gâteau au chocolat* wasn't wasted on me.

He pulls a laugh from his inexhaustible supply as we
take our seats, and he wonders aloud how it is that I can
remember the French names only for desserts or things
that involve chocolate.

"*Chocolat*," I correct, saying it with what I hope is a
convincing French accent.

He waves away my attempt at being seductive and tells
me that I should have been there for the practice run.
"Cockle Bruschetta," he says, like cockles were likely to
be the surprise ingredient they'd have the chefs use
tonight. "Then a choucroute Royale Alsacienne, done
not with sauerkraut but with a pickled mushroom…" He
closes his eyes like he's having sex and it is too perfect to
describe.

At least, I think he'd close his eyes during sex. It's not
something I know firsthand.

"And just this morning I had to go on a scavenger
hunt for tamarind paste," he tells me as I settle into my
seat and take in our surroundings. "Took me until nearly
noon to find it in this little Indian spice place on
Broadway down on the South Shore."

"The Taj? The one next to The Steak-Out?" I ask. I
remind him that was where I was at lunchtime, and it

was where I discovered the murdered man I've already told him about.

He stops helping me off with Bobbie's shrug and asks me if I'm sure. I tell him it's not the sort of thing that one forgets. And then I could swear he shudders.

"You all right?" I ask and he gets all defensive, like I've impugned his manhood or something.

"I suppose you talked to the police," he says. I tell him that yes, they interviewed my mother and me. But, because the chip on his shoulder is the size of Shea Stadium when it comes to Drew Scoones, I don't mention just who "they" were.

"Well, luckily you didn't see anything," he says, slipping out of his jacket and carefully folding it behind him on the chair.

"Just a dead man," I say a bit sarcastically, since he seems to think that watching someone cook a fancy French meal trumps discovering a dead body.

I could see his argument if we were at least going to taste the results. And if they were chocolate.

He suggests that we leave our stuff on our seats and go backstage to see his friend Nick. We exit our row in the opposite direction and, after convincing the powers that be that we are vital to the survival of Earth, we are permitted to go behind the scenes to look for Nick and Madison Watts, owners of Madison on Park. Howard has described Nick in detail, but has never even mentioned Madison before tonight, so I am taken aback when he allows himself to be greeted with kisses on both cheeks by an elegant thirtysomething-just-younger-than-me woman who seems as surprised to see me as I am to see her kissing the man I've come in with.

She's dressed all in black, like, well, like a black swan. Or like Mrs. Danvers, from *Rebecca* with Joan Fontaine. And let me tell you, if I were crumbs, I'd know better than to stick to her outfit. You know how interviewers always ask stupid questions like, "If you were a flower, what kind of flower would you be?" Well, Madison Watts would be a rare orchid that you know would cost thousands of dollars and would die if you looked at it wrong. And it would be your fault, not the flower's.

Or maybe a Venus flytrap.

Something intimidating.

Yes, if I had to find one word to describe Madison Watts, it would be intimidating.

"Madison," Howard says, and my ordinarily warm, garrulous date has suddenly gone cold and distant. "I'd like you to meet Teddi Bayer."

"Your…?" Madison says, as if daring him to introduce me as his girlfriend. She waits, not giving him an out.

"Nick around?" he asks instead.

Madison eyes me critically while I try not to stare at her perfect complexion and huge gray eyes. I struggle to remember if I put on lipstick before Howard picked me up and figure it's probably gone by now, anyway. I am wearing one of Bobbie's crocheted tops with the matching shrug from last year and a pair of Ann Taylor pants which, I admit, are a good five years old. I feel mismatched, underdressed, out of style and fat. Where are this woman's Hadassah arms? If Nick is such a great cook, why doesn't her figure show that she ever, ever eats?

I'd credit Madison with an uncanny ability to reduce me to shame and self-loathing, but heck, nearly anyone can do it. It's not like I don't try. I'm sure I look good when I look in the mirror at home, or at the very least, *good enough*. And then I get where I'm going, see someone wearing the right thing, someone whose hair looks like she just stepped out of the salon, someone whose makeup isn't smudged under her eyes, whose shoes apparently don't cripple her feet, and all I want to do is crawl back into bed.

With the slightest hint of an accent, Madison, who looks like she's primped all afternoon when I know she had to be preparing for the show, asks, "I know you, don't I?" Those exquisite gray eyes of hers narrow slightly, as if she's seeing through my disguise as a socially-acceptable, upwardly-mobile person who could pay for her own ticket and dinner if she had to. Which, luckily, I don't.

I tell her that I don't think we've ever met at the same time that Howard tells her that I am a decorator. "She's doing a lot of commercial work," he says. "Redecorating restaurants…" He pauses like he's suddenly put two and two together and gotten Reese's peanut butter cups. "You two should talk."

My heart thumps wildly in my chest. Doing Madison on Park would be quite the notch in my glue gun. I can almost see the wheels turning in Madison's head, too, and I smile at her like it's an open invitation for her to watch the same process in mine—as long as we come to the same conclusion.

"You look so familiar to me," she says, taking a step or two back and eyeing me from head to toe. "Have you been to the restaurant?"

I tell her I've been dying to come, but I've been so very busy. *And poor*, I think, but I don't tell her as much.

"She's doing The Steak-Out," Howard tells her and we all exchange one of those *oh, right*, looks.

"You weren't there today? When it happened, were you?" Madison asks, putting her hand on my arm as if ready to console me if I was.

And I admit that, unfortunately, I was.

"So sad about Joe," she says as someone official-looking approaches her and she has to excuse herself to see to something about the show. "We'll talk later," she says to me, and maybe it's just wishful thinking, but I get the sense she is going to let me do the restaurant.

"'So sad about Joe,'" Howard mimics as he looks around, I suppose for Nick. "She hated him just as much as the rest of us."

I'm about to ask him how he came to know someone from the Health Department when he brightens and points toward the back of the stage. "Look! There's Nick!"

Nick, who even with a chef's hat on his head only comes up to Howard's chin, pumps my hand until my arm goes numb. He is a cherub of a man, a little too chubby, a little too short, a little too bald to be considered good-looking, or even cute. But his eyes sparkle when he sees us and his pudgy hands clasp mine in a warm welcome.

"You're here! I'm so glad! Now go away!" he says cheerily. "I must set up *le mise en place*." I have no idea what that is, but I don't dare ask Howard because he's probably already told me three times and because if he tells me again I still won't care. "They're going to tell them the ingredients fifteen minutes before they're supposed to start cooking," Howard tells me.

"Yeah," I say. I am getting testy because all we've talked about is food, on every monitor is food, and I'm getting hungrier by the minute. I still can't believe we get to watch and not sample. "Like cockles."

Howard, not offended that I clearly think cockles—which I have only heard of in the nursery rhyme—haven't a chocolate bar's chance in a gynecologist's office of being the "designated food," tells me, "It could be anything, and he has to be prepared. I mean, he's got to have a million recipes in his head that need only the ingredients that are supplied, along with the spices and stuff he's allowed to bring with him."

I wonder for a moment about whether Howard would be more interested in me if I were a great cook, and whether Howard's interest would make Drew jealous. And then my reality check kicks in. Drew doesn't get jealous because Drew doesn't really care. *Remember this*, I tell myself.

I watch the TV screens as the chefs lay out their wares, line up their knives, peelers, microplanes.

"What's that?" I ask Howard, pointing at a stainless-steel gadget on one of the TV screens. He pulls his eyes away from Nick's setup for a second. "A culinary torch," he says dismissively before pointing out that Nick's is newer and bigger and that he usually uses a salamander for caramelizing sugar.

I know better than to ask what a salamander is.

The emcee is apparently someone from the Food Network. I have been able to cram raising kids, running a business, trying to date and coping with my parents into one life, but it's meant there's no time for the Food Network. Howard seems to find this impossible to believe.

"You've never heard of him?" he asks. "He's on after Rachel Ray." I look at him blankly. He asks if I am pulling his leg.

"I know Emeril," I offer gamely. "'Kick it up a notch,' right?"

Howard pats my leg affectionately and looks at me with something akin to pity while Mr. Food Network calls everyone to order and announces the rules.

"And now," he says—and Howard takes my hand and squeezes it like they're announcing the nominees for Best Actor in a Documentary Starring Food—"the ingredients."

Howard raises a fist and shouts, "Yes!" at the mention of duck. I smile at him as if I care, while I imagine how best to redecorate Madison on Park, and how to present my ideas in a way that will convince Nick and Madison to take me up on my offer. Like one of Rio's NASCAR races, Mr. Food Network tells the chefs to start their ovens. All around me people sit forward in their seats.

Around me, but not *me*. I'm thinking about traditional colors that go with oak, and how forest green has been so overdone. I want Madison on Park to take people by surprise. Not dead-guy-in-the-bathroom surprise, but something that will distinguish it from every other nice restaurant they've ever been in. I try to picture deep red with the oak. I like it, but I feel it still needs something to make it pop, to give it pizzaz. Touches of a pale chartreuse? A bold lavender? A deep purple?

A sharp whack jerks me from my reverie, and Howard tells me that the chef at the second station couldn't cut the rind off an orange, never mind the head off a duck. I watch Nick's monitor and see Madison put her hands on her hips and stamp her foot like Nick is purposely not getting on with it. There's something Lady Macbethian about her as she directs Nick's cleaver to some exact spot on the poor duck's neck.

Howard says something about a perfectly cooked foie gras with poached pear and a port wine reduction sauce, but I'm trying to imagine the chartreuse and finding it unappetizing.

Maybe because now I'm associating it with dead duck.

Meanwhile, no one seems the least bit concerned that knives are being tossed about the stage with dangerous abandon. No one except me and a fire marshal stationed just off to the right of the stage. Sure—he and I are well acquainted with disasters. I arrive in time to report them and he gets to clean up after them.

An oven door is slammed, followed by an outraged shout about a soufflé and another about a rising cake.

A time warning is issued and the chefs go into double time. The monitors look like someone's hit the fast-forward button on TiVo.

And I decide to go with the deep purple. Maybe it's all the surrounding drama.

At each station, one chef is tending the stove and the other is at the chopping block. Almost every monitor shows vegetables being julienned with knives the size of light sabers.

A sudden gasp. Mine. Blood seeps onto the cutting board on Monitor Number Three—Nick and Madison's station. Howard rises from his seat as Nick rushes to Madison's side, wrapping her hand in a dishcloth and raising it up.

Someone in the crowd announces that he is a doctor. A half dozen others jump to their feet and announce that they, too, are doctors, throwing specialities around the room like baseball statistics.

"I'm a plastic surgeon."

"I'm a surgeon."

"I'm a urologist."

A *urologist?*

Two or three doctors head for the stage, one even leaping up without bothering to use the stairs. And then Madison starts to scream, like she's just realized what happened, and someone, I'm not sure who, knocks over one of those crème brûlée scorcher things. And suddenly there are flames leaping from the stage and people in the audience are screaming and Howard's looking at me like it's all my fault and he shouldn't have brought me.

People clamber over seats despite the fact that all the flames are confined to the stage and that the fire marshal is ordering everyone to stay calm. Someone keeps shouting about the nightclub in Rhode Island, and several lawyer-types are yelling something that sounds like, "Sue, sue!"

Twenty minutes later, after we have been drenched by the automatic sprinklers, a police car has taken Madison, her severed fingertip and Nick to a hospital, and I have managed to pick the little padlock on Nick's travel case with a bobby pin, Howard and I are gathering up his knives and tools.

"Wish you hadn't touched that," a familiar voice drawls and there, in the flesh, twice in one day, is Drew Scoones.

I drop the knife. "My mother's right," I say. "You are a stalker."

Drew tells me to feel free to put the knife away, now that my prints are all over it. I assure him that, despite the fact that I was here, there wasn't any crime.

"The woman just cut herself," I say. "Heat of the moment," I add, pointing toward the ceiling from whence, hair plastered to my forehead, I have been reduced to looking like a drowned rat.

He looks at the debris-strewn floor and hands me what I think is a citrus reamer. "So what is it with you and disasters?" he asks.

CHAPTER 3

Design Tip of the Day
"When we think of *fooling the eye* we tend to think
only of trompe l'oeil, but there are many more ways
of tricking the viewer than simply painting scenes
on walls. There are faux finishes. There are fiber-
board tables hidden under the fanciest of cloths.
And of course, there are metallic paints and gold
leaf, reminding us that 'all that glitters is not gold.'"
                                        —TipsFromTeddi.com

Until now the best thing about going out with Howard
has been the food. I mean, only the finest restaurants, and
all at *Newsday*'s expense, as long as I let him order for me
and sample what's on my plate. I mean, how great is that?
I thought it couldn't get any better.

Only it has. Now the best thing about going out with
Howard is that I get to tell Drew Scoones, when he calls
this afternoon, that I am busy dressing for dinner at
Madison on Park and can't really talk.

And no, I can't possibly see him.

Perhaps he'd like a raincheck? I say cooly.

He says it's not raining. "Gonna see old Nine Fingers? She gonna be there?"

I tell him that I don't know, that again I'm sorry, but like I said, I'm busy.

"Oh, don't worry about me," he says. "I'm sure I can find something to do. It's not like I'll be sitting in my apartment pining, sweetheart. I can always go hang out in a pool hall, drop in at Hooters, find somebody to keep the old bed warm."

I tell him I'm sure he can, while I hold earrings up to my ears and pick a pair of long, dangly chandeliers that Bobbie would tell me are so "last year."

I don't know why he feels he's got to be mean to me.

"Won't be quite the same, though," he says, like he doesn't know why, either.

And I say, "I wish we were still friends," then gasp when I realized I've said it aloud.

"I'm still your friend," Drew says and his voice is so low and soft that it does that thing to me I don't want done, deep in the pit of my stomach. So I tell him that I've really got to go, but just before I hang up the phone he says that maybe he'll just spend the night working on my murder investigation with old Hal instead of me. And he adds that he's surprised I'm not more interested.

And, of course, I don't hang up. "It's not *my* murder investigation," I say in my own defense. "I didn't even know the man. And I want to just put it behind me. I don't like feeling like a murder magnet."

Drew is pretty silent, no doubt giving me time to play

the whole scene out again in my head, to smell that sharp bitterness that filled the men's room at The Steak-Out, to see the look of surprise on the dead man's face. And, in some small, petty recess of my mind, to remember that the dead man is the reason Dana's bat mitzvah may wind up being held in some Korean restaurant where kimchee accompanies every dish.

"Well," Drew says, "you might ask your friend tonight if he isn't interested. I'm pretty certain he knew him."

Howard is stunning in his navy sports jacket and his khaki shirt, which he wears open at the collar so that he is not overly formal, but still well-dressed. The man truly knows how to put himself together. He looks out of place in the parking lot that serves both the strip of stores and restaurants on Park Avenue in Rockville Centre and the local Long Island Railroad station. Spring is in the air, and there is just the slightest warm breeze, promising the summer to come. My skirt with the sequins scattered over the flowers catches the breeze and propels me toward Madison on Park, where Howard says that Madison wants to talk to me.

The restaurant is dim—usually a sign that they are hiding worn carpeting, frayed linens and a chipping paint job, but, maybe because of the soft music playing in the background, the place still manages to pull off a romantic air.

It's warm, in that homey sort of way where you get the sense that people come here fairly often, but only as the default choice. Despite its reputation, it doesn't look to me like the kind of place you'd celebrate a new job (unless you're me and the job is redecorating the place), or that you'd take your boss if you wanted to impress him. It's upscale, but just barely hanging on by a thread. It's comfortable, sort of.

In fact, that's what's wrong with it. It's not anything *enough*.

It's one of those places you agree on when he doesn't feel like Chinese and you don't feel like Italian, and Thai sounds too exotic and a hamburger too ordinary. Judging from the diners, it's nobody's first choice, but everyone can agree on it.

Madison, her right index finger heavily bandaged, greets us at the door as though we are long-lost relatives from the old country. She is what my mother would call "on." I think it has to do with being in her element.

"What a fiasco," she says and laughs a tinny laugh. "Well, at least the publicity hasn't hurt us any." She shepherds us through the half-empty restaurant to a spot against the back wall. It's apparent to me that Madison on Park can't live on its six-year-old Zagat rating much longer.

A waiter appears and pulls the table out for me. I slide into the banquette while Howard takes the seat facing me and asks Madison how Nick is taking last night's disappointment.

She says they'll surely never forget it and looks down at her bandages. She leans into the table and says quietly,

"If it didn't hurt so damn much, I'd cut off another one just to keep the sympathy diners coming in."

Howard looks just as appalled as I feel, and Madison seems to sense her mistake. She once again laughs her tinny laugh to signal she was only joking and then disappears toward the kitchen.

I pick up my menu, open it and am surprised by the offerings. The choices are exotic. The prices are through the roof. I'm thrilled because I now have a bead on what the restaurant needs. Forget homey. Forget comfortable. You don't pay these kinds of prices just for the food, you pay them for atmosphere.

And if there's one thing I know how to create, it's ambience.

I close my eyes, imagining this place with chandeliers rather than high hats, fabric walls rather than paneling, a fabulous window treatment. When I open them, I catch the faintest glimpse of someone through the window, just now walking out of view. Though I didn't see his face, I'd know that leather jacket anywhere. So when Howard asks me if there is anything I see that I want, I nearly choke on my water. When I can catch my breath I tell him, as I always do, to order for both of us.

Howard orders the inzimino, which he tells me is calamari, spinach, chickpeas and nero d'avola served on a crouton. I don't have a clue what nero d'avola is, but I say, "and for me?" which tells him I'd only eat his choice at gunpoint, and even then I might not. He suggests the foie gras and braised duck terrine, and I give him my *please take pity on me* look. He orders me a tricolor salad and then goes on to order three different entrées of which he requests *petit* portions for us to share and taste. Like I would really touch a braised pork shank with pepperoncini and wild mushrooms over a ragout of root vegetables.

While he orders, I watch Drew Scoones pantomiming outside the window. The best I can tell, he's asking me to go ahead and ask Howard something. I shake my head. Howard catches me, shifts around in his seat so that he can see out the window, and asks what I'm looking at since Drew is no longer in view.

I tell him the window treatment is dreadful. He turns back to me. Drew comes back into view. Howard turns for another look. Drew manages to disappear again.

If Drew wants to know what Howard knows, he can ask him himself. What does he think? That Howard is a murderer? As far as I know, Howard's never done an illegal thing in his life—if you don't count the turn he made against the light the night that Drew followed us and pulled him over to give him a ticket.

And that was entrapment.

And Howard is not duplicitous—except maybe the whole trolling thing on JDate when we were first going out. But I don't count that since he thought he was flirting with me and not with my mother, who'd registered me without my knowledge or participation.

So what if he knew the Health Department Inspector? He's a food critic. Shouldn't he know the man who makes sure he isn't going to get food poisoning doing his job?

"So, Teddi, about The Steak-Out..." he starts. "I wanted to ask you—" But Nick comes over, his chef's hat askew, and interrupts him.

"Howard's girl," he says, nodding at me and grabbing up my hand to shake it. "Good to meet you again. Madison see you yet?" he asks, but he doesn't wait for an answer. Instead he asks Howard if he can talk to him alone for a minute, apologizing to me as he asks.

Howard, looking horrified, says, "No," really weirdly. Like just "no," without any "sorry," or "something wrong?" or anything. I remind myself that another of my New Year's resolutions was to stop seeing perfectly ordinary things as suspicious. Just because Drew Scoones put a bug in my ear (or wherever he put it) is no reason to let my imagination run away with me.

"I have to powder my nose, anyway," I say, putting my napkin beside my plate and coming to a stand.

Nick apologizes again and says he only needs a minute while Howard reaches out his hand to stop me from leaving the table. Drew is still watching, now from across the street, and I can just see relating this to him and listening to him guess that Howard's credit card was refused.

I pat Howard's hand and get up from the table. The layouts of most restaurants fall into two categories. Cheaper, funkier ones often have their restroom toward the side or front of the place. The ones that want to appear classier, more exclusive, have them in the back, near the kitchen, because they aren't afraid of what a patron might see. The layout of Madison on Park and The Steak-Out are nearly identical—loos near the kitchen, only the placement of the Male/Female rooms are reversed.

Which explains why I am frozen in my tracks in front of the restroom doors, feeling slightly nauseated and just a trifle dizzy.

"Are you all right?" I hear someone say, and turn to find Madison standing beside me. "You look kind of green, dear."

I assure her I'm fine, but my hand just won't reach out and grasp the doorknob. I feel sweat break out on my upper lip.

"Shall I get Howard?" she asks, seemingly caught between leaving me to possibly fall down in a dead faint and wanting someone else to deal with it.

I explain about The Steak-Out and being the one to open the men's room door and find the body.

"Oh, you poor thing," she coos over me solicitously. Or, should I say, salaciously. She, like everyone else, no doubt wants the gory details. "So sad about Joe. Who would do a thing like that? In a men's room, no less. Leave it to a man, right? I swear, it's the sort of thing you see on television. A regular mob hit, or made to look like one, I'd say. So sad."

"So you knew him?" I ask, wishing I could pull my antennae in. None of my business. *None of my business.*

Still…

"Don't tell Nick," she says, lowering her voice dramatically. "Especially now. But this was before I even knew Nick, anyway. Joe and I...we were kind of an item for a while. Not that anyone knew. We kept it hush-hush. I mean, a restaurateur and the health inspector. It could be misinterpreted."

"You owned this restaurant before you knew Nick?" I ask.

"Not this one," she says. "Another restaurant. In Boston, in fact. Nothing like this one. And I was just a chef, anyway. I'm embarrassed to even tell you the name."

She can tell me who she slept with, but not where she used to cook. Howard always tells me that chefs take their knives to bed. Now I believe him.

My cell phone rings. It's the theme from *Home Alone*, which means one of my kids is calling from home. I apologize to Madison, who didn't even appear to notice, and I take the call. It's Jesse, who tells me that his father wants to borrow my car. Only he doesn't call him "my father." He calls him "your ex-husband."

Rio gets on the phone. Before he gets past "How ya doing?" I tell him he cannot borrow my car.

"You really get a kick out of busting my balls, don't you? In front of our kids, too. You don't even wanna know what I need it for?" he says like it's an accusation.

I tell him I don't. "Unless one of my children is bleeding on the floor and you need to take him or her to the hospital, you can't borrow the car."

"It's something like that," he says. "And I only need it for a couple of days."

I ask him what he means by *it's something like that.*

He says one of his kids needs to go the hospital.

"I'll be right there," I tell him, signaling to Madison that I'm sorry, waving to Howard that we've got to leave. He's deep in conversation with Nick and I decide I can get home faster with Drew and his siren. I should never have left the kids alone. I am a terrible mother. I should be arrested for child abuse.

Only, then who'd raise my kids?

I dash out of the restaurant like a maniac, searching for Drew, while I try to get a straight answer out of Rio.

I should know better.

"*Who* is hurt?" I demand. Drew appears from nowhere. "What's happening?" he demands.

The kids, I mouth. "Rio, I swear to God I will kill you if you don't tell me, this instant, who is hurt and how they are hurt."

Drew hustles me toward his car.

"Nobody's hurt," Rio says. "I didn't say anyone was hurt. Did I say anyone was hurt?"

I put up my hand to stop Drew, who looks pretty pale for a man who sees dead people on a daily basis. "If no one is hurt, why are you taking my kids to the hospital?"

"I didn't say *your* kids," Rio says. His voice changes like he's cupping the phone. "I said *mine.*"

"What? My kids aren't your kids?" I ask before I realize what he's saying.

"I'm gonna be a father again," he says. I lean against Drew's car. My legs have turned to gummi worms. Relief?

Jealousy? Drew leans into me the better to hear Rio's news. "The kids are gonna have a new little sister, sometime in the next couple a days."

"Put Jesse on the phone," I tell Mr. High Sperm Count while Drew laughs at me and Howard comes charging toward us.

"Mom?" Jesse says, and my heart goes out to this middle child of mine who is always caught in the middle.

"Listen to me, Jesse," I say as evenly as I can. "Go into my office. In my desk, in that little drawer behind the door that opens for the printer, is some money. Give your father fifty dollars and tell him to use it for a cab to take Marion to the hospital when the time comes. Do not, I repeat, do not, give him the keys to my car."

Jesse asks if I'm sure he should give him the money and I tell him softly that we do not take out our anger at his dad on a pregnant lady and her new baby. Hell, how else is he going to learn to be a good man? A mensch? Surely not from his father.

When I hang up, the men at my side seem to have nothing to say.

"My ex is going to be a father again," I say, trying to sound breezy about the whole thing. "What does that make me?"

"Mad?" Howard asks.

"Even crazier than usual?" Drew suggests.

"I mean, Marion is my kids' stepmother, or will be if Rio ever bothers to marry her. But we're already divorced, so what would his baby be to me?"

"A thorn in your side?" Howard says.

"A pain in the ass?" Drew suggests.

"I'm glad you two are so thoroughly enjoying your-selves. Too bad it's at my expense."

Both men stand around with their hands in their pockets as if they don't want to touch this situation lit-erally or figuratively.

Finally, Howard asks Drew what he's doing here. Drew claims that he was hungry, saying that even cops eat, and somehow the three of us wind up back in Madison on Park like we're the best of friends.

Nick comes by to tell us to order freely. Everything is on the house. He brings a bottle of wine, which Howard tries to decline as too generous, but Nick insists.

Drew, making some *Everyman* statement, orders a beer.

With some difficulty, Madison pulls up a chair and all of us reach to help her a moment too late. She waves away our belated attempts as if to say "It's nothing," and declines the offer to join us in any wine, our gazes con-necting as she does. Then, as if brushing the moment aside, she asks me what I think of the decor.

I try to find something nice to say and mention the romantic air. Drew looks amused.

"You can be honest," she says. "God knows, they're always saying honesty is the best policy."

"So, what kind of name is Madison, anyway?" Drew asks. I don't know if he is somehow implying that the woman hasn't come by the name honestly, or just making conversation. I never can tell exactly what

Drew is up to, which is how I wound up in his bed in the first place.

Anyway, she explains that she was born on Madison Avenue to Yugoslavian immigrants. I want to say, "So there."

I tell her the restaurant has good bones, but the colors are off, and so much more could be done for the place with very little expense. And then I tell her that I would be happy to do the work at cost since the restaurant would be a great showcase for my talents. I tell her that Bobbie and I are still establishing our credentials and that it would be worth it to us to give her a great deal.

"A win-win situation," Howard calls it while Drew indicates that his phone is vibrating and that he has to go.

"Ask them about Joe Greco," he whispers in my ear as he gets up to leave. I glare at him while he shakes hands with Howard and takes Madison's uninjured left hand. "You take care now," he tells her as she rises along with him and sees him out, greeting new diners at the door.

"So what did Nick want to talk to you about, anyway?" I ask Howard while he waxes on about braised remembrance farm greens, whatever they are.

"Wanted to tell me about the health inspector being murdered," Howard says. "I told him I already knew from you."

"Why did he want to tell you about Joe Greco?" I ask. Howard doesn't ask me if that was the man's name. He just says that Nick always treats him like he's "in the business," what with him being a food critic and all and that I shouldn't go reading anything into it, the way I always do. "It's not like he had anything to do with it," he adds.

"Fine," I say, dropping it in favor of talking about decorating Madison on Park.

"Can you really keep the cost down?" he asks me. This from a man who is having caviar-encrusted salmon on the house.

"It doesn't look like they're hurting," I tell him, imagining Scalamandré silks on the window with layer upon layer of passementerie.

Howard looks around the room. "Appearances," he says, "can be deceiving."

CHAPTER 4

Design Tip of the Day
"Family photos can personalize your space, but they
have their place. Limit your office to two or three,
and save your rogues' gallery for a hallway or small
wall where they can be studied in relation to one
another and serve to reveal how you came to be who
you are."

—TipsFromTeddi.com

I hit "post" and the tip appears on my Web site. Unfortunately, the two photos that are supposed to accompany it disappear. If only it were that easy to dispose of a couple of the people in my life. And their baby-to-be.

Family, even ex-family, sure can make your life interesting. For example, there's my mother, who certainly makes life…interesting.

And I wish Bobbie would stop laughing about what that mother of mine did, because she's spitting soda on my kitchen counter and my laptop, and because what happened at my parents' house is not really funny. But you be the judge. I stopped by my parents' house to check on my mother—you know, see how she was doing after finding Joe Greco and all. She answered the door and told me that my father was "washing his hands."

While I hit computer keys in an attempt to find what happened to the pictures of my bathroom wall and Bobbie's husband, Mike's, credenza, which are supposed to illustrate my point about family photos, Bobbie tells me she thinks that so far my story is "the first normal thing you've ever told me happened in your mom's house."

Of course, since it's my mother's house, it doesn't stay normal for long. My father took forever, and it turned out he wasn't in the bathroom, but in the kitchen, really *washing his hands*.

Bobbie whines that I already told her this part. She's holding up earrings to her ears and checking out her reflection in the glass of my kitchen cabinets, seeking my opinion, which she will ultimately ignore. "Tell me again how your mother told him she bought him the ring."

"And that he shouldn't let me see it because I'm so poor and I'll think she's being extravagant?" I ask, copying and pasting the pictures back where they belong and indicating the dangly earrings over the studs while I tell the story. "It's so totally my mother. So I tell my dad that she didn't buy it, she stole it from a dead man. Which doesn't help get the ring off his finger and now he's desperate to get it off like it's cursed or something. Only the harder he tries, the tighter it gets."

"Windex," Bobbie says in that matter-of-fact, doesn't-everyone-know-this way she has. "They use it in jewelry shops when you can't get the diamonds off your hand." I tell her we could have used her at my mom's house.

"Instead, we had to go to the emergency room because his finger was swelling up," I tell her. "Four hours later, after my mother has made up half a dozen cock-and-bull stories for every nurse and physician in the hospital about how the ring was smuggled into the country by her Russian ancestors, he's handing me the ring."

"And he wasn't furious with her?" Bobbie asks. I tell her we've all learned that there isn't any point in being mad at my mother. It doesn't bother her in the slightest and it just drives us insane.

"Anyway, now I'm the one who's got to get rid of the thing," I say, pushing Joe Greco's diamond pinky ring across the kitchen counter toward Bobbie with one finger while I peruse the questions posted on my site—in the hopes that I can answer one of them. I'm amazed that people out there are actually seeking *my* advice. Especially when Bobbie opts for the diamond studs instead of the longer earrings.

"Sell it," Bobbie says, flicking the ring back toward me as I settle on the question of how to remove blood stains from draperies. "You could use the money."

I remind her it isn't mine to sell and type in a question of my own. *I hate to ask, but how does one get blood on the draperies in the first place?* I know the right thing to do is to just turn it over to the police, but my mother's had enough trouble with them, and then again, Drew is already calling it *my* murder. I push the ring back toward her and it dances off the counter onto the floor and caroms off the baseboard.

"But it would give you a good excuse to see him again," Bobbie says while I stoop to pick it up off the floor.

I tell her that I'm afraid that is precisely how it will look. Like I took the ring so that I could "produce evidence" and get involved with him on a case again.

Frankly, if that didn't seem so embarrassingly obvious, I'd consider it.

"And maybe it's some family heirloom or something," I say, though it looks like a pretty generic Zales sort of thing.

"Okay then, Miss Goody Two-Shoes, give it back to the dead guy, why don't you?" Bobbie says as if she doesn't care much one way or the other, while I type *The best way to deal with blood stains on draperies is to take them to the dry cleaners and let a professional do it. However, if you are sure they are washable, you could try an enzyme presoak and then wash as usual. Good luck!*

"Give it back? How?" I ask her, closing down Windows and shutting off the computer. "Put it in an envelope and mail it to heaven?"

"I don't know," Bobbie says. "Why don't you just take it to his funeral and ask him if he still wants it."

I don't know what else there is to do but that. "Right. We have to give it back to him at the funeral."

Bobbie chokes on her soda. "*We?*"

I tell her that if I'm going to put the ring on a dead man's finger, the least she can do is come along as moral support.

She says she'll bring bail money in her enormous new Michael Kors bag.

Four days later the police release the body and Bobbie and I traipse into Queens for Joe Greco's funeral. Bobbie insists that I drive because she hates Queens Boulevard. "It's city driving," she claims. Somewhere in the *Secret Handbook of Long Island Rules* it explains when the Borough of Queens is the City (like when you have to drive through it) and when it's not (like when you want to buy nice things—is there a Bloomingdale's in Flushing, Queens? A Nordstrom's in Astoria, Queens?).

In my purse, which sits on the floor of my Toyota by Bobbie's feet, is Joe's ring. Having had his ring for several days now, I'm on a first-name basis with Joe. Which is closer than I am to my mother, who isn't talking to me because I've taken her *booty*. I keep telling her that the word has a different meaning these days, but since she isn't talking to me she isn't hearing me, either.

I know this whole thing is a mistake. But sometimes, even when you know something is going to go badly, there's nothing to do but go ahead with it, so, despite all the misgivings, I join the line of cars waiting to turn into the parking lot at the Anthony Verderame Funeral Home in Flushing.

In front of me is a black Mercedes like Howard's, only bigger. In front of that is a black Cadillac Esplanade.

Behind me is a black sports car with a silver jaguar lunging for the tail of my dented red Toyota RAV4. Every other car appears to be a black Lincoln Town Car.

Bobbie and I exchange glances that question whether we could be any more conspicuous. The line crawls, and if our car is a tip-off that we don't belong here, the preponderance of men in black suits with dark glasses heading for the funeral steps really cinches it.

"We should not do this," Bobbie says emphatically. "This is a mistake."

The line of cars turning into the lot has multiplied into two lanes and we are part of the inner one, next to the curb. We couldn't leave if we wanted to. Which, despite the looks we are getting from the mourners, I don't.

"At least we shouldn't park here, so that we can make a quick getaway," Bobbie says, and she has a point. Of course, there isn't one available spot on the street as far as the eye can see.

I tell her she is worried about nothing. I don't tell her that my heart is pounding so hard I can hardly breathe around it, that I am drenched from my armpits right down to my waist. I also don't tell her that I still haven't come up with a plan beyond getting in the door.

We park the car, leaving our keys with the attendant, and climb the steps to the chapel.

It occurs to me that the casket could be closed, an eventuality I hadn't planned for. Of course, that assumes I've planned at all, beyond "bring the ring to the funeral."

A man whose chest strains the confines of his size 48 suit welcomes us. He points out Joe's mother. I expect an old Italian woman in a black dress with her stockings rolled below her knees. Mrs. Greco doesn't disappoint. The man offers to take us over to pay our respects. It sounds like one of those offers you don't refuse, and I nod my thanks.

"I'm so sorry," I say to Joe's mother, and of course, I am, because there must be nothing harder for a mother than to bury her child, no matter how old he is. I don't tell her how I come to know this, how my mother's life was ruined by my younger brother's death and what it's done to the rest of us, but I do tell her that I know. She tells me Joe was a good boy. A good son. And she introduces me to her other son, Frank, who is bigger than the usher who greeted us.

Frank, towering over me, asks me how I knew Joe.

"We'd see each other at The Steak-Out," I say, and sense Frank's body stiffen, so I add, "occasionally," to sort of soften the statement.

"Wednesdays?" he asks. I don't know what the right response is.

"Sometimes," I say. "Just a lunch every now and then."

"Like once a month," he says. I get the sense that we are talking in code, only he's a cryptographer and I'm talking Pig Latin.

His jaw is working overtime and the grip he has on my arm tightens as he leads me toward the casket. I look back at Bobbie, who gives me a what-do-I-do-now? face. "My friend," I say, pointing toward Bobbie, but Frank's hold on my elbow is firm and unyielding.

"You'll want to say goodbye," he says firmly, all but ordering me to look into the casket at poor, dead Joe. This is what I wanted, after all, isn't it? The chance to look in that casket and replace Joe's ring.

"Well, I…" I start to say, realizing I should have put the damn thing in my pocket instead of my purse. I pretend to tear up, though it's not hard to force out tears when you're scared to death, and I open my purse for a tissue.

Naturally, Frank offers me a clean handkerchief. I have to say that Mrs. Greco raised her boys right, damn her. I cough into the handkerchief until I sound like I'm about to die on the spot.

"I think I've a lozenge in my purse," I tell Frank and root around until I find the ring.

I cough one more time and put the ring under my tongue as I do.

Now all I have to do is not swallow it before I look into the casket, cough it into my hand and then touch dear, dear Joe one last time.

I realize I can't do this with my eyes closed, and so I look down at Joe. The hole in his head has been plugged up, and if my mother could see him now, spiffy in his gray suit, serene in repose, she'd tell me how wrong I was to let this one go.

Frank puts his arm around my shoulder. I smile at him, lips closed, ring beneath my tongue, and I wish he'd give me a little space. Sniffling, I bow my head and look over at Bobbie, who is still standing with Mrs. Greco. I signal her as best I can that I'm stuck with Frank at my side, and spit the ring into Frank's handkerchief.

"Is your mother all right?" I ask Frank loudly, hoping that Bobbie will get the hint. I fan my face with the handkerchief to clue her in about what she can do, and the ring falls out. I look down and cover it with my foot, claiming it's my lozenge.

Frank offers to get it, and just as he begins to bend down Bobbie starts fanning Mrs. Greco and calls Frank's name. "Your mother," she says, and Frank is gone as fast as a guy who makes Refrigerator Perry look small can vanish.

I bend down, pick up the ring, and lean over the coffin. "Frank," I say, and then realize I'm bidding a fond farewell to the wrong Greco. "Joe," I start again, reaching my hand into the coffin and touching Joe's hands, which are placed low on his lap.

They are clammy. Cold. They feel waxen. I manage to slide the ring on as far as the first knuckle. And then two men approach the coffin from different sides.

Softly, patting his hands with one of mine, I say, "I'll miss our lunches."

"Not as much as he will," the man near Joe's head says.

I'm still holding Joe's hands. My left hand is trying to push the ring on and my right is trying to hide what I'm doing. The ring refuses to budge. If I let go now, it will look like I was trying to get the ring off, not on.

If I don't let go, with his hands basically on his crotch, it will look like I'm sexually assaulting a dead man.

I could try to faint, but I'm not the world's best actress. Beside me, both men appear to be waiting for me to finish saying goodbye to Joe.

"Oh, my God," I hear Bobbie shout. "She's fainting!" I turn, along with everyone else, to see poor Mrs. Greco sliding to the floor.

I jam the ring as far as I can up Joe's finger and turn.

"Get out now," one of the men whispers at me, and I take off, grab Bobbie's hand, and we run out of the chapel like Jimmy Choo is giving out free samples down on the corner.

The parking lot is hopeless, so we hobble a few extra blocks to catch the LIRR heading for home. Ordinarily, women from Long Island only use the railroad to get to and from the city, and even then, the rule is pretty much only for Wednesday matinees and only if you're too old or too poor to drive in. Don't get the wrong idea. There's nothing wrong with the railroad. The cars are clean and the service is good. I don't understand it, either. It's just one of those *Long Island Rules*.

I figure we can take a cab home from the station and go back tomorrow for my car. And we hide in the ladies' room until we hear them announce the train.

"How in the world did you get Joe's mother to faint?" I ask Bobbie after we've caught our breath. She claims that luck was just with us.

As we slip into the railroad car and the doors slide

closed behind us, I notice a man in a black suit watching us. He rubs at his nose and I see there are two fingers missing on his right hand.

I tell Bobbie it looks like our luck has just run out.

CHAPTER 5

Design Tip of the Day

"I always recommend that clients splurge on their bedding. A person spends something like one third of his or her life in bed, and that's too much time to be relegated to second-class status. With good quality sheets and towels available reasonably at every outlet mall and on the Internet, why wake up feeling like you've spent the night at Bob's Cabins Off Interstate 6 instead of The Plaza on Central Park?"

—TipsFromTeddi.com

My car is waiting outside my house the next morning with a note on it. "Courtesy of the Nassau County Police Department."

Which can mean only one thing. I'm going to have a lot of explaining to do.

When I come back in the house, Dana is in the kitchen whispering to Kimmie, the nicer of Bobbie's twin daughters. Kimmie nudges her, and Dana throws her a look before telling me that Drew has called and said I should wait for him.

"I wouldn't let a man tell me what to do," she says as she gathers up her book bag and heads for the open door.

"How about a police officer?" Drew says in response, and laughs when Dana reddens and pushes past him, Kimmie in her wake. "That one's gonna be a handful," he tells me, like he's raised any kids of his own.

"Yeah, well," is all I can say. That and *it would have been nice if you'd given me enough warning to put on some make-up and decent clothes.* Of course, I don't say that.

"Just like her mom," he says, looking me over from toe to head. "A real handful."

I ask if he wants coffee and fumble with the maker.

"What I'd like is to know what the hell you were doing at Joe Greco's funeral."

That's it. He doesn't say more.

"Saying goodbye?" I suggest.

He just waits.

"I was one of the last people to see him alive," I say. "Closure?"

"Just how well did you know him?" he asks, and his tone implies I was having sex with the man on a regular basis.

I tell him I didn't know the man at all. Not even his name.

"Never saw him with his pants down?" he asks.

"Only dead," I remind him, like if he's trying to trap me, he's failed.

"Lunches on Wednesdays?"

This is clearly a clue, but I say nothing.

He takes out a small tape recorder and places it on the counter. I hear myself telling Joe I'll miss him.

I repeat that I didn't know the man, though I admit that it does seem fishy.

"Everything with you seems fishy," he says. "But until now you've always been honest with me and didn't play games."

I tell him I'm being honest about not knowing Joe, but the way it comes out it sounds as cagey as it is.

"I'm asking you, as a police officer, what you were doing at Joe Greco's funeral, crying over his dead body."

"Are you jealous?" I ask. It's a dangerous question, but it could take us off the subject at hand, and give me time to think.

He tells me he's not jealous, he's angry. "I've put myself on the line for you, Teddi. Not once, not twice, but enough times to get the whole damn department betting on what you'll do next. You know what it took to ditch Hal this morning so that I could take care of this alone?"

I ask him what he's talking about, but my skin is already crawling.

"The Department's a club, a fraternity. Christ, it's a legal gang. It's got rules, codes, and there's no such thing as secrets." He looks embarrassed, but seems to shake it off. "And you, Teddi Bayer, are one interesting woman."

"What does that mean?"

He tells me that I'm as smart as I am interesting, and he doesn't mean it as a compliment. "So you figure it out. And while you're thinking on it, you want to explain your relationship with Joe Greco to me? Or to some guys down at the station?"

I tell him again that I have no relationship with Joe Greco, but I can see that isn't going to be enough.

I tell him I was returning a ring. He asks what kind of a ring. I tell him a diamond. I'm so angry I'm letting him jump to every wrong conclusion he can.

"Joe Greco gave you a diamond ring?" he says. "You need a sugar daddy that bad, kiddo?"

I tell him that my mother didn't think he was too old for me and he just laughs.

"Your mother, as we both know, is a whacko."

I nod. "Whacko enough to use a men's room when the ladies' room is occupied. Whacko enough to take a dead man's ring from where it was left on a sink ledge in that men's bathroom. Whacko enough to give it to her husband, and whacko enough to be mad at her daughter for taking it back and returning it to the dead man's finger."

Drew just sighs. Then he asks if I have any proof.

"That my mother is whacky? I have a police detective's assessment."

He gives me a sick little smile.

"And then there's the hospital report from Sunday when I took my father there to have the ring removed from his finger when he couldn't get it off. Will that do?"

"Was that so hard?" he asks me, and the hand on the counter is balled in a fist. "When the hell are you going to realize I'm on your side?"

"Against whom?" I ask, and I'm trembling because I don't want to need him on my side. I don't want to need anyone on my side. I want to stand alone, be left alone. "I didn't ask to be part of this mess. I was just in the wrong place at the wrong time with the wrong person."

Drew comes to his feet and pushes me against the refrigerator. I can feel Alyssa's latest drawing behind my back. He presses himself up against me and kisses me like he is making up for three months of being AWOL. He kisses my mouth, my cheeks, my neck. He kisses my eyelids until I'm forced to close my eyes, and he kisses my forehead so tenderly that if he wasn't pressed against me I'd just melt in a puddle on the floor.

And then he pushes himself away from me. "Damn it to hell, woman," he says. "You could have just given me the ring."

I could have, I think to myself. But I wouldn't have gotten kissed like that if I had.

He shakes his head at me. "Damn it," he says again, grabbing up his jacket and heading for the door.

"Drew," I say, wanting to tell him about what Frank Greco said about Wednesdays, like Joe met someone regularly, and what the other man by the casket said, but he doesn't turn around. He just waves his hand over his head.

"Damn it all to hell," he says again and then slams my door.

At 10:00 a.m. I call two potential clients and then answer a bunch of questions on my Web site about shelving, including why Miss Stake's shelves look like the library's instead of her sister's. I tell her to arrange the books by size instead of alphabetically, and to pull all the spines to the front edge of the shelves. And she wants to know how to stop them from making the room look smaller (paint the backs of the units the same color as the walls and put very few items on them).

Then I meet Mark Bishop, my carpenter, at The Steak-Out.

Mark is young, big and strong, and he's built well enough that seeing a bit of his butt when he bends over is still a treat. He's got a million girls calling him and showing up to "help him work," and he is two hundred percent male.

The best part is that he's a tease and a flirt, always coming on to me, always pretending he'd throw over all his little chickies for one roll in the hay with me.

He takes one look at me today and he can see that I'm already done in. "Come to papa, gorgeous," he tells me, and I let him give me a big bear hug. "When are you going to give in and let me take care of you?"

I tell him that on what I pay him, he can't afford to take care of me. "Who's talking about financially?" he asks with a wink.

"I saw Drew Scoones this morning," I tell him. Having heard Bobbie's description of Drew in the past couple of months—which included words like *creep*, *louse*, *user* and *stud*—he's ready to go beat the man up.

"Just say the word," he tells me, like I haven't been stupid enough when it comes to Drew.

I can hear Tony, the owner of The Steak-Out, shouting from the kitchen and I tell Mark it's time to get to work. I open my portfolio to show him the designs I've worked up.

Even though it's a steak house, I didn't want to do the usual Western theme. No Ponderosa, no O-K Corral. Instead, I want to do a gentlemen's club look. After all, it's men who think they can eat a side of beef without consequence—not women, who daintily order a nice salad nicoise. So I figure that Tony needs a setting in which men feel like men. Big men. Chairman-of-the-Board kind of men.

Meanwhile we can hear Tony shouting. "I got spoilage," he's yelling. "Three times in one week is too much for perishables. Last week you came Tuesday, you came Wednesday, you came Friday..."

I show Mark my favorite sketch. I ask if it doesn't look like the kind of place Richard Bellamy would take his son to celebrate his commission in the army. Mark looks at me blankly and I realize the kids are right—I've been watching too much PBS since Rio left. It's not likely that Tony will know his Upstairs from his Downstairs.

Tony is still shouting. "You think I can forget Wednesday? I'm not gonna forget Wednesday ever, a dead man in my restroom. Guns I find in there, drug pipes and tubes. Ladies' personals I don't want to think about. Used condoms. I thought I saw it all."

Hmm. Guess I'll leave the Bellamys out of the conversation. We try to ignore the shouting going on in the kitchen and concentrate on my drawings. At least, I do.

"Wednesdays I get fish, I get linens. I get flowers that will still be fresh for the weekend. Last Wednesday, I get produce from you schmucks that I don't need and I won't pay for." He slams out the kitchen door to find Mark and me standing in the restaurant.

He apologizes for his language. Mark and I pretend we couldn't hear him. I point toward the window to indicate that I just came in and as I do, I think I see someone watching me. I go closer to the window, wondering when Drew Scoones actually does any police work.

There's no sign of him, so I shrug it off and show Tony some designs I've worked up for him. The first is a hacienda style, with a sort of stucco-and-log wall with a fireplace. He doesn't seem thrilled, which is fine with me. I know you never lead with your best design because no one wants to take what they are offered first.

I show him another room, based loosely on the Cartwrights' place from *Bonanza*. This is more to his liking, and I'm a little nervous that he'll go with it.

"And then there's the upscale English Club look," I say, pulling out what I consider the pièce de résistance. "Although it may be too classy for the clientele you service now. But it could be perfect for the one you're hoping to attract once the renovations are completed."

Tony's eyes light up. They swell with tears. He closes

them and puts his fist against his chest like this is too much to wish for.

I explain my theory about how he needs to appeal to men, the real carnivores these days. Scotch served neat. Bourbon served with branch. Rye and whatever the heck it is men drink rye with. A couple of drinks for the ladies, but only as an accommodation. No cutesy-poo chocolate-kiss martinis. He should court business lunches as well as dinners. Make it a place for serious conversations by setting off private areas where men can do business deals.

He loves the idea. Of course, I tell him, it will mean some construction, and this is where Mark takes over, talking time, money and permits.

"The best thing to do," he tells me after Tony goes off to tend to some crisis in the kitchen, "is to hire an expediter to get the proper permits through and passed. It'll take a little money under the table, but that's life."

I know I'm naive, but sometimes these things just smack me in the face. "Are you telling me that I have to pay someone to obtain permits that I have to pay someone else for?"

He chucks me under the chin. "For such a sexy woman, you sure are cute. Money makes the world go around, gorgeous, and greased palms turn the wheels. Happens all the time."

I tell him he's pretty jaded for such a young kid and he laughs at me.

"That guy who got killed down here?" he tells me. "Bet

you anything he was on the take and he tried to stiff the
mob their share of it."

I tell him that this is Long Island, not New Jersey. And
that it's real life, not *The Sopranos*. And then I think about
the men at Joe Greco's funeral and recall my ex-husband's
association with *The Nose* and other men with animal and
body part appellations from whom he borrowed sums of
money without telling me. And I wonder who's the one
with the imagination—Mark or me?

I mean, thinking about Frank Greco's reaction—that
was really something. Clearly he believed that Joe was
meeting some woman on Wednesdays and Frank didn't
like her. Well, I think he didn't like me, actually, but was
it because he thought I was the bag woman?

Assuming any of that is true, there was no one with
Joe on the day he got killed, which was a Wednesday, so
is that because he was slated to be whacked? Whoever
killed him knew he'd be at The Steak-Out.

So many pieces to this puzzle…

All the way home I fight my usual flights of imagination. Checking the rearview mirror, I convince myself
that only three of the cars behind me are actually following me—instead of the usual ten I imagine. I tell myself
that not everyone whose chest looks like it could store
hockey equipment takes steroids, and not everyone who
takes steroids is an "enforcer." And that maybe Joe Greco
was a bouncer on the side and the men at his funeral were
all bouncer friends, which would explain why they
looked like they'd enjoy breaking knee caps. Mine.

My cell phone rings and I have to dig in my purse while I navigate the Seaford-Oyster Bay Expressway. It's the *Looney Tunes* theme, so I know it's my mother calling, and I'd just let it ring, but until now she wasn't speaking to me at all, so in the interest of progress and family peace, I figure I'd better take the call.

"Burned," she says when I manage to answer the phone. "To the ground. Now what are you going to do?"

CHAPTER 6

Design Tip of the Day
"Smoke damage is best left to the professionals. In addition to soot and ash removal, professionals can deodorize by using ozone treatments to clean the air. Yes, it can be expensive, but if you're lucky, your insurance company should be picking up the tab."
—TipsFromTeddi.com

"Mom?" I say as I try to make my way over to the right lane so that I can get off the expressway and onto the parkway, and wishing I'd taken side streets so that I could just pull over until I get a straight answer out of my mother. "What burned?"

"You ever wonder if you're just unlucky?" my mother asks.

"Often," I admit.

"You got stuck with me. You got stuck with Rio…of course, that was your fault, not bad luck. Most of what happens to you is your fault. Except me, of course."

I ask her again what burned down. "Just tell me it wasn't my house," I say.

She tells me *that* would be easy. We could come and live with her.

"Oh, God! Tell me it's not *your* house," I say, flipping the plan and imagining my parents coming to live with my hormone-driven daughter, my overprotective son and a six-and-a-half- year-old who thinks she rules the world.

My mother concedes that I am a very busy woman, that I am trying to support a family—inexplicably without any help from my father, and says she knows that I prefer country music. "But don't you ever listen to the news?"

"I would, but so often I'm on the phone…"

She tells me I shouldn't talk on the phone so much, but when I offer to hang up and turn on the radio, she is insulted.

"Sheldon's of Great Neck burned down," she finally says.

All I can think of to say is, "It did not." No one's luck could be this bad.

My call-waiting clicks.

"We'll find you a place," Howard says when I take the call. "I promise."

Oh, yeah. Someone's luck could be this bad.

Mine.

And the good times just keep rolling. Drew Scoones's car is waiting in my driveway when I pull in. Maggie May greets me at the door, which, I suppose, beats being met by no one at all.

"Hello?" I call into the house. "Anyone walk the dog?"

Dana calls down that she has too much homework,

she's studying her *haftorah*, and the dog isn't hers. "No one has to walk a hamster," she says in an *I'm-so-smart* tone that only a nearly thirteen-year-old can master with so little effort.

Alyssa reminds me that she isn't allowed. "I'm only six," she says.

"And a half," both Jesse, coming in from the direction of my office, and his sister Dana add, warning her that her time is fast approaching.

"Drew's here," Jesse says, as if that's a good reason to let the dog's bladder burst. "We're working on your computer."

The first thing I am going to buy when I get paid for the Steak-Out job—if I don't need still more money for Dana's bat mitzvah—is a computer for Jesse. Nothing strikes fear into the heart of a mother who uses her computer for work faster than hearing one of her kids say, "We're working on your computer."

"On what?" I ask, which is a mistake because the truth is that right at this moment I don't really care all that much, which doesn't stop Jesse from launching into a ten-minute explanation of some project for school without Drew making an appearance.

As two can play at this game, I announce that I am going to take Maggie for a walk and drop my briefcase by the door.

No matter how wound up I am, five minutes of dog walking with the Magster always calms me down.

We circle the block once before Maggie's best friend, Samian, comes bounding out the door of 22 Gregory

Lane and the two do their happy dance around each other, sniffing butts, nuzzling ears, rolling on their backs in the grass with joy.

"Samian!" Eleanor Heinis comes out of her house with a dishtowel in one hand and a plate in the other, complaining that her cockapoo will be the death of her yet. "It's hard to be mad at him when he looks so freakin' happy," she admits, clearly disappointed that she can't work up a good mad at the dog as he crushes her impatiens.

"You know that guy?" she asks me, gesturing with her chin at a long black car going slowly down the street. I turn, but it speeds up and I don't get a look at the guy.

"Probably looking for the Haitkins's house," she says. "Every time there's even the hint that someone might want to sell, the real estate salesmen descend like vultures." She reaches down and separates the dogs, who seem to know that spring is mating season even for the fixed.

And the lonely.

I wonder how long I have to stay out before someone—read: Drew—comes looking for me. I think it's a lot longer than this, and decide to take a second turn around the block, say goodbye to Eleanor and tell Maggie to do the same to Samian.

By the time we've circled the block two more times, seen the same black sedan a time or two, conversed with the new neighbors who complain to me that some dog has been pooping on their lawn and who don't seem to believe me when I swear it's not mine, I've almost convinced myself that I don't care that Drew Scoones is in my office. Stretching the truth to the extreme, I tell myself that I'll surely find an even better place to hold Dana's bat mitzvah than Sheldon's of Great Neck.

I never wanted to have it at Sheldon's in the first place, but at the time I agreed to it I was still married to Rio, who was intent on pleasing my parents at every turn—not because he cared about them, but because he had to work with my father every day at Bayer Furniture (*the home of headache-free financing and hassle-free furniture buying*) and Sheldon's was the best we could afford that my parents would find acceptable.

Anyway, I'm nearly calm when I round the corner and see Mark's truck parked in the driveway behind Drew's navy blue RX-7.

Once upon a time I had a normal life, I think to myself. *Oh, wait. No, I didn't.*

Dana meets me in the driveway. "How come I don't take after you?" she asks me. "I mean, you've got two hot guys standing in our kitchen giving each other dirty looks. And I have dorky Steven Schwartz and he can't even come to my bat mitzvah because he has to go to his stupid sister's wedding. My life sucks."

"And, honey," I say, putting an arm around her shoulder. "It's about to get worse." I tell her about Sheldon's burning down.

The last thing she says as she storms into the house

is, "Good! Then I don't have to have a stupid bat mitzvah at all."

Ha. As if the *Long Island Rules* would let me simply cancel the whole affair and then continue to live among civilized people instead of having to move to some yurt in upstate New York.

In the kitchen, as promised, are two hot guys. And they are, indeed, giving each other dirty looks. Drew says that he takes it I've heard about Sheldon's.

Mark says something like, "So what are you going to do about it?" only he doesn't direct this question to me, but to Drew.

"Arson squad is investigating it," Drew says. "With the shutdown by the Board of Health their guess is insurance fraud."

Mark grunts. "Great. So how does that help Gorgeous over here? How's that gonna give her a place to have the party?"

"Oh, *Gorgeous* will land on her feet just fine," Drew says, using Mark's name for me sarcastically. "She always does."

From upstairs Dana yells that she isn't having a party. "Just forget it," she screams at us.

Alyssa wanders into the kitchen unfazed. "I'm keeping the dress and the shoes," she tells me. "Grandma will take me out somewhere and I'll be beautiful."

I think my mother may be right about certain characteristics and tendencies skipping a generation. Alyssa is one hundred percent June's granddaughter and about ten percent my own.

Jesse materializes from thin air. "Is the bat mitzvah off? Because Danny Tahany is having this thing at his house and—"

See why I like walking the dog?

I tell everyone that the party is not off, just moved. To where I don't know, but I will take care of it. "I will take care of everything," I say through clenched teeth, adding that Alyssa will keep her dress, Jesse will not be going to Danny's, and, raising my voice so that Dana will hear me, she'd better keep practicing her *haftorah* even if Steven Schwartz won't be there to hear it.

"And what," I ask Drew and Mark, while Maggie does her *I-peed-and-I-want-a-biscuit* dance around my feet, "can I do for you?"

Mark puts up his hands and backs up a couple of feet. "Not a thing," he says. "Just brought over the estimates for The Steak-Out." He gestures toward a file on the counter.

I stare at Drew, waiting.

"Wanted to let you know about the arson squad," he says, but there's clearly more he has in mind.

"And?" I say while gesturing for Jesse to see to Maggie.

Drew looks at Jesse and Alyssa. "You want to see me to my car?" he asks, jerking his head in that general direction. Mark says that his truck is blocking Drew's car and that he guesses he'll be going. He says it like it's a question—do I want him to go?

Hell, I want everyone to go. I have to start calling

catering halls so the people can laugh at me for wanting to book a place three weeks from now.

Mark leaves. I walk Drew to his car. "So who is this guy?" he asks me.

"Mark?" I ask. "Didn't you see him this morning down at The Steak-Out? He's my contractor. He does carpentry for me. Put the closets in at the Kramnicks', raised the ceiling for me at the Penner place. Why?"

"First off, I wasn't down at The Steak-Out this morning. I do have other things to do besides watch your ass, attractive as that might be." He looks back at the house. "So what do you know about this carpenter of yours?"

I tell him that I know he is good at what he does, that he is reliable, pleasant, and he works cheap, which, while I'm building up a base of satisfied customers, is important. I say he's neat, creative, and we work well together.

"That's it? All you know about him are his work habits?" he says, like how could I not have had the FBI run a check on him. "He seemed pretty comfortable in your house. You have him over often?"

"You didn't come over here to ask me about Mark," I say, putting an end to the discussion. "What did you come for?"

He raises his shoulders up in one of those don't-come-crying-to-me-when-he-turns-out-to-be-a-serial-killer motions and says he came to offer me a ride over to Sheldon's to see what they're doing about other arrangements, deposit returns, that sort of thing. "I thought you might need some help getting your money back."

I remember all too clearly going to Sheldon's with

Drew, feeling like it was the start of something between us, something more permanent than our couple of rolls in the hay. And I remember that night and the things he did to melt away every inhibition I might have had about being older than him, having stretch marks, the whole nine yards.

And I remember waiting to hear from him after that. And waiting for him to return my calls.

"I can handle it myself," I say, thinking I've handled worse.

The next morning I open my e-mail to find two new clients e-mailing me for estimates. Both are local, and one has attached a picture of the den from hell. Her subject line reads: "HELP!" What she wants is a "look." Any look. And, frankly, anything would be an improvement.

I e-mail her that I'm sure I can help, explaining that her problem is that she has pieces of nondescript furniture from virtually every period—castoffs from various relatives would be my guess. From what I can see in the picture, there is a pair of old Italianate end tables flanking a herculon sectional with a boomerang coffee table in front of it. You wouldn't have to put *Psycho* in the DVD player to wind up with nightmares in this room.

But there is, behind the couch, a great-looking, full-size carousel bunny. Possibly museum quality, though it's hard to tell in the picture.

I tell her I'd decorate around the bunny unless she's

into midcentury stuff, which I admit is very in now. In that case, we could save the coffee table and get more teak stuff. If she doesn't want to go that way, she could sell the coffee table on e-Bay for a decent amount and put that toward a more garden-room look—white wicker or rattan, pastel colors drawn from the bunny, etc.

And then I decide that unless she hires me, she's gotten all the free advice I've got time to give.

The second query is just as promising as the first—help with a new baby's room before the baby makes her appearance. It's a small room and, provided she can be flexible, I tell the woman I can get it done before the baby is due. Though I warn her that babies have been known to show up early and the child might have to spend a few weeks in her mama's room.

Two potential clients is a good day's catch, and I have to be satisfied with that anyway because Dana's bat mitzvah arrangements can't wait. After I close down the computer and gulp down a cup of coffee, I head for Sheldon's of Great Neck.

There's still a sign that says it's the Premier Place for Your Special Day, but even a phoenix couldn't rise from what's left of Sheldon's. The entire left side of the building is gone. There's just a pile of charred timbers and bent metal beams. Tossed near the road is the skeleton of a chandelier, the glass drops either melted or picked clean by scavengers.

A handsome sign rises from the ashes like the American flag atop Kilimanjaro. On it, the word *Office* is embossed in black and outlined in gold. A big gold arrow points toward a construction trailer parked in Sheldon's parking lot. I go up to it and knock.

The same blond woman who took my deposit two years ago is there, all smiles and eager to help. Okay, she seems a bit less eager when she learns that I am there not to book for some date long in the future when the place is rebuilt, but to get my deposit back.

"You mean people are really coming in to book a place that's a pile of ashes?" I ask.

She points to watercolor renderings of *The New Sheldon's—Better Than Before*, and I think the arson squad would be very interested to know just when these renderings were made.

"Wow. Quick work," I say, and she says that the remodeling was planned ages ago, only the thing is, I know remodeling, and these building plans were not based on the catering hall that was there. She tells me that their promotional pricing—pre-rebuilding—is just incredible and that people are snapping up dates like shovels before a snowstorm.

"Two couples have even postponed their weddings to take advantage of the preconstruction pricing structure," she tells me, tapping a folder in her out-box.

"Well," I say, "that's so nice. I wish I could take advantage of that, but my daughter turns thirteen this month and I really can't see throwing her a bat mitzvah party when she's fifteen years old."

Without missing a beat, Miss Bookitnow suggests

going with just the service for her bat mitzvah and throwing her an incredible Sweet Sixteen. "Everyone's doing it," she assures me. "And we would apply your deposit to the Sweet Sixteen and—"

I cut her off at the pass. "I want the money back now. It will be hard enough to find someplace else to hold a party for one hundred and forty guests in just three weeks, and I'm sure they'll charge me a premium to do it."

Miss Bookitnow assures me that I will never find a hall. Just what I want to hear. I am sure that there are places where people pitch in and help each other in situations like this, or make helpful suggestions about possible solutions. Long Island isn't one of them. The first rule in the *Secret Handbook of Long Island Rules* is that you can't. *Can't what?* you might ask. Doesn't matter. There's a law against it, or it's impossible, or it simply isn't done.

The second rule is that if you do manage to do it, it won't turn out as well as your neighbor's and you shouldn't have tried it in the first place. This is sometimes called the *I Told You So Clause*.

I tell her that while I'm sure it will be difficult, I have a friend who might be able to help. Apparently no stranger to "helpful friends," she nods knowingly and turns to her computer, where, by some miracle she calls *remote storage*, all her files are still intact.

"Name?" she asks.

I tell her it would be under Gallo, since I was still married to Rio when I booked the hall.

"Dana Gallo Bat Mitzvah," she says, and it sounds so

silly for a Gallo to be having a bat mitzvah. "May 27, receiving line 1 :00 p.m., dinner at 3:00."

I tell her that's me, or technically, my daughter.

"Rio and Teddi Gallo, parents, signed the contract," she says.

I tell her that yes, we did.

"And Rio Gallo picked up the check for five thousand seven hundred dollars yesterday afternoon," she says dismissively. "Your husband has it, Mrs. Gallo."

I tell her I don't have a husband. That Rio and I have been divorced since last fall. That I am the only one they have been dealing with since we booked the place two years ago.

She doesn't care. She repeats that Rio was a signatory, that Sheldon's of Great Neck has fulfilled its obligation and that our business is concluded.

"On a personal note," she adds, "I found Mr. Gallo an extremely handsome and charming man. I'm sure you'll have no trouble coming to some equitable solution."

Yes, I think. I will wring his neck, and he will fork over my check, or I will send Mark over to his love nest with a nail gun.

"Can you put a stop payment on that check?" I ask, though knowing Rio, he's already cashed the thing at the nearest bank.

Miss Bookitnow shakes her head and says something about it being just as much his money as mine. "Probably more so," she adds.

"You want to tell my thirteen-year-old that?" I say.

* * *

It's somewhere in the low sixties today, but I turn my air conditioner up full blast because I now know the meaning of *fuming*.

I also know the meaning of *broken* when the a/c spits hot air at me mockingly.

I call Rio's cell phone and get no answer. I think about my possible alternatives.

I can let my parents pay for the bat mitzvah, but not only is that not fair, I'd have to let my mother make all the decisions. My brother, David, who is flying in with his family from the Bahamas for the occasion, has warned me against this. Apparently, because my father insisted on paying for David and his wife, Isolde, and baby, Cody, to come to the bat mitzvah, my mother decided it was all right to change their plane reservations to suit her schedule and to cancel their hotel arrangements. David and his family will now be staying at the Bayer residence in Woodmere.

Even if I could be sure my mother wouldn't take over Dana's big day, I'm not sure my father could afford it.

Option two, I can call Drew and try to have Rio arrested. Gosh, that would be a nice birthday present for Dana, putting her father in jail.

And I'm not sure for what, anyway. Miss Bookitnow was right—it was his money to begin with. It may have come from my father, but Rio earned it working at Bayer Furniture—on the days he wasn't sneaking out to screw Marion, anyway.

Or I can find Rio, reason with him, and get him to return the money to use for the bat mitzvah.

With little hope, I go with Door Number Three, and force myself to call my ex's home number.

"Sorry we can't take your call, but we're off to the hospital. Yup, Marion's popped and the kid's ready to meet her Papa. Stay tuned for height, weight, all that good stuff. Beep."

"I...I..." I stammer and then hang up. *Nice for you, you meathead*, I think as I pull onto Jericho Turnpike.

Maybe I should make a quick stop at Precious Things, where I used to sell my hand-painted furniture and now buy a few custom pieces for my residential clients. The owner, Helene, is Howard's sister, and last year I saved her life when her assistant and a smuggler tried to kill her. Neither of these facts nets me a discount because, as Helene says, "you do it for one and you've got to do it for all."

Since I'm passing it, since the kids are in school anyway, and since if I go home I may slit my wrists, I pull into the store's parking lot.

Helene welcomes me with open arms. Literally. She hugs me and kisses me on both cheeks. I wonder what she wants.

"I've missed you," she tells me. I remind her I was in last week checking on Mrs. Goldberg's order.

"But only for a minute," she whines. "We should go out to dinner, you and me and Howie, don't you think?"

I think I've never heard him referred to as "Howie," and that he'd probably punch anyone he heard call him that.

"You and he are still getting along, aren't you?" she asks anxiously.

I assure her we are, while noticing a fabulous new round hassock with tassels that would perfectly complement Mrs. Goldberg's love seat without needing to be special ordered. A leather tray on it would turn it into a coffee table to die for. I tell Helene it's lovely and ask how much.

"Whatever you want to give me for it," she says. I wonder if she's been diagnosed with some mysterious and fatal illness Howard hasn't mentioned to me. "I mean, we're practically family."

I'm not going there, so I tell Helene I think I can charge Mrs. Goldberg two hundred and fifty dollars for the hassock, so I couldn't pay more than two hundred for it. That's our rule, Bobbie's and mine, when we aren't getting paid on the clock. Make twenty percent. Unless we can't, in which case our rule is make ten percent.

Unless it's so perfect that I'd practically pay the client to use a piece, in which case I give it to her at cost. But don't tell Bobbie.

Helene says she paid a hundred dollars for it and I can have it for that. When I hesitate, not because I'm bargaining but because I'm shocked, she lowers the price to seventy-five. "I'll tell the distributor it was damaged but that I can fix it if he lets me keep it for that."

I tell her a hundred is fine.

"And you'll stand by Howard," she says out of the blue, like that's the quid pro quo. "Should it come to that."

It's a nice hassock, but I have the sense I'm signing my life away.

"He's a good brother," she reminds me. "A great food critic. And you have to know by now that he's a really nice man, Theodora."

"Teddi isn't short for Theodora," I say. "It's just Teddi."

She looks suspicious, like I just don't want her to call me by my real name. I offer to show her my license, and tell her the same thing I've told other people—that they probably charged by the letter on my birth certificate and my father went for the bargain when my mother wasn't fully conscious.

Helene ignores my explanation in favor of telling me to think about where'd I'd be today if it weren't for her and Howard. I'm too polite to remind her that she'd be six feet under if it hadn't been for me.

She brings it up herself, saying that it wouldn't happen today because now she's got a gun at the store. So if someone were to come in and try to rob her—

I remind her that the people who tried to kill her, and me, didn't "come to rob her." They actually worked for her. And I advise her that if someone should come in to rob her she should give them whatever they want. Nothing is worth your life.

She appears to consider this for a moment. "I have some very valuable things at the store," she tells me.

If she does, she's got them well hidden. "What could be more valuable than your life?" I ask her.

She doesn't concede easily.

"I'd give away anything but my kids," I tell her. "In fact, they could have my ex-husband."

She tells me that she doesn't have kids, but that she'd risk her own life for her brother's and raises an eyebrow to me as if to ask whether I, too, would risk my life for Howard.

I say something about how morbid we've become and suggest we change the subject. She agrees.

"Let's talk about more important things," she says. I wonder what's more important than who you would lay down your life for, but I let her lead.

Then she takes my hand and asks me how things are going for me now, holding me steady in her gaze as though she's been holding her breath since the last time we discussed my personal life, which has to be about a year ago.

I tell her about Sheldon's of Great Neck and the way she lights up, you'd think she'd won a makeover at Elizabeth Arden.

"But Howard can take care of that with a phone call, dear. He has connections in the restaurant business, after all." She starts dusting the counters furiously, not meeting my gaze.

"You mean, being a food critic," I say, scooting out of her way before she dusts me along with the furniture.

"Of course I mean that," she snaps at me. "What else could I mean?"

I beat Alyssa home by moments, call Mrs. Goldberg to tell her about the wonderful hassock I've found, and post a Tip from Teddi on my surprisingly popular site. I'm on the phone with Bobbie when Lys comes in the door.

"He's at the hospital," I remind Bobbie, who wants to talk about Rio instead of Mrs. Platt's dining room, which is what she was supposed to spend her morning on. "They don't let you keep your cell phones on in there. Besides, he's probably passed out in the delivery room."

Bobbie accuses him of hiding there. "She's probably not even pregnant. Just think, he could get money out of you and sympathy and stuff. He knows you're a sucker for a baby."

"Not when that baby is getting the five thousand dollars that belongs to one of mine," I say.

Alyssa plops down on the kitchen floor and pushes Maggie out of her face. She swipes at her cheeks, though I don't think her tears are genuine. Still…

I tell Bobbie she should suggest salmon to Mrs. Platt because it is more sophisticated than the peach she wants us to use, and that I have to see to Alyssa. I lower myself painfully onto the floor. It's the perfect day for me to start feeling arthritic—the day that Rio becomes a new dad. I ask Alyssa what's wrong. Did she have a bad day?

"I'm not Daddy's little girl anymore," she tells me, and she gestures for me to get her a tissue.

"That's not true," I assure her, wiping her nose while hating Rio Gallo with every fibre of my being. "You'll always be your Daddy's little girl."

"I'll be like Dana," she tells me. "Daddy's always telling her what she should do and asking why she doesn't do this or that. I'm supposed to be his baby, and now he has another baby. It's not fair."

"What have I always told you about life being fair?" I ask her.

"That if life was fair, I'd be Dakota Fanning," she parrots. Then she tells me she doesn't even know who Dakota Fanning is.

I decide that tonight after the kids are asleep I will go to Rio's apartment and get Dana's money. And I will remind him of his duty to our kids.

And he will tell me to make up my mind. Do I want him out of their lives or in them?

I have roughly eight hours to figure out the answer.

CHAPTER 7

Design Tip of the Day

"I can't overemphasize the importance of safety in decor. You need to incorporate lighting and handrails into your general design so that your lovely foliage-covered walkway by day doesn't become the *alley of death* at night. Your bathroom should provide a night light for both guests and for good aiming by the unfair sex. Your stairways should have railings for the old, the infirm and the drunken.

—TipsFromTeddi.com

"Where are you?" Drew demands when I answer my cell phone. I don't dare tell him I'm in my car outside Rio's apartment waiting for him to come home from the hospital. This is surely later than the man ever stayed by my side when I had his kids. In fairness, he had to get home for the older ones, but I don't feel like being fair.

"Out." The night is cold and I start the car and turn on the heat, but nothing happens. In the distance another engine roars to life, dwarfing mine, and I figure whoever it is, I bet they have heat. Feeling idiotic, I flick on the air-conditioning. The car begins to warm up.

"I freakin' know you're 'out,'" he says, and I can hear something jiggling in the background, maybe the change in his pocket while he shakes his leg. "Jesse said he was forbidden to tell me where you went."

"And that stopped him from telling you?" I ask. I am amazed. Jesse idolizes Drew. I thought he'd tell him anything, even where he's got his father's old *Playboy* collection—which he thinks I don't know about—stashed.

"You're not with your friend Howard," he says. I turn off the car and ask him just how he knows that. He tells me not to ask.

"Are you tailing Howard Rosen?" I look in my rear-view mirror and see no sign of Rio, who I expect will come back in a cab.

"Me?" he says. "No."

I'm not as stupid as he thinks. "Okay, are you *having* Howard tailed?"

"Me?" he says again. "I told you, no."

We could go on with twenty questions all night, but it's Drew's turn.

"And you? Are you being tailed?" he asks me. I tell him that if I were, he'd know where I was, wouldn't he? "Not if we're not the ones tailing you," he says.

"And just who would be tailing me?" I ask.

His answer? "Just tell me where you are."

I tell him. He tells me that while I'm not stupid, I'm

doing a stupid thing. Okay, what he really says is "Teddi, that takes the shit-brain cake, you know? Not that you generally have shit for brains, but in this case…" And then he tells me to hold on, because he probably thinks, correctly, that I am about to hang up on him, but that I'll wait until he's back on the phone so that I can break his eardrum doing it.

I watch a car come slowly down the street. *Be Rio*, I think. *Be Rio*. It never ceases to amaze me how ironic my life sometimes seems—especially when I'm terrified.

"You see a cruiser?" Drew asks me, and I'm too scared to do the hang-up thing I've planned to.

A moment later the squad car pulls up alongside mine and a uniformed officer gives me a wave.

"Yeah," I say, the moment gone. He tells me that the cops will keep an eye out for me, and circle the block until they see me leave. I say they seem pretty obvious in their Nassau County patrol car and Drew says that's the point.

"You see 'em, so will anyone who's where he doesn't belong. And they'll get tired of waiting and take off."

"Who will?" I ask.

Instead of answering, Drew says it's probably nothing. Just a precaution. But, as Drew says, I'm not stupid.

"Were there undercover cops at Joe Greco's funeral?" I ask.

Drew tells me that maybe there were.

"How many?" I ask him, remembering a man on either side of me at the coffin, one of them telling me to run.

"If there were any undercovers," he says, "and I'm

not confirming that there were, it would have been one. Just one."

The only thing worse than being paranoid is finding out that someone really *is* following you.

For a change, I'm in Bobbie's house. I'm there getting her take on the plans for The Steak-Out. She says I'm hiding. She should only know the half of it.

"So he says he'll give me the money back tomorrow," I tell her about my conversation with Rio last night when he finally showed up. Okay, so he didn't "show up." He called and I picked him up from the hospital because, having had to take Marion there twice, he'd used up the cab money I gave him.

"Not to mention what it cost him to go to Great Neck to steal your deposit," Bobbie reminds me.

"Of no consequence," I tell her. I don't tell her that he expects to bring the baby to Dana's bat mitzvah, which is enough to make me cancel the whole thing—something it's looking like I may have to do, anyway.

So far, I've two viable options. The Korean restaurant on Hempstead Turnpike, which my mother thinks I'm only joking about, and Jillian's, which is a kind of Chuck E. Cheese for grownups. So *viable* may be overstating the case a tad.

Can you really hold a bat mitzvah party in a Korean restaurant? Would you be the Jewish equivalent of ex-communicated if you served hot pepper paste instead of horseradish with the gefilte fish?

What *is* the Jewish equivalent of excommunicated?

At any rate, I don't think we'll be having kimchee and gefilte fish.

At least, I hope not.

And somehow I can't see my father doing the *motzi*, the prayer over the bread, while strangers are bowling and playing video games all around him. I get a visual of my father lifting his wineglass and some guys in T-shirts with pictures of wooden screws with "you" underneath them raising their long-necked beer bottles in salute.

I am screwed. I am so screwed that I actually hear myself telling Bobbie, "Rio claims he can get a place for the bat mitzvah. He says that he can take care of it."

Bobbie snorts and I realize how unlikely it is that Rio can fix this. We hear the screen door slam behind Bobbie's daughter Kimmie, who comes running in from my house to tell me that Detective Scoones is there.

"So?" Bobbie says.

"So he asked me to come get Teddi," Kimmie says. I feel around with my feet for my moccasins with kitten heels that Bobbie tells me are *so last year* while Bobbie makes noises of exasperation and instructs Kimmie to tell Drew that I'm busy.

"He said to tell you that he brought the Russian babka you like from that bakery near Waldbaum's," Kimmie says and magically my feet find my shoes.

"What are you?" Bobbie says. "One of Pavlov's dogs? I'll buy you babka. Sit down."

But I don't, because Bobbie's babka won't come with Drew Scoones staring at me above it.

I go running across the lawns and slow before I reach the door so that I can appear to just saunter in. Drew is waiting, looking serious, and he tells Jesse to go do his homework. Clearly a prearranged signal, since Jesse doesn't argue.

"Tell me everything you know," he tells me, gesturing for me to sit at the kitchen table and not the counter, which means we're here for the long haul.

I tell him he knows everything I know. I ask if I remembered to mention how Frank Greco asked about Joe's Wednesday lunches. "Mark thinks it was some sort of mob hit because everyone knows that all the inspectors get paid off and that they in turn pay off higher-ups. Or something," I add. "That could have been his standing Wednesday date."

"It's a good theory, but it wasn't a mob hit," Drew tells me. "Not that Greco wasn't into the mob, but good. It's just that we know they didn't rub him out."

I really thought the only time the words *rub him out* would be uttered in my house it would be via the TV. "How do you know?"

"How did I know someone was watching you last night?" Drew asks me. "Snitches, moles, the usual suspects. Oh, this was supposed to look like a mob hit, but it wasn't close enough. Our best guess it is that it was either an actual amateur or the assailant wanted the police to think it was an amateur."

"Is this where I'm supposed to say 'curiouser and curiouser'?" I ask.

Drew doesn't answer. "You get the job at The Steak-Out?" he asks instead. I tell him I did. And that I'm doing Madison on Park, as well. "Sweet," he says, reminding me that he really is too young for me, anyway.

"Why *sweet?*"

"No reason," he says.

But I'm not liking the sound of this. I am so not liking it that I'm not even eating my babka. And it's chocolate babka at that. *Russian* chocolate babka.

"That guy, Mark? He usually go with you down to Rockville Centre?" he asks offhandedly.

"Am I in danger?" I ask. "I mean, I've got three kids, and…well, and nothing else really and—"

He looks at me with something close to tenderness. Okay, more like amusement than tenderness, but he tells me he wouldn't let me be in harm's way.

I tell him that's not good enough. That I don't want any part of any police investigation, that I didn't know Joe Greco, that I'm just an interior decorator and a mom and I had enough excitement last year, thank you very much.

And he tells me that's fine.

"Too bad about your friend Howard, though," he says.

And of course, that's got my attention. It's the old, *just when I thought I was out, they pull me back in.* "What about Howard?"

"Well, you know he's involved somehow with Madison on Park, right?"

I say I know he's friends with the owners. Drew crosses his arms over his chest, waiting. "So what?" I say.

"Seems Joe Greco was holding Madison and Nick Watts up for megabucks," Drew says.

"So they were paying off the health inspector. I thought all the restaurants were paying him off. I remember when my father had his store in the Bronx he was always paying off the fire inspector. He said it was the way the world worked."

"It happens," Drew concedes, "though we've cleaned a lot of it up. But this was not the run-of-the-mill hold-up. I'm talking money that had to cripple even a successful restaurant. Blackmail on a pretty grand scale, it looks like."

"And you're telling me this because…?"

Drew plays with the edge of the babka. He breaks off a piece and puts it on my plate to keep the first one company.

"Just keep your eyes open, Teddi," he says. "Could be your friend is in tagliatelle up to his well-moisturized neck."

Mark and I are measuring for short walls at The Steak-Out, trying to create private, intimate areas where before there was just a big, open space, and I am trying to remember that my business here is decorating, not snooping.

Unfortunately, I can't find my off switch. So while Mark is making little jokes about what he'd rather measure, his every comment a double entendre, I am noticing the way the kitchen staff is watching us, the way Tony is fidgeting, the way everyone jumps when the back door opens.

"Produce," a delivery man calls in, then drops a carton with a thud.

"Watch it!" Tony yells at him, picking a browning head of lettuce out of the carton and shaking it in the man's face. "You think I'm gonna pay for this? I'm closed this week, anyway."

"Take it up with Carmine," the delivery man says and the restaurant gets really quiet.

"Who do you think Carmine is?" I whisper to Mark, who nods in the direction of the front door where a man in a fancy suit is waiting for someone to open the door for him. Mark steps in front of me and I try to see around him, but he shifts his weight.

"Time for us to go," he says, trying to maneuver me toward the door and still keep me out of Carmine's line of vision.

Tony unlocks the front door and one of Carmine's entourage opens the door for him. "Doing a little remodeling, I see," Carmine says to no one in particular. "That's nice. This place was beginning to look like a crapper, you know what I mean?"

Tony doesn't answer him. He just looks trapped.

"So you're the whatchacallit? The *interior designer?*" Carmine asks me, wiggling his head back and forth.

Mark says we were just leaving and tries to scoot me around Carmine and his pals, but they block the door.

"Don't hurry off," Carmine says. "We were just going to have lunch. Why not join us?"

"The restaurant is closed for renovations," I say, and Carmine says, "Is that so?" And he looks at Tony, who bows and scrapes and offers them his office.

Carmine nods like this is acceptable to him, and the group moves toward the back of the restaurant, Carmine's men looking suspiciously in every direction and all but throwing rose petals beneath Carmine's feet. They all look like extras from *The Sopranos*, and I feel like I've seen one or two of them before.

"Wow," I say to Mark when the last one waddles out of sight. "I thought Pussy was swimming with the sharks."

"You're out of here, Gorgeous," he answers, all but lifting me off my feet as he grabs up my briefcase and hustles me toward the door.

I tell him I'm not going anywhere and try to wriggle my way out of his vice grip. "Hey," I yell at him when he refuses to let me go.

"Hey, yourself." He looks at me as if he's just noticed how small I am next to him at the same moment I've noticed how big he is next to me. And he releases me so quickly I almost fall over in Bobbie's Manolos.

"I'm sure he just comes in here so he and his buddies can eat for free, like when Tony goes to what's-his-name's place," I say, straightening myself up and dismissing Mark's worries and our near embrace. "It's not like I'm in any danger. It's the middle of the day, for Pete's sake."

Mark reminds me that it was the middle of the day

when I found Joe Greco murdered. And it was here. And he thinks I ought to leave.

"I'll stay and finish up today's work," he says.

"And while you do your work, I'll do mine," I say, pulling out several upholstery samples and spreading them out on one of the large tables to see how the ambient light will affect them.

Mark seems tentative, but we can hear the staff in the kitchen banging pots and pans and joking around about not needing to clean under the lids. We hear nothing from Tony's office.

"I thought they came for lunch," I say, measuring the wall as I sidle a little closer to Tony's office without Mark noticing.

I can't help wondering what's going on behind Tony's door. A shakedown? Did Tony pay off Joe Greco, and Joe Greco pay off Carmine? And now Carmine wants his cut even though Joe Greco is dead? And wouldn't Drew want to know if that's the case?

I inch closer to the office door. Mark is sawing some beadboard panels and is intent on his work. Of course, his sawing makes it much harder to hear, but every now and then he stops to measure and…

I am leaning against the door. As Mark saws, I carefully turn the knob just enough to crack the door open slightly. I figure when he pauses I may be able to catch a word or two.…

The sawing stops and I lean forward just a little. I feel a hand on my shoulder and let out a shriek as I jerk away.

"What the fuck?" Carmine says as I fall into the room, a guy in a jogging suit right behind me.

"She was snoopin'," he reports, pushing me farther into the room.

I look at him like that's the most ridiculous thing I've ever heard. "I was measuring the door," I say, though there is no tape measure in sight. "To replace it with something more, more…"

"*We* were measuring for the door," Mark says, coming into the room with his saw blade still spinning.

"Come on in," Carmine says, gesturing with a hand to both of us. "Come on. It's okay. I don't bite."

I take two more steps into the room with Mark glued to my butt. One of Carmine's men closes the door behind me.

"Don't bite, get it? That reminds me. What happened to lunch, Tony? Wasn't you going to get us something to eat?"

Tony nods and all but backs out of the room while I look around as if I'm planning on redecorating the office, too. I gesture to Mark that a piece of ceiling tile is missing.

"So, a decorator, huh?" Carmine asks me. "And you don't do nothin' else? I mean, besides the regular stuff, like goin' to funerals?"

So it wasn't HBO where I saw these guys. I decide to ignore the comment. Something about discretion being the better part of valor. "And you're…?" I ask, and feel Mark poke me in the back.

"Carmine D'Guisseppe," he says, extending a meaty paw. "I'm an investor, of sorts, right boys?"

There's lots of "yeah, yeah, an investor" mumbles and laughs. I have the feeling if he said he was a tightrope walker the men with him would say, "yeah, yeah, a tightrope walker."

"Did you invest in this restaurant?" I ask, and I can hear Mark sigh behind me.

Carmine says he really invests more in people than in places and he asks how my decorating business is doing, as if he'd like to invest in that, too.

I tell him that I can't complain, which is what all Jewish business people say because if business is good they don't want to put a *kinahora* on it and if it's not, well, really, is that someone else's affair, I'd like to know?

Tony has managed to make antipasto appear despite the fact that the restaurant is closed, and Carmine gestures to Mark and me to sit. Of course, there are no more chairs and a look from Carmine sends one of his men scurrying off to get us each one.

"You like decorating?" he asks me once I'm seated and he's passed me the antipasto platter.

I decline the food and tell him that I do.

"Bet you learn a lot about people, doing up their places, huh?" he asks.

I tell him it's mostly about people's tastes, and channeling their choices to take into account color and scale and I'm babbling but he doesn't seem to mind.

"You do anyone I might know?" he asks.

I figure that since the answer is "no," I don't have to clarify just what he means by "do."

"So I bet you can tell things about people right off the bat," he says. "By their likes and all."

Mark says we really have work to do, and we should get to it. "One thing all customers have in common," he says, "is that they want the work done fast and us outta there."

Carmine ignores him and continues our discussion. "So what can you tell about me?" he asks.

I don't need to tell you this isn't something we covered at Parsons. I explain that when I start a project there's a lot of intake—the client tells me about himself, I ask some questions and we go from there.

"Ask me anything you want," Carmine says, spreading his hands wide like he's got nothing to hide. I don't say a word. "Go ahead. Anything."

Kill anybody lately? More specifically, Joe Greco?

"You do houses, right? I mean, you don't just do restaurants, do you?"

Mark stands up and says he's got to get back to work and he needs me to show him just where I want the largest of the banquettes. Carmine nods at the man by the door and he opens it for Mark, but when I stand, he shakes his head and asks me again about doing houses.

"I can see you got lots of taste," Carmine says as Mark forlornly leaves the room. "I'm thinking my house could use a little more taste."

I tell him that most houses could, and I suggest that a

great way to achieve taste without bothering with a decorator is to just eliminate. "Usually more stuff equals less
taste." I'm making this stuff up as I go along. "Fewer
colors shout class."

Carmine nods like what I'm saying makes a lot of
sense. "I knew a woman once, only color she liked was
beige. Only she didn't call it that. It was egg something…"

"Ecru," I say, having learned all this at the knee of my
mother, the Countess of Class. "It's a little paler than
beige. Taupe's a little grayer."

"Woman had more class in her pinky than I got in
my whole body. Like you. You got class. It's in the
blood, I think."

"Yeah, the blood," one of his cronies echoes and
Carmine shoots him a look like he's said a dirty word in
front of a lady.

"I don't know about that," I say, not argumentatively,
but the last thing I want is to have inherited my mother's
fondness for taupe or ecru. "But I do know the kind of
woman you mean. My mother is so fond of beige we refer
to her as the Queen of Ecru."

"But that ain't her real name," Carmine tells me.
"Right?"

"No." I laugh. "It's not."

"So it's…" he prompts me. Everyone waits for my answer.

"June," I say, and Carmine seems satisfied. He nods
like he knew she wasn't really Queen Ecru any more than
Dana Owens is really Queen Latifah.

"So whaddya think about doing my place?" he asks.

We actually did discuss refusing clients at Parsons, only I can't use the *our tastes wouldn't be a good match* excuse after he's told me I'm classy. That would imply I thought he wasn't. I can't say I'm out of his price range. I try the third option.

"Much as I'd like that, I'm a slow worker and I've got a half dozen clients waiting for me to do their homes, as well as several businesses. I couldn't possibly get to you for several months."

He's just staring at me.

"Many, many months," I say.

"Mr. D'Guisseppe doesn't like to wait. He—" one of his men starts to say, but a look from Carmine cuts him off.

"Why don't you give me your card," Carmine says, and he reaches into his breast pocket, stopping my heart. "And I'll give you mine. That way, should any of your clients happen to change their minds..."

I tell him that my cards are in my handbag and that I'll get one. Jogging Suit Man opens the door for me, and Mark, who has been standing on the other side of the door, hustles me over to the work table. "You're not giving him your card," he hisses at me while Jogging Suit Man waits with his arms crossed over his chest.

I point to a spot on the plans and say that the wall should go there. I have no idea what I'm actually looking at, but since Mark isn't looking at the plans, it doesn't really matter.

A minute later I'm exchanging cards with Carmine D'Guisseppe and he's looking me over like I'm on the menu and he's considering me for dessert. Or maybe for a first course. "You're a pretty girl," he says. "You'd never know you weren't a kid anymore. So you get your dark eyes from your father," he says.

"In fact, I do. My mother is—" I am about to say blond, but instead out comes "—ecru."

"Boss," one of the men says, and both of us turn to the doorway, where two Nassau County policeman are standing. Well, one policeman and one policewoman— Bobbie's sister, Diane.

Carmine asks if he can help them, and Diane says they are just here to check on the building permits. She asks if Carmine is the owner, and Tony, appearing from nowhere, tells her that it's his place.

"And you are?" she asks me, willing me with her eyes not to say "your sister's best friend, you idiot." It takes biting my tongue, but I don't. I'm getting better at this playing my cards close to the vest, ever since Drew claimed that every thought I've ever had was broadcast across my forehead.

"I'm Teddi Bayer. I'm the interior decorator," I say, extending my hand sociably. "I'm sure all the permits are in order." They ought to be. We paid the expediter enough to push them through.

Diane manages to extricate me from the office, asking to see some form I think she's just making up. She all but drags me outside where she points at permits for effect while she yells at me. "Are you insane? Do you have a death wish? Is that it? Giving Carmine D'Guisseppe your card? Why not just give him the keys to your house?"

"Google me," I say, and it comes out much like *bite me*. "I mean, anyone can find me. There's no such thing as anonymity anymore, Diane, and you know it. If that man wants to find me, he only has to look me up in the Yellow Pages, put me into Google…"

Diane says I don't have to make it easy, but she knows I'm right.

"What are you doing here, anyway?" I ask her. "I mean, you're not really checking into permits, are you?"

Diane cagily claims she is, which means that, of course, she isn't, that Drew sent her to check on me. I can't decide if I'm flattered or annoyed.

"He says you don't have the sense God gave a flea," Diane tells me with an apologetic shrug.

At least now I know how I feel about her showing up.

"And giving him your business card, Teddi. Really," she goes on, but I interrupt her.

"Why run if you can't hide?" I ask. "And besides, would you advise I get on the man's bad side?"

Diane tells me that Carmine doesn't have a good side.

"Everyone has a good side," I say.

"Tell Joe Greco that," she says with disgust.

Later that afternoon my mother, Howard and I are all sitting around my kitchen table. Remember that Sartre play you had to read in high school, *No Exit*, about hell being three people who hate each other locked in one room?

I'm living it.

My mother is using my landline and Howard and I are each using our cell phones, calling every restaurant on Long Island that seats more than 125 people.

My mother is berating Howard. "You eat in restaurants every night of the week. You do them favors—they don't owe you one?"

Howard explains, for the zillionth time, that he cannot use his position as a food critic to obtain favors, not even for me.

"I'm not asking you to do it for Teddi," my mother tells him. "I'm asking you to do it for me."

Howard bites his tongue and gives me a look that shrieks "I'm going to kill her."

My father comes in with two bags from Trader Joe's and plunks them on the table. "Our problems are solved," he announces while my mother grimaces at what he's brought.

"Nuts? Dried fruits? You call this sustenance? I should have gone myself," she tells him.

"Cajun pistachios! Yes!" I say, not because I like them, but because my father deserves to be appreciated for bothering to get us anything at all.

"I said," he announces loudly, "'our problems are solved.' Doesn't anyone want to ask me how?"

My mother unearths a box of Joyva raspberry jells. "This is good," she tells him, as if he hasn't said anything at all.

"How, Dad?" I ask, because I love the man and I'm polite, and not because I think for a second that "our problems are solved."

My father waits until he has everyone's attention. This involves waiting for my mother to pass around the candy and open two bags of nuts. "The Indian place up the block, The Jewel, or whatever it's called?" he says. "They can accommodate us and they do vegetarian, so it would be kosher."

My mother doesn't roll her eyes. She doesn't say he's off his rocker, or that there are few places less appropriate for a bat mitzvah, unless it's an Arab restaurant. She just pointedly lets her finger run down the list in the Yellow Pages and dials another number while taking note of how many jells I'm consuming.

Howard says the food there is good, as if it's really a viable alternative. I switch to the nuts, figuring protein is better than sugar.

"And we can all wear saris," my mother says, slapping my hand as I reach for more nuts. "Since your dress won't fit you, anyway. And instead of reading the *haftorah*, maybe Dana can do a belly dance."

"It's not better than pork at the Chinese restaurant?" my father asks Howard, who puts up one finger like he has an idea.

He dials the phone while we watch him with bated breath. Bated breath and a handful of cajun pistachios. I'd rather solve this problem myself. I'd rather not have someone—especially a man—swoop in and fix this for me, but at this point in time I'd actually support another male on the Supreme Court if Howard could take care of this.

"It's Howard," he says into the phone while we watch him. "Put Nick on."

My hopes go down the tubes. Madison on Park is one of those boutique restaurants that seats seventy-five people, tops. I hear Howard tell Nick he needs a favor. I hear him explain the situation, and I watch his face for signs that Nick is willing to break down the side wall of his restaurant, rent the place next door, and serve 140 dinners for free. I figure if he says that, I can get the tooth fairy to be the DJ.

"You ever do that before?" I hear him ask Nick. "How much to rent a tent? Wow." And then he says he'll float it by us and get back to him.

I push the nuts away because I have a feeling I may have to fit into the slinky bat mitzvah dress I bought to show the world that Rio was an idiot for cheating on me.

"Well?" my mother finally says.

Howard directs his words to me and to my father. He starts by telling us that Madison on Park is too small to hold all our guests for the meal. "But, if the tables were replaced by a few little round ones, and the hors d'oeuvres were passed, it could work for the cocktail hour."

"And then?" my mother demands.

"And then the party could be held in a tent behind the restaurant." Howard loosens his shirt collar slightly, and I get the impression there are problems involved that he doesn't want to bring up unless he's got to.

I pretty much tell him he's got to.

"What's behind the restaurant?" I ask. "Besides the municipal lot?"

Howard confirms that there is nothing but the parking lot, that we'd need to get special permission from the town, that there'd be a fee, and there'd be the rental of extra tables, the tent, flowers to hide the parking meters…but that Nick will do the food for cost.

My father wants to know why.

"Because he's my friend," Howard says, and I notice he doesn't meet my father's eyes, but looks at a place on the wall above my father's head before he adds, "He and his wife."

My mother wants to be sure she's got this straight. "You are all seriously considering having my grand-daughter's bat mitzvah in a Long Island Railroad parking lot. Is that right? With parking meters at every table?"

Howard says that with flowers and ribbons they could be made to resemble Maypoles, and since the party is at the end of May, we could play up the theme.

My father reminds us that The Jewel is still an option. "And the Korean restaurant."

I am at the Vs in the phone listings. Besides several pizza parlors, I think I'm out of options.

"What if it rains?" I ask Howard. He assures me that the tents have sides with arched windows in them that can be rolled down. He says that Nick thinks he can get us a deal from the rental people.

"You and Nick seem pretty well-connected," my father says. There seems to be suspicion in his voice.

Ha. Join the club.

CHAPTER 8

Design Tip of the Day

"I adore the element of surprise, though one must always keep in mind that there are all types of surprises. A heavy wooden table surrounded by delicately twisted iron chairs from Mexico can be a wonderful treat for the eyes. An orange shag rug in a pale blue dining room? Not so much. Some surprises work. Some don't."

—TipsFromTeddi.com

I pull up in front of Mrs. Goldberg's house with her wonderful new hassock in the back of my RAV4 and turn off the engine.

"I have to go," I tell my mother, who is on the cell phone talking to me while she has her pedicure done by Mary, one of the best pedicurists on the South Shore. "Talk to Mary."

"She doesn't speak English," my mother says, and I can hear Mary sputtering in the background and saying her English is better than George Bush's.

"I'm at my client's," I say, and I see Mrs. Goldberg coming out of her house, her arms waving at me.

"I forgot you were coming," Mrs. Goldberg tells me, and as I hang up my phone, I hear my mother say I probably got the appointment wrong. "I'm so excited I don't know if I'm coming or going!"

Her blue eyes are sparkling and she can hardly stand still by my car. It's always a joy to come to Mrs. Goldberg's because she offers hope for the future. I mean, if she can remarry—not to mention redecorate—at nearly eighty, isn't there a chance for the rest of us to find happiness?

"We won a trip, Martin and I," she tells me. "And we don't even remember entering the contest. Martin says I must be getting senile, but I think he's the one who forgot. I never enter contests. I was going to say 'because I never win,' but this time I did.

"Unless he entered and won, in which case I still don't win."

Another reason I like coming to see Mrs. Goldberg is that she makes me believe that given enough years, one day the babbling I do will seem cute.

"Las Vegas! Did I tell you the trip was to Las Vegas? That's where Martin and I tied the knot, you know."

I tell her I didn't know as I get out of the car and open the back doors to get out her hassock/coffee table. "Isn't it perfect?" I ask her.

"It is, it is," she says with a sigh. "If it wasn't for this trip…"

I ask her what she means and she tells me that one of

the provisions of the contest is that you cannot change anything in your home for six months.

"Isn't that the strangest thing you've ever heard?"

It would be, if it wasn't the second time I'd heard it today.

"You learn anything?" Drew asks me when he calls late that afternoon.

I tell him I learned that when Carmine D'Guisseppe wants a decorator, telling him you're too busy isn't likely to stop him.

Drew finds Carmine's technique questionable, but not illegal. At least, not if he actually delivers. What he really wants to know is what I've learned about Joe Greco's murder. Or, more precisely, what I've learned about Drew's prime murder suspect.

I'm telling him how the mafia works and all he wants to know is what Howard might have said?

I tell him I don't know what he's talking about.

"Don't pretend to be dense," he tells me. "It doesn't suit you and I know better. I just wish I could have been a fly on your kitchen wall this afternoon."

I tell him that if he had been, he'd have witnessed Howard coming to the rescue, and that Dana's bat mitzvah is all set.

"Don't tell me," Drew says. "At Madison on Park, right?"

I hate it when he's right. I hate it more when he's smug about it.

"Why am I not surprised?" he says. "Your whatever-you-want-to-call-him is in up to his eyeballs and he and his 'friend' will do whatever it takes to keep you off track."

"We've gone down this road before," I tell him. "Only that time you were out to get my friend Bobbie. Now you're out to get my friend Howard. Don't you get tired of harassing my friends? Can't you find suspects on your own?"

"Can I help it if you associate with the wrong people?" he asks.

I ask him if maybe he's just jealous that I have friends.

"Jealous?" he says and laughs a nasty laugh. "You know better." I hear hoots in the background and realize that all his detective buddies are hanging on our every word.

"I'm hanging up now," I tell him.

"Hate me all you want, Teddi. But keep your eyes open."

Wish he'd told me to keep my eyes open months ago, before I slept with him, I think as I hang up and try to find the holes that were in my ears just yesterday when I went to put earrings in them.

I glance out the window and see Howard's Mercedes pulling into my driveway. Not only was Drew's call irritating, but now I'm late for my "date."

Sometimes it feels like I've got quotation marks around my life.

Howard tells me that since it's Monday, Madison on Park is closed. So he's invited Nick and Madison to join us for dinner. "Thought we'd try out this great new place in the city," Howard says. "Nick wants to see if he can get some new menu ideas."

I hate traipsing into the city for a meal, and I'm not thrilled that we are going to be spending the evening with Nick and Madison because I know that I will feel like a spy—a fat and dumpy spy—especially when Drew calls me tomorrow and demands to know what I learned.

Howard turns on his radio and presses the CD button. The car is filled with something that resembles a death dirge, which Howard directs with an imaginary baton. I ask if we are meeting the Wattses at the restaurant and am dismayed to learn that we are picking them up. I had wanted to talk to Howard about whether I should really go through with having Dana's bat mitzvah at Madison on Parking Lot, as I've begun to think of it.

Nick helps Madison into the seat behind Howard while I get out of the car and move into the backseat beside her because that's the way couples sit on Long Island. Men in the front, to control the radio and talk about stocks or sports or best routes to wherever we're going, and women in the back to converse about clothes, jewelry, sales and men.

I smile at Madison, who squeezes my arm with her good hand while telling me how glad she is to see me.

"We have so much to talk about," she says like now we're the best of friends. "That's why I thought the long drive into the city was worth it. I mean, you're decorating the restaurant, we're doing you're daughter's bat mitzvah... I feel like we've been friends forever, don't you?"

Uh, no.

"Or that we know each other from somewhere…"

I hate when people play Jewish Geography, known to the rest of the world as the where-do-we-know-each-other-from game. Which is exactly what happens next and concludes the way it always does.

"Well, you must have a clone," Madison says. "And I just have one of those faces everyone mistakes for someone else's."

We talk for a while about the look she has in mind for the restaurant, with lots of her deferring to my opinion, which makes me uncomfortable because, after all, it's not my restaurant. And there's always the inevitable, "But you said…"

She loves the idea of dark red and purple. "So royal," she says. I tell her about the new wave of restaurant decorating that involves using pillows on chairs and banquettes and the possibility of changing the pillows with the seasons for a fresh look.

"Velvets in the winter, cool silks in the summer," I explain. She loves that, too.

She asks what I'm planning on for The Steak-Out, since she doesn't want to duplicate their look, and I tell her it's completely different, that hers is more romantic, high-end, sophisticated, aimed at couples coming in to celebrate rather than men closing deals. She says that since I'm giving her such a good deal, she doesn't feel right making demands. I remind her that Madison on Park is her restaurant and if she isn't satisfied, I won't be happy, either.

She assures me she's going to love it, and that she will be honest and up-front with me about her opinions. That squared away, she seems to feel free to move on to other topics, such as…

"It must have been awful, discovering that body." I notice that she slips a finger into her waistband as she speaks. It's one of those poo-poo, keep-away-the-evil-spirits-from-the-unborn-child things that came over with our ancestors in steerage from Eastern Europe. I'm about to say something when she smooths out her skirt to hide the movement she thinks I might have noticed. "It must have been incredibly upsetting."

I really don't want to talk about it, but it's clear she does. Well, since she had a relationship with Joe Greco, I guess she finds it irresistible.

I try to imagine this elegant woman with fat, old Joe Greco. And I think about the blackmail that Drew seems to think was occurring. Could Joe Greco have been threatening to tell Nick about their affair? Didn't Madison say she dated him before Nick was in the picture?

I tell myself that this is none of my business and that my job is to decorate Madison on Park, not indict it. And then I look over at Howard and imagine Drew going after him because of me. Howard would last fifteen minutes, tops, in a jail cell.

Not that I think, even for a moment…

"So did you see Howard when you were there?" Madison asks. "I mean, how wonderful that he could be there to comfort you after such a horrific event."

I tell her that Howard wasn't there.

"I thought he said that he was right next door," she says, clearly confused. "Didn't you say that was where you finally found the tamarind concentrate, Howard?"

Howard says he didn't see me, and Madison puts a hand on her hip. "Then I don't know what took you so long," she says. "Men! We have an expression in Yugoslavia—send a man to the kitchen for a spoon and he comes back half an hour later with a knife."

I think, *Unless it's in the dishwasher, in which case you'll get nothing because they refuse to open one of those*, but I don't say it because I don't like to criticize men as an entire gender. Individually, however, I could rant for hours, especially about a certain new father. But by now the conversation has moved on to how to decorate a parking lot, a venue I never thought I'd have to turn my talents to.

I wonder if you can rent AstroTurf? It would be nice to have a garden party feeling if we're going to be outdoors.

I've reprogrammed my phone so that when Rio calls, it plays "I Hate Everything About You," which is funny when I'm with Bobbie, but pretty embarrassing with clients.

The music fills the car. I apologize for not having turned it off, explain how with children you have to be available, explain that this isn't the kids, and finally just answer the damn phone.

"What?" I catch the look Madison exchanges with

her husband at my abrupt greeting. Sorry, but rotten ex-husbands who make life miserable don't get cheery hellos.

"Madison on Park?" he says. "I thought you were pressed for cash, giving me a lousy fifty bucks when—"

"I'm not going to discuss this now," I say.

"Well, don't expect me to fork over that refund for some highfalutin, over-the-top—"

He's shouting and everyone in the car can hear him. "Isn't the baby sleeping?" I ask. "Don't you have to be quiet?"

He tells me he doesn't know what "the kid" is doing. He's not home.

Ah, the Rio I know.

"About the money, Ted," he says and my heart sinks. "I don't have it. And if you want to get technical, it's really your fault."

Of course it is. It always was. "How do you figure?"

"Your father took me off the insurance plan, without even telling me. How the hell was I supposed to know Marion wasn't covered?" he asks.

"You thought he'd keep you insured?" I ask incredulously. "And that he'd insure your girlfriend so that the child you had with her after you and she tried to—" I stop myself before I say any more in front of Madison and Nick, though Howard knows the whole story by now.

He knows how Rio and Marion worked together to try to drive me right into South Winds Psychiatric Center, where I could share a suite with my mother, who didn't take to the idea at all and, when she found out the plan, took one of Rio's own guns and shot him. A little better aim and he'd be a soprano now—the singing kind, not the whacking kind. She'd probably be in jail, too, if I hadn't found the loan papers he forged my signature on and blackmailed him into not pressing charges.

And after all this Rio has the nerve to whine that my father should have at least told him he was cutting off the insurance.

I ask if Dana's money is gone. He swears he'll pay me back and I don't bother asking when or how.

Great. I'm having my daughter's bat mitzvah in a parking lot, I won't be able to pay for flowers or the tent or anything without charging it all and paying God-knows-how-much interest, and I am in a car full of people who can hear every word we're saying.

"I have to go," I say, and I think I hear our daughter in the background. "Have you got Alyssa with you?"

"You wanna talk to her?" Rio says instead of answering, while Howard looks at me as if to ask if I want him to turn the car around.

He puts her on and she says her daddy is going to take her out for Carvel. She says something about Jesse being upstairs and not wanting to go. And then she hangs up.

I stare at the dead phone in my hands. Daddy is such a sport, taking the kids out for ice cream on Dana's bat mitzvah money.

"Her ex," Howard explains to Nick and Madison.

"Schmuck left you with kids," Nick says, and makes a hand gesture you don't have to know Italian to understand. "A man who does that should have his balls cut off."

I decide not to tell him that I was the one who kicked Rio to the curb, because the image of Rio with his balls cut off is, at this moment, rather appealing.

The next morning I am going through my old pocketbooks hoping that I left a big bill hidden in one of them. Okay, I am going through my mother's castoffs, hoping *she* left a big bill in one of them. I'm wishing that I had a nickel for every refundable deposit bottle I've thrown into the recycle bin or the trash over the years, and realizing that is exactly what I would have if I'd taken them back to the store.

I've gone over my accounts receivable a hundred times since last night and if everyone pays me on time, a huge *if*, I can manage the tent.

I call Rio to ask if there is any portion of Dana's refund left and explain how we're going to have to pay the town for the parking spaces we use for the afternoon, hidden, though the meters will be under ribbons and flowers if I can afford them.

"In Rockville Centre?" Rio says. "And the town's who you pay?"

I tell him that's what we were told when we called. He, of course, makes a big deal about who *we* is, while he bounces his new baby on his knee and then tells Marion to take the kid so he can talk.

"I didn't want Marion to hear this," he whispers, "but I can fix this for you. You remember my buddy, Sal?"

"The Nose?" I ask.

"That's Nicky," he says.

"The Snake?"

"Sammy."

No other animal names or body parts come to mind.

"Sal was the guy I bought your engagement ring from, remember?"

What I actually remember is that inside my ring were initials that weren't mine or Rio's, and being told the ring had been "returned." I remember believing it, too.

"His friend is married to the girl down there. You know, the one who you pay your tickets to."

"I don't get tickets," I tell him, to which he replies, "Yeah, well the rest of us aren't so perfect," which makes me feel like Goody Two-Shoes.

"Anyway," he says, "she can fix it so you don't have to pay one stinkin' dime. Nada. Nothing. I told you to leave it to me, didn't I?"

Experience tells me that disaster is written all over this one. In indelible ink.

"You're playing on my field now, Teddi, with my balls. I'll take care of this whole thing. It's the least I can do."

Amen to that, I think, trying to erase the image of playing with his balls on his field or anywhere else. "So you'll speak to her, see what it takes and get back to me, right?"

He assures me he will. He reminds me that his kids mean everything to him, which is probably the only honest thing he's ever said to me. And, knowing that Rio could sell valet parking on the Long Island Expressway,

I figure that if this girl is young, and he sees her in person, she'll no doubt throw in some free fishing licenses before Rio's through with her.

I bring up his various parking tickets and moving violations and the fact that the police seem to be keeping tabs on him. "Do it by the book, Mario," I tell him. I call him Mario these days rather than Rio, the nickname I gave him, lest I forget that he is not the man I fell in love with and married.

"I don't know any other way," he says, and I don't know quite how to take that, but I don't have time to argue with him because my mother and Bobbie are coming over to help me work on the centerpieces for the tables. Okay, Bobbie is coming to help and my mother is coming to carp.

"You should have hired someone to do this," she says as she walks in the door with her hands up, fingers spread wide apart. "I'm not sure my nails are dry."

I remind her that her nail appointment was at nine and that it's now after noon. She says that it's humid out and, not that I'd know, but that makes the drying time longer.

"Oh, Teddi'd never know that," Bobbie says as she comes into my kitchen through the back door. "She only custom-painted furniture for years."

My mother gives her the patented June-Bayer-thinks-you-are-an-idiot look which, amazingly, she can still deliver despite all the Botox and Restylane.

I have set up supplies on the table in the dining room,

covering it with craft paper to protect it from our work. As I lead my little workforce in, my mother comments that she supposes that the fact that the kitchen table isn't being used means we aren't going out for lunch.

"Lunch?" I assumed that she and Bobbie ate before they came over so that we could actually get some work done.

My mother stretches her neck out and scratches it gingerly. "What are you serving?" she asks.

"Let's do Chinese," Bobbie suggests as the phone rings. "We could call it in and I could pick it up."

"How much longer does it take to eat it there?" my mother says as I answer the phone. If they didn't hate each other, I would swear they planned this little dialogue to make me crazy.

Oh, been there, done that.

"Hello?" I say, wondering who "private caller" is.

"Is this Teddi Bayer Design Services?" a woman's voice asks.

I tell her that it is, and kick myself for being so distracted when the phone rang that I didn't realize it was my business phone. I ask her how I can help her. It sounds better than asking how I can direct her call, don't you think?

"Please hold for Mr. D'Guisseppe," she says.

I put my hand over the mouthpiece and whisper to Bobbi that, *oh my God*, it's Carmine D'Guisseppe.

"Hang up," my mother says, and tries to wrest the phone from me. "Hang. It. Up!"

"No," I tell her, batting her hands away and signaling

Bobbie to hold my mother, which she makes it clear she isn't about to do by backing away with her hands up.

"Do not talk to that man," my mother says. "He's a gangster. A mobster."

I hear a soft chuckle from the earpiece.

My mother reaches out her hand. "Give me the phone," she says. "I'll talk to him."

I ask him to wait just a moment and hiss at my mother that he didn't call her, he called me.

My mother asks if I'm defying her.

"Hell, yes," I tell her. "Now go sit down and behave. I have a business to run here."

To my surprise, my mother sits. I'd have ordered her around years ago if I'd known it would work.

"I'm sorry to keep you waiting, Mr. D'Guisseppe," I say. "You caught me in the middle of something. How can I help you?"

He tells me I can help him by not taking that tone with my mother. "Show some respect," he cautions me.

I tell him he doesn't know my mother. She gives me the death stare and leaves the room.

"Irregardless," he says.

In the interest of not antagonizing a potential client, not to mention a mafia don, and considering she's no longer in hearing range, I agree and apologize.

"I know," he says softly. "She can be frustrating. It's a mother's job. You don't frustrate your children?"

I think of the argument Dana and I had last night over the theme we'd originally planned for her party—

American Idol—and what was going to be possible under the circumstances now: nothing.

"How can I help you?" I ask again, this time sounding friendlier, like we suddenly understand each other, which, of course, we don't. My mother wanders back in, fingering the silk flowers on the table with contempt.

"I was wondering if, maybe fortuitously, your schedule has opened up any," he says, like he hasn't opened it up himself.

I tell him that while it has, *fortuitously*—and I use that word like it's a code so we both know that I know that it wasn't *fortuitous* at all, but *D'Guisseppeous*—I'm overwhelmed with preparations for my daughter's bat mitzvah and I really can't take on any new work until the bat mitzvah is over.

"The bat mitzvah," he says. "That's like a party, right?" I tell him how a party follows the service, which is the real bat mitzvah, like he cares. He asks polite questions, I give vague answers.

And then he asks to speak to my mother.

"I'm sorry," I say, pinning her to her chair with a look, a trick I've tried to steal from her for years and have only now succeeded. "But she's not here anymore."

I can't tell if my mother is relieved or annoyed.

Maggie May has taken to scratching at the door and I'm guessing it's the fact that Samian's fancy has turned to her and she doesn't want to miss out on any loving, however ineffectual it might be.

I understand and sympathize. All the more, in fact, when I open the door and Drew is on my doorstep.

"I have to walk the dog," I tell him, and he waits while I grab a sweater and then falls into step beside me. "Before you ask, I don't know anything more than I did the last time we talked."

"Fair enough," he says, but there's something on his mind.

"What?" I ask.

"I do." Okay, words I'd like to hear from him someday in another context. "Know more than the last time we talked, that is."

"And you're telling me because…?" I ask, calling Maggie out of Eleanor Heinis's bushes and wondering if she'd be able to tell Maggie's poop from Samian's. Maybe if I'm lucky Maggie will just pee so I won't have to clean it up while Drew shakes his head at me for taking the dog in the first place.

He says he didn't say I'd be interested. He's the second man in my life to play me like a fiddle and I don't like it much better this time around.

"Noose is tightening," he says, picking up a stick and tossing it like Maggie is going to run and catch it. He's got a few things to learn about women, I think.

Maggie, a disgrace to her gender, runs after the damn stick.

"Seems half the South Shore was paying off *your friend Joe*," he says. "The more we investigate this guy, the more dirt we turn up—literally as well as figuratively."

I remind him we knew he was on the take already. He tells me that we only *suspected* he was a blackmailer until yesterday.

"And now we know?" I ask, then want to kick myself for using *we* when Drew smiles.

"Know who, know what, know why," he says.

"Gonna arrest someone?" I ask, and there's this trembling in my chest when I do.

"Unlike being the blackmailer, there's no law against being a blackmail victim," he says, studying the horizon.

"But it's a motive," I say as we head back toward the house.

"It's a motive," Drew agrees.

"Whose?" I ask after we are silent for a while. Drew looks me dead in the face, and I don't want him to answer.

"Evidence or supposition?" I ask.

"Irrefutable," he tells me.

"Ha," is as clever as I can get. "Far be it from me to get in front of the train you're using to railroad this nameless person, but did you know that Madison Watts and Joe Greco had a torrid affair back before she married Nick?"

I can see from his expression that this is news.

I consider telling him that I strongly suspect that Madison is pregnant, but decide not to, I think because I don't want him to have sympathy for any suspect who might take his mind off Howard for five minutes.

"Did you find the gun?" I ask, skipping to means.

Someone forgot to put a hold on the Dumpsters and they were picked up that afternoon, he tells me.

"Don't they usually get the Dumpsters at, like, 4:00 a.m. from businesses?" I ask.

"Not when someone's ordered a special pickup," he tells me, and gives me that "good girl" look, but resists saying it because he knows how much I hate it when he patronizes me.

"Trace the call?" I ask. He tells me the phone records indicate a throwaway cell phone, one of those pay-in-advance jobs. Harder to track down, but not impossible. They are working on it.

I suggest that someone could buy a phone in someone else's name. It's a stupid thing to say because it looks like I know whose phone it was, and whose phone would I know but Howard's?

"I'm just saying," I say, opening my screen door and realizing that for the zillionth time I've left the door open while I'm out with Maggie.

Drew gives me his usual offhanded "be careful" and heads for his car while I stand just inside my house listening. Are those footsteps? Or just my imagination? Probably my ex-husband robbing me blind, I tell myself.

Drew is pulling out of the driveway when I see an enormous butcher's knife sticking straight out of my kitchen counter. I take two steps toward the kitchen, see a note, pierced by the knife's blade, waffling in the breeze. And I hear what could be my den door slam.

I let loose one of those shrieks that would wake the dead, and I go flying out of my house and into the street to catch Drew before he's gone.

Brakes squeal and I feel the impact as though it's happening to someone else. Only it's me who's suddenly lying on the pavement listening to Drew call for an ambulance. And I hear myself telling him that I'm all right.

"What the hell were you doing?" he asks me, and he's grasping my arms just a little too tight. "I could have killed you. Don't you know that?"

My elbow is bleeding and my shoulder hurts like hell. Still I tell him again that I'm all right.

"What about your head?" He stares at my pupils and seems satisfied. He cancels the call for the ambulance and tells the dispatcher he'll take me to the emergency room himself. "Can you get up?" He puts a hand under my bloody elbow and I yelp.

"Someone was in the house," I tell him. "I heard a noise—"

He asks what kind of a noise, like I'm making it up so he won't be so furious with me.

"—a door slammed. And there's a note in my kitchen." I pause, and I know he thinks it's no big deal, that Bobbie probably left it for me or something. "And it's stuck in the counter with a knife."

Now I've got his attention. He wants to know why I didn't say that to begin with.

I tell him maybe because I'd just been hit by a car.

He wants to go in the house—I can see it. But he doesn't want to leave me out here alone. And he doesn't want me to get up just yet and he doesn't want me in the house, either.

Of course, I could just be projecting.

He asks if Bobbie is home. I surmise not, since her car isn't in her driveway, so he asks me for her cell phone number and dials it. He explains to her how I've had a little accident—or more accurately, *that* I've had one. I don't think he wants the tongue lashing he'd get from her about hitting me. He says he's going to have a patrol car wait for the kids and that he doesn't want them to go into the house. Can she come home and wait for them, as well?

I hear Bobbie ask if I'm all right and demand to speak with me. After assuring her that I'm fine, I ask her to please do as Drew says.

She says I'm scaring the stuffing out of her and all I can say is, "Me too."

CHAPTER 9

Design Tip of the Day
"Sometimes it's necessary or desirable to split a room into two or more spaces. This is where room dividers come in handy. The trick is to make the dividers interesting themselves by using screens that hold pictures, glass blocks, two-sided bookcases. I always advise against curtains, unless you're doing the sixties look and can get away with beaded ones. Avoid cloth ones at all costs."

—TipsFromTeddi.com

The hospital appears very unimpressed with my situation until Drew, agitated, flashes his badge. Suddenly my injuries seem to merit some attention, especially when it is clear that I'm not the detective's wife, but his victim.

The nurses at the desk in triage want to know if I was running away when the accident occurred. I tell them I was actually chasing the cop. One nurse takes a look at Drew and says she understands. If she wasn't married, she'd chase him, too.

Out of the corner of my eye, I see Drew preen.

"Get over yourself," I tell him. "She doesn't know you as well as I do."

"She gets testy whenever I run her over," Drew explains to the other nurse, who has no sense of humor and asks if this has happened before.

Drew says that he's wanted to several times, but that this is the first time he's actually done it, and then he pats my shoulder and I gasp.

"Shit," he says, crouching beside the chair in which I'm sitting and gently stroking my thigh. "She needs to see a doctor. She needs the shoulder x-rayed, along with her arm. She needs some pain medication and—"

"—he needs a sedative," I finish for him.

"What he needs is to calm down," the nurse tells him before asking me, for the second time, for my insurance card.

"You ran into the car," he tells me while I try to fish one-handed through my purse for the card the nurse is demanding. "Like a deer, smack into the path of the car."

He grabs my purse out of my hands and starts rummaging through it, taking out half-eaten candy bars, tampons with their paper covers falling off and finally my wallet. As he replaces the tampons, looking fairly disgusted at their condition, he says something about how it's no wonder I'm testy.

"Maybe it's because I freakin' got run over," I say. "Some people use their rearview mirrors when backing up," I add.

"Some people—" he starts, but the nurse, who's had

enough of us, tells us to go through the emergency room doors and someone will show me where to wait for the doctor.

I start to tell Drew that he doesn't have to accompany me, but his look cuts me off. Before I get any ideas that he cares about me, he says that he feels responsible, and that he wants to make sure I accurately tell the doctor what happened.

"How I ran into the path of the car," I agree, making it sound like we've concocted the story instead of that it's simply the truth.

I am sitting in a cloth cubicle on a gurney in a hospital gown that Drew helped me into, feeling foolish, tired and exposed. Every now and then someone pokes his or her head in and asks how I'm doing, checks my vitals, and disappears with the promise that the doctor will be in shortly. Drew makes jokes about how short the doctor will be when he finally comes in.

Eventually, his patience exhausted, he goes searching for a nurse, or a doctor, or maybe a shot of scotch. After he's gone, I lie back—carefully, because my shoulder feels like I've been hit by a...

Oh, yeah. I have been.

My elbow is bleeding. It's not bad enough to be scary, like I'm going to bleed to death before they see to me, but it's bad enough to sting like hell. I try to close my eyes, only I keep hearing footsteps back and forth and nearer and farther and I can't help watching the floor beneath the curtain like I'm checking for vacancies in a ladies' room.

White rubber soles. Shoes covered in surgical caps. Sneakers. High heels Bobbie would approve of. More white rubber soles. Flip-flops. Black oxfords which stop outside my cubicle. They face away from my curtain. Pocket change jingles.

The shoes turn and suddenly there is a hand pulling the curtain back. A hand with two fingers missing. A face pokes in through the opening where one curtain meets another.

A familiar face. One I saw only a couple of days ago at Tony's and, I guess, before that at the train station.

"You okay?" he asks.

I nod that I am.

"You're sure?" he asks, as Drew comes up behind him and inquires whether there is anything he can do for the man. Okay, he asks him what the hell he thinks he's doing in here.

The man shrugs his shoulder and says something about being in the wrong room, maybe even the wrong hospital. And then behind him a pretty young woman asks if maybe the party might be over so that she can see the patient now?

"You the doc?" the man asks, clearly surprised, but willing to take her word for it if she says she is. Which she does. "Mr. D'Guisseppe would appreciate your taking good care of her," he says, gesturing in my direction.

She says she takes good care of all her patients, but before she even gets out the whole thought, Carmine's friend is gone and she's staring at a one-hundred-dollar bill in her hand.

"You do collect 'em," Drew says to me, shaking his head. "Every walk of life."

"Magnetic personality," I say, and then let out an ungodly screech as the doctor examines my shoulder.

She wants it x-rayed, she wants the cut on my elbow flushed out, she wants Drew to leave the room. I could tell her that with Drew, you rarely get what you want, but I let her learn for herself when he flashes his badge, explains there was a car involved, possible charges, blah, blah, blah.

Which is to say that she loses interest quickly in his explanation and my ailments.

They wheel me into the hallway to make room for a woman they think may be having a stroke and leave me there.

Hours later, Drew escorts me into the house. I look like an escapee from the remake of *The Mummy*, and Alyssa immediately begins to cry when she sees me. Dana is visibly shaken and insists on bringing me a cup of tea, which is weird because I don't drink tea. I let her, because I can see that she needs to do something for me. Bobbie helps her, as though it takes two people to turn a burner on under a kettle and throw a teabag in a cup.

Jesse paces. I can see he's angry in the same way that his father used to be angry when the kids or I got hurt—*this should have been preventable. I should have prevented it.*

"Tell me again what happened," he says, sounding too much like Rio for comfort.

"Maggie got loose and ran into the street," I say, just as we have rehearsed on the way home. "I stupidly ran out after her and a car clipped me. I'm fine. I just feel like an idiot for not being more careful. I'd punish any of you within an inch of your life if you did such a stupid thing."

Jesse wants to know if it was as simple as I say, then why was a detective waiting in the house when they got home from school? Drew says it's because I have friends in high places, but Jesse isn't buying it. His mother didn't raise any dumb children, I guess.

"What happened to the kitchen counter?" he wants to know. I pretend I don't know what he's talking about but Bobbie shakes her head like the jig is up.

"Oh, that," I say. Everyone waits.

Finally Drew says that he was showing off, making me some lunch, and the knife got away. It is so clear that no one believes him that he just shrugs and shoots me a look that says, *I tried.*

Jesse asks if his father did it. I tell him that of course he didn't, but I'm not sure what else to say, so I start complaining that my shoulder really hurts and Drew suggests that I get into bed and he helps me up the stairs. He sits me down on the edge of the bed and slips off my shoes.

"Is it really bad?" he asks me and I tell him that it just aches. "You wanna get out of your clothes?" he offers, pretending to mean more than just helping me out. When

I stand like an idiot just staring at him, he offers to get Bobbie or Dana.

Too tired and achey to even try getting undressed, I tell him to just pull back the covers and when he does, I lie down on the bed. I don't think it really hits me until now, but I could have gotten killed this morning—by whomever was in the house or by Drew's car.

When I start shaking, Drew pulls the covers up to my chin and tucks them gently around me. "You're all right," he says, and he lies down on top of the blanket without shaking the bed at all.

Bobbie appears at the doorway and offers to take the kids to her house for the evening. "Then we can all come back and sleep here so you won't be alone," she offers.

Drew assures her I won't be alone, ignores Bobbie's little gasp, and goes on to thank her for taking the kids. I give in to the muscle relaxers they gave me at the hospital and shut my eyes for five minutes.

When I wake up it's dark and the clock reads 3:17. Drew is sitting in a chair by the window, half dozing. I call his name.

"I was hoping you'd snore," he says. When I don't answer he explains I wouldn't look so cute and vulnerable if I was snoring loudly. I tell him he can lie down on the bed if he wants to, but he says he'd better not.

"I'm on duty," he says.

"Like you can't have a drink?"

He smiles at me. "Yeah, like that."

I tell him no one's offering him a drink or anything

else. He says something about a drunk not going into a bar if he knows what's good for him. I'd feel irresistible if there wasn't drool on my pillow and I wasn't still in my shirt with the sleeve cut off. And if my jeans weren't unzipped just to make me more comfortable.

"What did the note say?" I ask.

"Exactly what you'd want it to say," he tells me, coming over to sit on the edge of the bed. I try to scoot over a little, but it hurts too much. He offers me another dose of medication and I nod, asking him to first tell me what it said.

"The detective read it to me over the phone. It said you should stay out of it," he says, putting the pill on my tongue and helping me with the glass of water. "Just a friendly warning."

I ask if he thinks my *friend* is Carmine D'Guisseppe.

"You've got to admit, you've got a lot of 'friends,'" he says, putting quotes around the word.

"Yeah, everybody loves me but you," I say.

He tells me the medicine is talking and I should go to sleep.

"It hurts," I tell him. He offers to get me an ice pack. "No. What you did. Dropping out of my life like that. It hurts."

I think he says that it hurts him, too. "You're better off this way," he says, and he adjusts the pillows behind my head and under my arm and he pulls the blanket up to my chin.

"How many women have you said that to, I wonder."

He kisses me lightly on my forehead as I fight the fog

of the medicine. "Go back to sleep, Teddi," he tells me again.

"But I need to know," I whisper as he brings his chair closer to the bed.

"None, okay?" he says as he looks out the window before sitting down beside me.

"*None* left the note? Who's *None*? Why is he warning me?" I ask, only it comes out slurred and Drew claims that there's nothing for me to worry about with him there. That I'm safe with him there.

"That's what I'm worried about," I tell him, and I hear his low chuckle just before I drift back off to sleep.

After making sure I am all right, Drew takes off the next morning, assuring me he's already checked on the kids and watched Bobbie put them on the bus. He says she's planning on checking in on me from time to time and that he's got to get to the precinct. He tells me the house is being watched, adds "by the good guys," and I wave him away, fall back to sleep and am awakened by the phone somewhere around noon.

While I read a note Bobbie's left on my nightstand that says to call if I need anything and tells me the muffin she's left is full of powerful antioxidants that will help me heal faster, Helene tells me she has two customers who are interested in hiring me.

She's never funneled clients my way before and I am suspicious, but thankful, what with Mrs. Goldberg canceling and another client postponing. And maybe still a trifle groggy, too. She suggests we go to lunch and I tell her that I'm a little under the weather. Why I don't tell her the whole truth I'm not sure.

Anyway, she is full of concern and insists she'll bring lunch to me. Three quarters of an hour later, I'm slowly, painfully making my way to the door in yesterday's clothes to find her standing there, a policeman beside her.

Her mouth drops open at the sight of me and she sputters about why the police have stopped her and what's happened to me all in the same breath.

"She's a friend," I tell the uniformed officer. "It's all right."

I tell Helene there have been a number of robberies in the neighborhood and the police are just being vigilant. She seems to buy it.

"And you? What in God's name happened to you?" she asks as Maggie and I let her in. I give her the same story I gave the kids and she glares at Maggie, who looks properly contrite. Then Helene proceeds to give me a lecture on "better the dog than me," which doesn't stop until I begin to sway.

Solicitously, she helps me into the kitchen and sits me down at the table, ordering Maggie to a corner while I answer the phone and assure Bobbie that yes, I'm all right and she needn't come over.

"Oh, you *are* good," Helene says as she glances around the kitchen while pulling containers of prepared food from Ben's Delicatessen.

I murmur my thanks and pretend not to be annoyed that all this time she's been selling stuff to me she's thought I didn't know my Adams from my Eakins.

"Sandwiches. Pastrami or turkey?" she asks me with one in each hand. "Soup. Matzoh ball or chicken? And I've got potato salad, coleslaw and those fabulous pickles they have."

When talking about the Victorians' philosophy of decorating, the saying goes that for them, "too much was not enough." Well, the same can be said of Long Islanders and food. Portions are mammoth, choices are infinite, and status depends on how far over the top you go.

In a restaurant you have to order not one, but several appetizers—for the table, like it's another diner, and it's very hungry, at that. You need bottled still water and wine, not to mention Pellegrino and Perrier. It's always a good idea to order an extra entrée because someone might not like what they ordered, and don't worry, everyone will have a little.

And desserts? How about one of everything and we'll all share?

The only thing is, I don't think you're supposed to actually eat the stuff, because how could you do that and stay as rail thin as the women in the best restaurants always are? I know there's a *Long Island Rule* in there somewhere, I'm just not sure what it is. Maybe it goes back to the days when your bubbe claimed that people were starving in the old country. Maybe we're all providing for them.

At any rate, I thank Helene and choose just the soup, figuring that I can leave the rest for Jesse and the girls to devour after school. She says I need to eat to keep up my strength, unwraps the pastrami sandwich for me and puts it on a paper plate she unearths from the depths of the bag. I pull a small corner off a slice of pastrami and discreetly feed it to poor, abused Maggie under the table.

After Helene gets herself settled, she makes it clear she's got something on her mind. I sigh wearily and feign exhaustion, hoping she will just go away, but she doesn't.

"A detective came to see me this morning," she says and my eyes snap open. "He wanted to know about Howard."

"What about him?" I ask.

"You were the one who figured out who killed Elise Meyers," she reminds me. "I think it's your duty to help Howard. I think he's being framed."

I tell her she's being ridiculous, that he had absolutely nothing to do with Joe Greco's murder and the police know it. But there's something about the way she looks at me, something that says she thinks I'm being coy. And that I can be honest because she knows as much as I do.

Only the truth is that she must know more than I do. And, true to form, I can't help myself.

"Oh," I say, nodding solemnly. "There is *that*."

Does she know I'm fishing? And is this one of those "enough rope to hang myself" things, which in this case would be more like "enough line to hook myself"?

Desperately I add, "I mean, because of the restaurant and all…"

"Exactly. Because of Nick," she says, then quickly adds, "and Madison."

"Of course," I agree, though I don't know to what. I just know that every time someone mentions Nick, everyone seems to rush to add *and Madison*.

"I told him it was a bad idea," she says. "But would he listen to me? Of course not."

I ask why she thought it was a bad idea, playing with my sandwich rather than looking at Helene, who might recognize my confusion for what it is.

"Oh, only because of how it looks," she says, like how can I be so stupid?

"Oh, really," I say in my pish-posh voice. "No one would ever think—" Thankfully, she interrupts me, which is a good thing because I have no idea where I was going with the rest of that thought.

"Puh..lease! He could lose his job," she says as she tears a napkin to shreds. "I warned him, but he had to do it."

"His job?" I ask. So then, *not his freedom, not his life*.

"Well," she starts, and I think that now I'm going to find out what she's talking about. Only the doorbell rings and Helene clams up like a spring hinge. I struggle to get to my feet and she waves me back and says she'll get it.

"Glad you decided not to show up this morning," Mark says as he strolls into my kitchen. "Would have been nice, though, if you'd told me." Of course then he bothers to look at me and his face goes white.

"I'm all right," I say, but he isn't buying it.

"I'll kill him," he says. "If the police don't get him, I will. I swear it."

Helene is—naturally—jumping to the wrong conclusion. Well, after Mark has already jumped first. I explain that Mark is my carpenter and that we were working on the renovations to The Steak-Out before the accident. But Mark says that this was no accident.

I swear to him that it was. I tell him the story about running after Maggie, who seems so offended at being handed the blame time after time that she comes out from under the table, farts, and with a glare at all of us, leaves the room.

"And this was what?" Mark asks. "A coincidence? I don't believe in coincidences."

"Well, it was," I assure him. When he asks me how I can be so sure, I have to weigh telling him the truth against having him go off after Carmine D'Guisseppe. "I know who hit me."

Speak of the devil, I say under my breath when there's a knock on my screen door. But it's not Drew. It's my parents, instead. I don't know if I'm relieved or not. When you live in Grand Central Station, does it matter which train comes barreling at you on its way to derail?

"Shouldn't you be in bed?" my father asks, while my mother sizes up Mark and then looks at Helene with contempt.

"You look like hell," my mother says when she finally gets around to me.

I make introductions all around, and my mother makes a face at Helene's offering and tells her that Ben's has gone downhill. This, of course, is news to my father, who lives on Ben's corned beef—lean because of his heart. She tells Mark she needs new closets and he looks at me as if to ask whether I want him to drop everything and accommodate her.

"We'll talk about it later, Mom," I tell her.

Helene seems to realize that our conversation is over and heads for the door. Mark sees her out while my father picks at my sandwich and my mother reminds him he has high cholesterol and that my sandwich will kill him.

"You're really all right?" Mark asks me when he comes back into the kitchen. "And you're sure that Carmine D'Guisseppe's got nothing to do with this little accident?"

The color drains from my father's face, while my mother takes only a heartbeat to climb onto her high horse.

"Oh, sure. A big, important man like Carmine D'Guisseppe goes around mowing down innocent house-wives—" She stops and considers. "I suppose you're not a housewife anymore, now that you aren't married," she adds.

"Big, important man," my father huffs. "Lousy mafia punk, you mean. Should have been arrested years ago for that Brooklyn thing." His voice peters out.

"What are you if you're not a housewife?" my mother asks me, ignoring my father, who is now mumbling to himself.

"I'm a decorator, Mom. Remember?" I say. "And since I was never married to my house…"

"No, you were married to an idiot, but I thought you'd

rather be called a housewife than an *idiot's wife*," my mother says.

I should have known I wouldn't win.

"You should be in bed," my father says, and with the Percocet buzz, I have to agree with him.

He offers to help me up the stairs.

"Why don't you help her?" my mother asks Mark. "You're bigger and stronger and younger than he is."

I could swear Mark's cheeks redden slightly, despite the way he's always making passes, giving everything a sexual connotation, and he says that of course, he'd be happy to help me into bed.

And yeah, then my cheeks redden, too, and we both look guilty as hell about nothing.

Upstairs, Mark gives me one of my pain pills from my nightstand and then helps me take off my shoes. He asks if I want help with anything else, feigning interest and oozing concern. I tell him that Bobbie will come by later and help me change out of my clothes and stuff.

"I could do that," he offers, and his Adam's apple bobs. "I mean, completely platonically. I'm not, like, coming on to you or anything. I mean, not now, since—"

"And with my parents downstairs," I add, because watching him be flustered and awkward after all the flirting he's done is irresistible.

"Right," he says. "Not that I'm not totally interested, Gorgeous, but I like my partners able to at least stand up before I knock them off their feet."

I smile, but it's hard to banter when you feel like hell.

And then he holds the covers for me and I slide under them and he tucks them up to my chin.

"Don't go up there, Marty," I hear my mother yell at my father. "Maybe he'll take pity on her and she'll get lucky."

CHAPTER 10

Design Tip of the Day
"Remember that variety is the spice of life, even in collections. They should always include pieces of like scale, but different shapes or colors, from subtle (all the same size rectangular frames with different matting sizes), to less so (a collection of blue vases in round, cylindrical, square). Always something to unify them (another choice would be items that perform the same function: teapots, ice-cream scoops, etc.) and something to distinguish them (otherwise your collection becomes the stock shelf at Macy's)."

—TipsFromTeddi.com

Jesse once asked me why life was such a circle. "Why can't it be more like an oval?" he said.

Today I know what he means. Despite the accident and the fact that three days later I still feel like hell, I'm chasing my tail like Dana's hamster on a bad day, what with bat mitzvah arrangements, courting new customers courtesy of Helene, drawing up still more plans for The

Steak-Out and for Madison on Park and investigating a murder that's none of my business.

Because, as they say, life—or the show—must go on.

Could somebody please shoot *they*?

Anyhow, when the phone rings and caller ID tells me it's Rio, I wish, like Jesse, that I could get off the merry-go-round.

"What?" And no, he doesn't deserve more courtesy than that.

I hear a baby crying in the background and Rio's voice is tense, like one more cry and he'll be on his way up to the cabin he shares with his pals in Neversink, where he claimed to be when he broke in to the house he used to share with me. Amazing how just the tone of his voice can bring me right back to that night in the kitchen when I shot him with his own paint gun.

"Thought you'd want to know I got the whole parking lot thing in the bag," he says to me, and then yells at Marion to quiet "the kid."

"Babies cry, Mario," I remind him. "In fact, you were better at comforting Lys than I was."

He tells me he can't exactly comfort "the kid" and talk to me at the same time, now can he?

I ask if she doesn't have a name.

"Of course she's got a name," he tells me. He doesn't tell me what it is.

"And?"

"And what?" he says. "I have to run Marion's baby's name by you? Like you care?"

To be honest, I didn't care until this minute. Now I care a whole lot because there is a reason he isn't telling me. I demand to know her name.

"Elisa. Marion picked it out. It's nice, huh?" he says.

I am flabbergasted. "Elisa? You have a daughter named Alyssa, who feels she's been replaced as your little girl by this baby, and you name her Elisa?"

"Hey, back off. Look at it this way," Rio says. "It's a compliment. Isn't that what you're always telling the kids when someone copies them? That's it's flattery or something?"

I tell him he will have to change the baby's name. He asks who I think I am.

"I think I'm the mother of your first three children," I tell him. "And I—"

"I love it when you do the mother bear thing," he says, and his voice gets gooey. There was a time that voice made me go gooey, too.

"It's a tiger, not a bear," I tell him. "And you haven't seen my claws in a long time, Mario Gallo. The last time I showed them to you we were in a lawyer's office."

He reminds me that we wouldn't be having this conversation but for my insistence that he stay with Marion to prove to the kids that he hadn't left them, but me.

I tell him he doesn't want to go down that road, thank him for taking care of the parking lot issue and tell him to let us know the baby's name when they choose a new one.

"Wait'll you see her," my ex-husband says. "She looks just like Lys did when we brought her home. You think Dana remembers Lys as a baby?"

I tell him I don't know, because this whole baby thing hurts. It's like Rio has a new life and he's left me holding the bag in the old one.

"We'll see at the bat mitzvah," he says and I can hear the baby's crying getting louder. "Don't give her to me, I'm on the freakin' phone," I hear him tell Marion.

"You're not bringing her to the bat mitzvah," I say, but I don't think he hears me because there is an ear-piercing wail at the other end of the line.

"I gotta go," Rio says while I'm shouting at him that I don't want that woman or her baby at Dana's bat mitzvah.

I don't think he hears a word I'm saying.

"Rio, do you hear me?" I shout.

"The whole neighborhood hears you," Drew Scoones says as he saunters into my kitchen.

"Don't you ever knock? You're a cop—haven't you heard of breaking and entering, or trespassing or something?" I ask as I slam the phone down on my old life.

He tells me he's not the one I'm mad at. Maybe not, but he's handy. And he's in the path of the runoff. Even Maggie has more smarts than to get in my way now. She's quivering under the table.

"Don't you work? Shouldn't you be out somewhere detecting?" I ask.

He smiles at me, cool and calm, which makes me feel like a harridan, fuming all the more.

"What do you want?" I ask. "And stop smirking."

He doesn't even try. "Bad day?" he asks.

I don't bother answering. I just stare.

"Well, Hal's waiting for me, so I guess I'll just go *detect*," he says, strolling toward the door. "Found the gun, by the way."

"What do I care?" I respond.

"Right. What do you care?" he says and pushes open the screen door. "And another thing you don't care about—Joe Greco never lived in Boston."

"Really," I say, pretending it makes no difference to me while I wipe down the counters with a dry sponge that isn't doing anything.

He confirms that Boston is where Madison Watts said they had their affair.

"So?"

"So no affair, no grounds for blackmail."

He lets the screen door slam with a slap behind him. "Maybe she was lying about the place," I shout out the door to his back. "Maybe she was covering up the fact that she was already married."

He doesn't bother to turn around. "Could be," he says as he strolls down my walk. "Of course, there's the fact that Joe Greco was in jail when Madison Watts was slinging hash in Lawrence, Mass."

"Could have been earlier, or later," I say. "Or somewhere else."

"Could have been a lie," he says back.

I ask why she would lie about that. What would she have to gain, tying herself to Joe Greco?

"Maybe she's covering for Nick, just like your buddy Howard," he suggests.

"Howard doesn't lie," I say.

"Everybody lies, Teddi," he tells me. And then, as if to prove it, he says he'll call.

But when the phone rings it isn't Drew, it's Howard, offering to come cook for us since my arm is still out of commission. I admit that I could use the other hand to dial up a pizza, but Howard insists, and forty-five minutes later (not long enough for me to look really good, but at least enough time to post a new tip and manage not to look like something the dog tried to bury) he is at my door with bags of food and supplies.

I offer to help with my good hand, but he refuses, calls out to Dana to come help, and tells her, when she shows up with attitude, that it will be fun.

Dana offers up Jesse or Alyssa, but Howard says he needs adult help, which works. Dana stands a little taller and says, "Whatever," which from her, these days, constitutes enthusiasm.

Howard insists that I sit while he and Dana unpack the bags. As they do, Dana announces her displeasure at each item. Maggie May loses interest when it's clear that nothing is for her and heads for the stairs to pester my other two.

"I don't eat anything with gills," Dana tells Howard. "That means fish or mushrooms."

Naturally, Howard is holding some weird mushrooms and Dana has dropped a package of hake on the counter. He tells her if she helps him cook he will make her sweet potato fries instead of the mushrooms and she can have some of the hot dogs he brought for Alyssa. Clearly the implication is that the fries and dogs were for the "kids" and she was one of the adults.

"I might try some of the fish," she says. "If it's mild."

Howard assures her that the fish will be divine, and the mushrooms out of this world.

"Mushrooms can kill you," she tells him. "Which is only fair, since people kill food, but I'm not willing to pay for everyone's sins."

Howard, who clearly would have made the perfect nerdy biology teacher, launches into a lecture on how to tell deadly mushrooms from harmless ones. He tells her which ones cause kidney failure, which ones cause disorientation, hallucinations, and so forth, until neither one of us wants to risk eating his offering.

"These Agaricus campestris," he assures us, "are perfectly harmless."

"We're—"

"Not allergic," Howard says before we can claim it. "I've taken you out to too many dinners to fall for that, Teddi."

"Not her," Dana says. "Me. And Jesse and Alyssa. We got it from our dad."

"Lying?" Howard says. "I'm sure you did."

I tell him that was uncalled for and he apologizes reluctantly. "I went to a lot of trouble," he explains, "to plan this meal."

Dana tells him he can cook it himself. "I'm calling my Dad to bring me pizza," she says and storms upstairs.

"Her chances of that happening are slim to none," I say after she's left the room. "Her dad doesn't have a car or enough money to feed his new family, let alone his old one. If that baby's not on breast milk it's in big trouble." But I don't insist that Dana come down and accept Howard's apology because first off, he was out of line. And second, if those mushrooms are tainted, I don't want the kids to die.

Not that I think for a second that Howard...

"I expected more from her, that's all," Howard says, washing the mushrooms in my sink.

I pull out a bottle of white wine from the fridge and put it beside the sink for him to open. "That she'd be disloyal to her father? That's not fair, Howard."

He sighs, like he needs to consider whether or not it is. "Okay," he says as he pulls the foil away from the cork. "But there are those people who deserve your loyalty and those who don't."

I tell him that I think one's own father probably fits that bill as I pull a couple of glasses from the cupboard.

He contends that some do and some don't. "A person ought to have to earn your love and your fidelity. I wouldn't lie for my father, I can tell you that."

"I would," I say easily. Not that I expect I'd ever have to, which makes it all the easier. And I'd lie for the sake of the kids.

As he pours me a glass of Chablis, he tells me children don't count. In fact, blood relatives shouldn't count. "Is there anyone else you'd lie for?" he asks me.

"Bobbie," I say without even needing to think. "Are we talking white lies, big lies, court of law lies, here?"

Howard pours himself a glass and takes a long, slow swallow.

"Big," he finally says, going back to cleaning the mushrooms.

"What about you?" I ask as he pulls out a black canvas roll with a silver logo on it and unties the ribbon holding it closed. Unrolling it, there is knife after knife, each sheathed in its own channel, each with its own purpose. The knives are beautiful, with copper-weighted ends and a very distinctive textured grip creating dots all over their handles.

They look ominously familiar.

"Howard?" I ask, hoping he'll answer the question, but he is fingering the empty slot between the sharpening stick and the biggest knife.

I swallow hard and ask if anything's wrong.

"No," he says. "I just seem to have misplaced a knife."

In my kitchen counter?

"I can't imagine where it is."

Try the police station.

I tell him I'm sure he can replace it and he answers that the knives are very expensive, he'll have to special order it and there'll probably be a wait because they aren't mass-produced. And that he doesn't want Nick to know he's lost one. They were a gift.

"These aren't your *run-over-to-Fortunoff-and-pick-up-a-couple* sort of knives," he assures me, pulling a long, thin knife out of its shield and testing its edge against his finger.

He reaches for the mushrooms.

"I hope you're hungry," he says, his look murderous.

I don't have the guts to tell him I've kind of lost my appetite.

CHAPTER 11

Design Tip of the Day
"While nostalgia definitely has its place in decorating, and your grandmother's candelabra most certainly deserves a place of honor on your dining room table, other things are perhaps better off jettisoned, let go of, relegated to closed boxes (a collection of them?), scrapbooks, or simply a carton in the attic, in trust for some future generation (when the style returns!)."

—TipsFromTeddi.com

David calls to tell me when he and Issy are due in. He hasn't been able to reach my parents with the information because no one answers their cell phones.

"They're at the day spa," I tell him. "They don't let you keep your phones on in there."

David thinks I'm joking. He can't believe my father is at a spa. I tell him there's a masseuse there who reminds him of Angelina, who used to be our housekeeper until my mother found out—apparently long after my brother did—that the woman was buttering more than just my father's toast.

And then *she* was toast. Out on her keister. Goodbye.

I'd have felt sorrier for Angelina if I hadn't felt so betrayed. Angelina had been like a mother to me, and now I couldn't turn to her for solace. Not to mention that the whole thing came out at the same time that Rio was trying to drive me crazy. One minute it was my parents' household coming apart and the next minute it was mine.

Of course, David was long gone by then, lounging on the same beach my parents had sent him to as a present for completing his Harvard MBA. I think staying in the Bahamas instead of coming back to work at Bayer Furniture might have been David's way of punishing my father for his transgression (witnessed by David at the tender age of ten), but maybe he just liked the sun and the sand.

"I'd never go to a spa," David tells me. He has spent a lifetime insisting he is nothing like our father.

"Never say never," is about all I can think of for an answer.

"All those years he mocked Mom for pampering herself and here he is, getting what, a facial?"

I'm not a big one for jumping on the *Dump on Dad* bandwagon, but I'm also not looking to fight with my brother now that we're finally talking to each other after all these years of him choosing to be estranged from the whole family. I tell him I think Dad's probably getting a massage, and that I'm sure he only went at Mom's urging. "She doesn't like to go places alone anymore," I tell him.

He says I could have gone with her.

"One of us wouldn't have come out alive," I tell him and he laughs.

"So, how are you doing with the plans?" he asks me now. He says that my mother has told him about Sheldon's of Great Neck.

I give him the oh, things are going great line, but he doesn't buy it.

"Mom says your boyfriend arranged for this other place."

I tell him Mom seems to think I have boyfriends hanging from the chandeliers and that I'm just too stubborn to cut any of them down and marry them. "Howard's just a friend."

He tells me that he remembers saying the same thing about Issy, who is now his wife. I promise to eat my words if Howard becomes my wife and he gives up the good fight.

I agree to pick him up at the airport, throwing in that I can fit it in between picking up the goody bag supplies (I'm doing I Went To Dana's Bat Mitzvah T-shirts in decorated denim backpacks with lots of candy and stuff in them) and picking up Dana's dress from the dressmaker where I took it to be taken in. Everything was already ordered and while I've had to alter just about every other aspect of the bat mitzvah, at least Dana will be happy with them, I hope. I'm wishing David will say that he can get to my mother's himself, but he doesn't.

Instead he tells me about how finding the right person

isn't easy. Don't you just love advice from someone married less time than you were, who thinks he knows all the answers? Then he tells me that marriage takes work (he's been working at it three years now, so he's an expert compared to my parents and to me). "On top of all that," he says, "do you have any idea how hard it is to raise sane kids in this world?" Well, assuming that he thinks he is sane, it doesn't necessarily take sane parents to produce sane kids. Apparently, it doesn't even have to be on their minds.

On and on he rambles, telling me that he's happy, hoping that I am.

I manage not to tell him he's got to be kidding.

"They won't play," I tell Bobbie about the bat mitzvah band as we make mockups of Madison on Park on the computer, changing colors and rearranging tables on this fabulous program I haven't quite mastered yet. I'll get it, I'm sure, but in the meantime it's like the floating tea party in *Mary Poppins*—I can't seem to ground the tables.

"They can't just back out. They have a contract," she says as we both shake our heads at each of a dozen shades of green.

"I told them," I say, going back to the purple and red theme that Madison liked. "You know what their answer was? 'You want angry, resentful musicians playing under duress?'"

Bobbie adds a chartreuse pillow to the banquette. It looks smashing. "What is their problem?" she asks.

I try chartreuse napkins, but they are too much, so I just edge the red napkins with it and it's just right. I tell her the band's problem is the parking lot. Apparently they have an image to uphold. "They say they have their reputation to maintain. Not one thing has gone right about this bat mitzvah. It's like it's a sign, or a punishment, or something."

I go through the litany, for the zillionth time, of all that has gone wrong with this bat mitzvah since Rio and I started planning it three years ago. Of course, *Rio and I* was the first thing that went wrong.

She sympathizes, she strokes, she loses interest.

"Fine, be blasé," I say. "But know this. I still haven't even gotten shoes for it."

This elicits a greater response than did the burning down of Sheldon's of Great Neck.

"Go!" she shouts at me, reminding me that it's an outdoor affair, which calls for sandals. "No stockings. We'll spray your legs with that tan stuff."

I tell her I wish I could go, but there's all this work to do. I say this sadly, with a sigh, like there's nothing to be done about it but to keep working and go to the bat mitzvah in, oh, I don't know, sneakers?

"I can finish up here," she offers quickly, sending me on my way. "And if you find a band at DSW, see if they count toward your rewards certificates."

The reason women love shoes is that you can't really look bad in them, unless you have that disease that swells

your legs over your ankle straps. If that's the case, I'd recommend very long skirts. But otherwise, all they can do
is possibly hurt, which is a judgment call—do you love
them enough to bear the pain? Can you wear them somewhere you'll just be sitting?

Jeans can be too tight.

Bathing suits—don't even go there.

But shoes? You never need to diet for shoes.

Bobbie helped me pick out my dress, and it's black and
white with a full skirt and fitted, strapless bodice and
looks very retro. She's told me exactly what shoes to look
for. Black patent high-heeled sandals with either white
dots or white piping. Very thin-soled—*limousine shoes*,
she calls them. Perfect. I can be driven around the
parking lot. Or we could rent limos for everyone to eat
their lunch in. A theme—why didn't I think of that
sooner?

"What's so funny?" someone asks, and I realize I've
chuckled out loud. I look up and it's Ronnie Benjamin,
my former and sometimes-even-now psychiatrist. She's
holding the most gorgeous shoes I've ever seen—very
high spectator-style heels in camel with black patent.
They have an ankle strap with a pinked edge and a very
round toe.

"They don't come in black and white, do they?" I ask
her, disregarding Bobbie's sandal instructions, because I
know that if she saw these shoes…

She tells me they don't, but they do have them in
camel and white and do I think she should get that pair,

as well. "Terrible admission for a shrink," she tells me, "but I'm absolutely addicted to shoes. Obsessed. I'd go for therapy myself, but I'd rather spend the money on more shoes." She shakes her head at herself.

I'd ask her what it is about women and shoes, but as I already said, it's the never-too-fat-for-shoes effect. And then again, it's how a pair of heels can make you feel. I mean, put on jeans and sneakers and you look like someone's mom on her way to the laundromat. Put on jeans and cowboy boots and you look like someone's kid sister on her way to a bar where she'll peel labels off long-necked bottles. Put on jeans and jeweled high-heeled sandals and you can go shopping in the Hamptons.

Which reminds me... "I need shoes for Dana's bat mitzvah."

Ronnie squeals that she loves shopping with someone else's money and *having* to buy is the best. No guilt. She and I stroll the aisles together, commenting on shoes and who would wear those four-inch platform espadrilles.

"I mean, the whole point of espadrilles is comfort, isn't it?" I ask.

"Not for the obsessed," Ronnie says, considering a pair with embroidery on the front and three ribbons to tie around the ankle. Subtly she segues into how I'm doing these days by mentioning that she hasn't seen me in a while. "Things good with you, then?"

I tell her the bat mitzvah saga, making it sound funnier than it is. I really do believe that in twenty years I'll be laughing about it.

Okay, then. Thirty, when my mother is dead or too deaf to hear me.

"And that guy you were interested in?" she asks. "That go anywhere?"

She means Drew. I explain how I'm "sort of" seeing him again, and how I'm "sort of" helping him with another investigation.

"Talk about obsessions," I say with a laugh. "I can't seem to resist sticking my nose in where it doesn't belong. But this one isn't my fault. I just happened to be at the restaurant when the guy got whacked."

Ronnie tells me she read about me in the papers. "Funny you should say *whacked*. Do you think it was a mob hit?"

"The police think it was only supposed to look like one," I say. I tell her about going to the funeral and about Carmine being there.

"Oh, my God," she says with a gasp and she stops in her tracks. "Then I'm Dr. Melfi." I can see she wants to take the words back as soon as she's said them.

I try to give her a reassuring look that says her secret is safe with me. "What was wrong with this patient we're not discussing?" I ask her. When she waves the question away with her hand, I add, "It could be important to finding his killer."

She tells me she couldn't say, that it's against the Hippocratic Oath.

Ever notice how close Hippocratic is to hypocritical?

"I do treat a lot of patients for OCD," she says. "You

know, like Monk. Counting things, repeating things, excessive hand washing."

Was the killer waiting in the bathroom for Joe, knowing that he'd come in to wash his hands? And is the man two aisles over looking at me or at the shoe in his hand? He doesn't look like the Teva type.

I reach for a pair of shoes beyond Ronnie so that I am on her right instead of her left and the man is over my shoulder. "You see the guy in the men's sandal aisle?" I ask her.

Ronnie looks behind me. "No."

I describe him completely, from his haircut to his clothes, to the cork-soled slip-ons he was holding.

Ronnie still says, "Nope," but now she's looking at me and not around the store. I turn around and the man is gone. I walk over the two aisles to see if he's just sitting down, which would explain why I can't see him. The aisle is empty.

"Problem?" Ronnie is behind me, and she can see there's no one there.

"Guess he's gone," I say, trying to make light of it and pretend I'm not looking out the window, searching for him in the parking lot.

"Was he that cute?" Ronnie asks me, but I know that isn't what she's thinking. And she's the last person I want to hide my thoughts from.

"I keep thinking that someone is following me," I tell her. "Wherever I am, I see scary men or black Lincoln Town Cars and think they are watching me. I think dear friends who come over to do me favors are trying to poison me. I—"

Ronnie suggests I come see her in her office if I'm really afraid that I'm paranoid.

"No," I tell her. "This is different. I don't think I'm paranoid at all. I think someone really is following me."

I say the same thing to Drew not an hour later, after I've returned home with camel-and-white spectator heels like Ronnie's, flip-flops with shells on them, and yet another pair of moccasins which Bobbie says I can drop off at Goodwill the next time I'm out.

You'll notice there are no black-and-white high-heeled sandals. Funny. Bobbie noticed that, too.

Drew poo-poos my fear that someone is following me. "You're a good-looking woman," he tells me. "Of course men are going to look your way."

"And then disappear into thin air?" I ask, letting Maggie out the back door and telling her to do her business and get back inside.

Drew feigns indifference. "Maybe after closer inspection…"

I tell him he's not funny, but he doesn't seem to care. He goes on about how from afar someone might mistake me for someone better-looking.

"But up close," he says, and now he's got his nose practically glued to mine, "you don't look like anyone else at all. Not these eyes, not this nose…"

I know he's going to kiss me. I know I'm going to like it. I know that it's a mistake, and I know that I don't care. Luckily he knows it, too, and he does care, and he backs up and opens the door, calling the Magster in. And now he's all business. "Find out anything useful?" he asks.

I tell him about Joe Greco having OCD and the killer probably knowing that and hiding out in the bathroom.

"We pretty much figured the killer knew him," Drew says, brushing some hair out of my face and sending an electrical charge down my body.

"And that it was premeditated," I add. "I mean, it wasn't some argument in the men's room, some chance meeting."

Drew nods.

"But not the woman he regularly met there, I take it?"

"Otherwise occupied, it turns out," he says. He looks at me like I should know with whom.

His cell phone rings. He checks it and says, "Gotta take this." As he walks out of the house I hear him say, "Yeah, Hal, go ahead," into the phone.

I touch my cheeks and they feel as though they are on fire. I tell myself it's just warm in the house.

Ha.

While Drew is outside on police business I check my e-mail and post some pictures on my Web site. I realize I never checked my phone messages and find one from Rio claiming to have secured a band. He assures me it's for real and that I can count on him.

Ha, again.

And there's one from Howard asking if by any chance I found his knife.

Why do all the men in my life make me laugh?

There are three messages from my mother about the bat mitzvah including one insisting I invite my dead great-aunt so her family isn't insulted. One message is for the kids, who my mother invites for a sleep-over, no doubt to take them to her beauty parlor for haircuts and whatever else she deems necessary before the big day.

"Good idea," Drew says, having come back in and heard the message.

"A night with my mother?" I ask. "Not."

He repeats that it is a good idea with a solemn emphasis. I don't like the sound of his voice. I ask if the kids are in danger and he swears that they are not. They'd be safe at my parents', I ask.

Drew assures me they would be safe there, here, wherever. That I'm not in danger, they aren't in danger, the sky isn't falling and I can turn off my worry machine.

Pretty scary stuff.

I decide to send the kids to my mother's to keep them safe. The idea that they will be safer with her is a scary one.

CHAPTER 12

Design Tip of the Day

"Window Treatments: Open, they should bring the world in, pull in the cherry blossoms, the pool, even the snowman outside. Closed, they should created a cozy, safe haven, removed from the rest of the world. This can be achieved with layers of window dressing, starting with either blinds, a shade or a sheer curtain for privacy. Add to that a valance, draperies, tiebacks, passementerie, etc. What is passementerie? It's all those wonderful cords, tassels and ropes you see in pictures of the finest hotels in Europe. Click on the link to Tinseltrading.com to get an idea."

—TipsFromTeddi.com

Drew Scoones is in a car across the street from my house. I can't see him, but I know he's there. Two hours ago he told me to turn off the lights and go to sleep.

Fat chance.

I hate being scared. I hate the way it makes my chest shudder and my hands flail and my lips itch. In fact, my whole body itches. Maybe I have hives. I feel my skin in the dark under the covers. Knowing Drew is out there makes me self-conscious. I want to tell him I'm just looking for hives.

I turn on the light. There is no rash. There is only Maggie May blinking at me. I turn the lamp back off. The phone rings.

"What's the matter?" Drew asks.

I tell him nothing's wrong.

"Okay," he says and hangs back up.

I decide that all the times I thought I was going crazy I was wrong. This is what it really feels like. Hearing things outside, inside, unable to lie still. I creep into Alyssa's room with Maggie on my heels and smell my littlest daughter's blanket. I stop in Dana's pit and tell her hamster to go to sleep or I'm taking away his squeaky wheel. I stand in Jesse's doorway and look at all the little boy stuff.

I love them so much that I ache, and the ache replaces the fear for just one moment.

I crawl back into bed and pat the spot beside me for Maggie. Then I call Drew's phone, even though he's told me not to.

"What?" he says.

"Are my kids fine?" I ask him.

"Of course they're fine," he tells me. "Go to sleep."

"Why are you out there?" I ask him.

"So you can go to sleep," he says. "And if you're not going to, I might as well leave. Then at least one of us can get some rest."

I ask him again if the kids are safe, if I'm safe. If my parents are safe. I sense I'm on his last nerve, but I can't stop myself.

And then he says he's got to go.

And it doesn't sound like it's just because he's fed up, or because his pizza's getting cold.

"Drew?" I ask, but he isn't there.

Will I be seen if I go to the window? Maybe, but it doesn't seem to stop me.

I stand far enough back so that I am in the shadows and peer into the darkness, where I can just make out the form of a man coming up my path, and I am so relieved that Drew is going to come inside and keep the boogie man at bay that for a second I don't notice the other man running across the street toward my house until he tackles Drew.

Or is Drew the tackler? I run downstairs and put on the outside lights. From the grass two men blink at me. I know them both.

"Get the fuck off me," the bigger one is saying while Drew straddles him and tries to cuff his hands behind his back.

"It's Mark," I say, coming out onto the porch in a nightie that's much too short to be seen in. "Let him up, Drew. Let him loose."

"I said, 'get the fuck off me,'" Mark repeats, and his tone is so low and menacing that I actually take two steps back and trip over a lawn ornament from the Rio-lives-here days.

I shout out, because naturally I fall on my bad elbow, and both men watch me trying desperately to hold my elbow while attempting to cover parts of me that shouldn't be on public view. And they both are giving each other sideways glances to make sure that the other isn't seeing something he shouldn't. Maggie is throwing herself against the screen door and barking like a mad dog. Of course, being locked in when I'm out, she is a mad dog.

And if my elbow wasn't throbbing and Drew wasn't trying to cuff Mark, it might be amusing.

Given these two things, it's not.

Mark shrugs off Drew, stands and comes over to me to help me up, while Drew, to my horror, pulls a gun and tells Mark to stop where he is. Mark tells him to go "ef" himself, and gets me on my feet, puts his jacket around me and says he's taking me inside. I think I've smacked myself in the mouth because my lip stings and I taste blood.

Drew tells Mark if he takes one more step it'll be the last one he takes. He *orders* Mark to move away from me, and I give him a little shove to encourage him because my father always said you don't mess with a man with a gun.

Okay, it was "you don't fuck with a truck," and I was learning to drive, but the sentiment is the same.

I am pleading for calm like I'm Rodney King. "Can't we go inside and talk about this?" I ask, licking my lip gingerly.

Drew tells me to get in the house. He orders me. And then he makes noises about arresting Mark, who says the idea is ridiculous.

"I was just checking on Teddi," he says. "I was going to make sure the doors were locked like I always do, because sometimes she forgets, or the kids open a door and then forget to lock it."

"Never," I say. "I never leave the doors unlocked."

Drew orders me in the house again while Mark says, "Last Tuesday, Gorgeous."

"You check my doors every night?" I ask, dumbfounded, while Drew escorts Mark toward his car and asks if Maracita isn't waiting up for him. From the glance over his shoulder I can tell that Mark is trying to gauge if I've heard Drew's question.

I turn to go in the house to get on some clothes when I hear a sharp crack in the night and something whizzes by me.

"Get down!" Drew shouts and before I can even react, Mark is lying on top of me and we both hear Drew's footfalls running down the street.

"Did he try to shoot you?" I ask as Mark's body presses into mine. It sounds sexy, but the cement is rough against my skin, Mark weighs twenty million pounds—all muscle—and I can barely breathe.

He eases up and tells me he should get me inside. He stands, and somehow I'm sort of hanging in the air in front of him, pressed up against his body with one of his arms. Three steps later we're in the house, he's locking the doors and asking me about the kids' whereabouts.

A minute after that, he's gone.

For close to an hour I fret, I sweat, I start to go upstairs, come back down, start to dial the police, start to dial Bobbie. Maggie follows me for half that time and then falls asleep from sheer exhaustion.

Finally the phone rings and it's Drew, warning me that he is coming to my door and that it's all right to open it. When I do, he and Mark are standing on the doorstep. Two patrol cars are parked at angles on the street, and a large man in handcuffs is being hustled into the back of one of them.

"Frank Greco," Drew says. "He thought you had his brother killed for holding out."

"Holding out what?" I ask. For a second I haven't processed the idea that Frank took a shot at me. Wanted to kill me. And then it hits.

I lean on the wall for support while Drew says that Frank admits to stalking me. "Couldn't shut him up," he says. Apparently Frank saw me give Joe the ring, put two and two together and decided that I'd led Joe on and then turned him in to the mob when he didn't *report all his earnings*. "Apparently they're even worse than the IRS," Drew says.

It seems a pretty flippant comment considering the fact that the man was trying to kill me. "You said I wasn't in danger." My temper is barely under control and it shows.

"I sent your kids away and I sat outside your house all night. What did *that* say?"

Not to trust you, I think.

I ask if Frank still thinks I'm responsible for his brother's death.

Drew looks at Mark and says, "No. Not anymore," while Mark rubs his left hand over the knuckles on his right.

"You can go home now," Drew tells Mark, dismissing him.

Instead of leaving, Mark strolls into the house and parks himself on one of the bar stools in my kitchen, saying he thinks he'll stick around. He's gotten an earful from Bobbie on the subject of Drew Scoones and I think he wants to somehow protect me.

And not from the bad guys outside, but from the one in my kitchen.

Drew tries staring him down. When that doesn't work, he makes noises about pursuing the investigation, running Mark in, blah, blah, blah, until I tell Mark that I'm tired and he ought to leave. Reluctantly, he cups my chin and glares at Drew as if he's daring the entire police force to stop him.

"You need me, Gorgeous, you call," he says loud enough for Drew to hear. "I can be here in ten minutes."

Meanwhile Drew has started pulling cups and saucers

out of my kitchen cabinets. He unearths a bottle of Kahlúa.

"Sit," he orders me. I don't argue. He makes coffee and pours in a healthy amount of liquor. "Drink."

"How could you not tell me I was in danger?" I ask when I am calm enough to find my voice.

"You wouldn't have been in danger if your stupid little friend hadn't come lurking around trying your doors," he tells me.

I ask him how he figures that. Mark wasn't the one who took a shot at me.

He tells me he had me covered, he had me protected. Frank never would have gotten off a shot if "your felon friend hadn't come calling."

"My *felon* friend?"

He admits he isn't sure that what Mark's done is a felony, but that he's looking into it.

"And what is it that he's done?" I ask, and I rub my lip carefully with my finger.

"He kissed you?" Drew demands like a jealous suitor. "Did he—"

I ask when kissing me became a felony, and instead of just telling him the truth, I tell him it's none of his business. He claims that, of course, it is. "Really?" I ask him. "How is that?"

He does the usual bit about how I don't know anything about this guy and he's checked him out and—

"You've checked him out?" I put down my coffee cup and stare at him. "What are you, the FBI?"

He tells me I'm upset.

"Somebody tried to kill me," I shout at him. "So yeah, I'm upset." I want to yell at him for doing a check on Mark, but I'm too close to tears to bother.

He pours more Kahlúa into my cup and encourages me to drink it. "I'm gonna spend the night here, Ted. And everyone at the precinct is going to know it, and I'm gonna kick myself to hell and back in the morning, but there's no way I'm leaving here tonight."

"And that has exactly what to do with Mark?"

"I'm not sleeping on the couch. That's what it has to do with Mark."

I think I say "oh," but I'm not sure. Maybe he hears "so?" because he continues.

"So you know what they're saying about you? The men I work with, ride with, depend on for my life? I can't afford to fight with them, Teddi. It's bad enough they think I'm in your panties every time I leave the station…"

"No one is in my panties," I tell him. "Not uninvited. And if it's none of your business, it's certainly none of theirs."

"Is he or isn't he?"

I tell him Mark is my friend, and that he works for me. I tell him I shouldn't need to say more.

"Fine," he says, but he's anything but happy. "Just so long as you stay away from that guy."

"Because?"

"Because you're not the kind of woman who would commit adultery."

I remind him that Rio and I are completely, fully, legally divorced. "I am a free woman," I tell him.

"You're not the problem," he says. The light bulb goes on over my head as I drop my head into my hands. How is it I am so consistently wrong about men? And why do they all seem intent on hurting me?

We sit there a while, Drew tracing the back of my hand with the same finger that rested on a trigger a few hours ago.

"You're cold," he says after an eternity. "Let's get you upstairs and under the covers."

I don't move.

"Come on," he says, gently pulling me up out of my chair and looping an arm around me as he steers me toward the steps and tells Maggie to "stay."

"I could be dead, couldn't I? Right now, I could be dead."

Drew shakes his head. "Never happen. He'd have had to go through me," he says. He gives me half a smile and adds, "And I think he'd have had to go through your little friend, too."

I tell him to stop calling Mark my *little friend*. The man is probably six foot four and fills doorways without inhaling.

He eases me up the stairs and toward my bedroom. Maggie May is on our heels despite Drew's orders.

"Frank Greco was stalking me?" I say, still processing the whole night's happenings.

He tells me to let it go, that I'm safe now, and he sits me

down on the edge of my bed. "You always sleep in these little things?" he asks me, twisting his finger in the spaghetti strap that holds my nightie on. "Or is this just for me?"

I tell him I look like a wreck, but if the bulge in his jeans is any indication, he gets his kicks out of looking at wrecks.

"A person could strangle with all these strings around her neck," he says, and pulls the gown up over my head, taking great care not to raise my arm too high and hurt my shoulder, and tossing it somewhere behind me, claiming he's saved my life twice in one night.

Then he holds back the covers for me and I slip under them, close my eyes, and a moment later feel his weight on the bed.

"I hate that they know about this down at the precinct," he says, his hands beginning to roam over my breasts. "I don't want them to think—" he starts, and then it becomes clear that he doesn't want me to think, either. In fact, he doesn't want either of us to think at all.

And we don't. We just reach for each other, touch and taste and get lost in the sheets and our skin.

CHAPTER 13

Design Tip of the Day
"Things every nightstand needs: A good lamp. A box of tissues. Your phone. Your clock radio. If pressed for space, a lamp can be hung above the bedside table. Ideally, the table should have a shelf beneath it for additional surface space and a drawer to keep private those items the world (and your children) shouldn't see."

—TipsFromTeddi.com

When my mother calls at ten to eight in the morning, I have to reach over Drew to get the phone. He grabs me and pulls me to him and buries his face in my breasts while I agree with everything my mother says rather than listen to her.

"I have to go," I keep telling her, but her selective deafness has kicked in and she is telling me how I have to change the tablecloths for the bat mitzvah because the wrong lavender can clash with taupe, which, I presume, is the color of her dress, since it's the only color she wears.

She tells me she has to look perfect, fabulous, even better than she usually looks.

"I'm hanging up now," I warn her, but I don't get to do it before she assures me that the entire bat mitzvah is destined to be a disaster and that she and my father will be the laughingstocks of the Five Towns, that area of Long Island that consists of maybe twenty square miles surrounded by, and isolated from, the real world.

Drew takes the phone from my hand. "Say goodbye, Mom," he says into it, and I hear a gasp before he returns the receiver to its cradle.

"One...two..." The phone rings on cue, but Drew rolls me onto my back, pulls my hands up over my head and threatens me with handcuffs if I pick it up.

I remind him that my kids are at my mother's and that she isn't above pretending they are bleeding to death to get me to pick up the phone. We listen to my voice on the answering machine explaining that I can't take the call. Then we hear my mother shouting something about masked intruders.

"Go back to sleep, Teddi," my father's voice suddenly says. I hear my mother yell that I wasn't sleeping, for Christ's sake. "So do whatever you were doing," my father says and then we hear a click.

"You heard the man," Drew says, and picks up where we left off last night, teasing my body until teasing isn't nearly enough.

He strokes me everywhere at once, and every place he touches is on fire. He mumbles against my neck as he takes me and I hear, "I need," but what it is he needs is lost in his groan and my sigh.

A door slams downstairs and we both freeze.

"Teddi? Hello? Howard? Anybody here yet?" Bobbie shouts. "No coffee? Teddi, where are you?"

"Down in a minute," I yell, taking the covers with me as I get out of bed and stand at my bedroom door. "Do me a favor and make some coffee and let the Magster out," I yell before closing the door and turning the lock.

Drew lies stark naked and spent in the center of my bed. Smug, hands behind his head, he stares at me. "This secret thing...how's that working for you?" he asks as his beeper goes off.

"About as well as it's working for you," I say, amused that he moves the pillow to cover his privates before reaching for his phone.

I take some clothes and hurry into the bathroom, trying not to listen, or at least not to be obvious about it. "So either one of them had a motive, and they'd cover each other's asses," I hear him say. "Yeah, yeah. Get off the ass jokes and get me some facts, okay? Where do you think I am? I stopped for doughnuts, dickhead."

I rush to get my teeth brushed, don some clothes and run a brush through my very definitely bedheaded locks. When I return to my bedroom, Drew is dressed and pacing.

"I'll be right down," I yell to Bobbie, thinking that estimate might be a little optimistic, actually.

I busy myself with picking up last night's nightgown, and trying to straighten the room, which looks like a tornado whizzed through it.

Drew stops pacing. "You should have told me about Rosen having a piece of Madison on Park," he says. It doesn't take a heartbeat for him to read my face and know I have no idea what he means. "That your friend's a part owner? That he bought into it to save the place, then wrote an *unbiased* review of it? That he—"

And then he stops for another read of *Teddi's Truth-Telling Face*.

"You didn't know. The son of a bitch never told you, did he?" he demands. "Guess he didn't tell you Joe Greco was threatening him, either, then?"

"Teddi? Oh, jeesh! Is that Drew's car?" Bobbie's voice is closer. Maybe the bottom of the stairs. "Is he there? Are you…?"

Drew opens my bedroom door and is face-to-face with Bobbie, whose mouth opens slightly before she says something like, "Well, hello, Detective Scoones."

"Hello, Mrs. Lyons," he replies in kind.

"You two remember each other," I say, squeezing past both of them and heading for the stairs while recalling aloud how Drew had suspected Bobbie of murdering our first client, Elise Meyers, last fall. "This is the last friend you went after, as I remember."

Bobbie hurries after me. "What's that supposed to mean?" she whispers to me.

"Now Drew thinks that our dear friend Howard Rosen

is somehow involved in Joe Greco's murder." I glare at him over my shoulder.

"Guess he just doesn't like sharing you," Bobbie says loudly enough for Drew to hear.

Drew snorts rather than bothering to answer.

"Howard's due here in a few minutes to help me with the bat mitzvah decorations," I tell Drew. "Maybe you'd like to hang around and you can tell him yourself that you think he's a murderer."

"While he's putting together little bows and—" Bobbie starts to say, but I stop her. I started suspecting that Howard was gay several months ago, and now I'm sure, but I'm equally sure that he has no plans to come out of the closet and I don't want Bobbie to imply any such thing.

Our arrangement works for both of us. Every time my mother gets on my back about finding a new husband, or about my interest in Drew Scoones, I get to say that Howard and I are inches away from looking at gowns and rings. And when Howard's sister, Helene, pressures him, he gets to say that I'm the one dragging my heels.

"He's willing to help me," I tell Drew, slamming down three cups and pouring coffee for us all. "Something your macho pride would probably never let you do."

He tells me he doesn't need to tie ribbons and bows to prove he's a man. And then he lets his gaze stray toward my bedroom.

"It takes more than a penis to make a man," Bobbie pipes up. "That's what I tell my girls."

"And a lovely sentiment, that," Drew says, shaking his head at me as if to ask where I got this friend of mine.

I ask him if I have a friend he likes and doesn't suspect of some major felony.

He tells me, "Yeah. Me."

"I'm not sure we're friends," I admit sadly. "Friends hear each other, they trust each other's judgment…"

Bobbie says something about how Drew is one of those men who likes to isolate his partner—Drew winces more at the term *partner* than at the sentiment, I think—and cuts her off from her girlfriends and boyfriends.

Drew throws up his hands. "Is that what you think Howard is?" he asks me. "Your boyfriend?"

"He takes her out, he buys her dinner, he comes over here and cooks for her—" Bobbie says.

I wish she hadn't. It reminds me of the knife, and I know I should tell Drew, but he'll misconstrue it, he'll think Howard came into my house and stuck a warning on my countertop.

Howard would never ruin my countertop. Or his knife.

Drew grabs my arm and shoves me toward the front door. Okay, *shoves* is a little harsh, but it's no arm-in-arm stroll down the hall. "You know Howard's balls are not in your court, don't you?" he hisses at me. "You know that much, right?"

I don't have to answer him because *Tell-All-Face* is giving me away.

"You know that he and Nick are—"

Okay. That was a surprise and he knows it a second

later. "Nick is married to Madison and she's having his baby," I say.

"She's what?" Drew asks. "How long have you known that?" What he means is, How long have you known that and *withheld it from me?*

"I strongly suspect," I say.

He waits.

"When I was sure, I would have told you."

He seems engrossed in cleaning the backs of his teeth with his tongue.

"Does it make a difference?" I ask finally.

As always, Drew doesn't answer me. Instead he tells me that he's got to go.

I put an arm on his sleeve. "Do you still think Howard had anything to do with Joe Greco's death?" I ask.

He seems more sure of it than ever.

If I shouldn't play poker, than neither should Drew Scoones.

"Well, you're wrong," I say.

To which he replies, "We'll see."

"I thought we could at least count on Howard," my mother says, toying with ribbons but only managing to wrinkle them rather than make bows to cover the meters behind Madison on Park.

"Every other man you've ever dated has been a loser, but Howard was different."

I put down the tenth bow I've made. The wires are killers and amazingly, it's only the seventh one I've managed to cut my finger on. "*Is*, Mother, not *was*. The man is late, not dead." And is different, but I don't go into that.

"He's history, Teddi. Face it. If he really wanted to be part of this family, he'd be here making these ridiculous ribbon concoctions." My mother takes a cigarette out of her purse, frowns at me because I don't allow smoking in the house, and puts it between her lips unlit, talking around it. "There's an art to keeping a man interested, keeping him on the string."

My mother studies her nails as if the art involves a good manicure.

"There's a look you give a man that says it all. Says, *oh, don't worry about him, he's just my husband.*" She goes through the motions of smoking, blowing out her breath as though she has actually inhaled. "*It wouldn't even occur to him that someone might find me fascinating, the way I find you...*"

Her voice drifts off.

Bobbie gives me a *what was that all about* look. I shoot back one that says *darned if I know.*

"How long have you been married anyway, June?" Bobbie asks, as she twists numerous wire stems together to make several bows into one.

"A year too long," my mother says. "Ten years too long. Maybe forty-four years too long. Maybe my life could have been different. Better."

"You don't mean that," I tell her. "First off, you love Daddy. Secondly, then you wouldn't have David or me."

"Maybe," my mother says, "you should speak for yourself."

Bobbie shakes her head at me. A warning. Don't go there. She's doing her needle-Teddi-and-see-if-she-bleeds routine. I, of course, ask her what the hell she's talking about.

She tells me I wouldn't understand this, but that you get to a point in your life when you look back and wonder about paths not taken.

Bobbie looks up from her pompom making and asks pointedly, her big eyes blinking innocently, "You mean, like not marrying the man you married, finishing school, having a career, that sort of thing?"

Only my mother misses her sarcasm and says she means marrying someone else. Of course, in her day, not too many women chose not to marry and to have a career instead. Besides Florence Nightingale and Clara Barton, I mean.

I ask her if she's unhappy in her marriage. She looks at me like I haven't been listening, and maybe I haven't. I wonder how long I haven't heard her.

"You don't love Daddy anymore?" I ask, and I can't help remembering the TMI stuff my father told me about their love life. And feeling like I'm maybe nine years old and just realizing that sometimes mommies and daddies don't stay together forever.

"Of course I love your father," my mother snaps at me. "He's my best friend. He's loved me through more than a man should have to."

"But?"

"Who said but?" she says. "Did I say *but*?"

"You didn't have to," I start to say, only we're all really uncomfortable and luckily Bobbie breaks the tension.

"Look at this!" she shrieks, having put the artificial roses into the bow clusters the way I showed her. "It's gorgeous! We could give up the decorating business and go into party planning."

My mother and I stare at her. She looks at us blankly. "Well, we could!"

I remind her that we are holding my oldest child's bat mitzvah—a sacred, religious celebration of her coming into her womanhood—in a parking lot that an Italian restaurant shares with the Long Island Railroad.

And that I can't seem to get in touch with the man who has put all this together and seems to have gone AWOL.

I've tried Howard three times and gotten his voice mail at home and at work. I've even text-messaged him on his BlackBerry and gotten no response. Each time my mother has assured me that he is avoiding me. This is the coward's way of breaking up, she tells me.

I keep thinking about the knife in my counter appearing to be the one missing from his precious not-off-the-rack-at-Fortunoff set.

And not telling Drew about that because I know Howard would never want to so much as scare me, never mind hurt me.

When the phone rings I expect it's Howard. "I hope you're bleeding in the gutter somewhere," I say, "because that's about the only excuse I'll accept for—"

It turns out to be Lois Schaeffer, my newest client, wishing to change her appointment, only now she's a little iffy about when she'd like to reschedule. I'm thinking she's probably a little iffy about *whether*, too.

In order to convince her that we are absolutely the decorators she wants, I go into a song and dance about how I plan to brighten the rooms of her home, not with boring white walls, which will make everything seem dark in comparison, but by enlarging two windows, doing their treatments beyond their frames so as not to cut off any light, and hiding extra lighting behind wood valences to give the illusion that the world is brighter even at night.

My mother is frowning, as though I am talking pure nonsense. Bobbie looks like she's not convinced I know what I am talking about, either.

"We're going to focus on bringing more light into the room with indirect lighting and with the use of mirrors positioned to reflect each other to infinity. That will more than double the effect of the lights because they will reflect the light ad infinitum."

My mother throws the ribbon she's been mauling into the center of the table and heads for the door with her cigarette and her lighter. Bobbie admires her own handiwork while I flounder on the phone.

"Oh, that's my call-waiting," I say, and press Mute on the phone. After a good two minutes I go back to Mrs. Schaeffer and apologize. "Would Tuesday work for you? I have someone on the other line who is very anxious to get going and I could give her my only appointment this week, on Tuesday, or I can put her off until next week if Bobbie and I can come over Tuesday and show you some mockups. But if that doesn't work for you, she'd really like—"

Mrs. Schaeffer bites and I don't even feel guilty about it. Okay, a little guilty, but I know that Mark and I can make that house feel like it's on the water in Malibu if she just gives us a chance.

Bobbie and I are doing the little happy dance when my mother comes back in and says something about the kind of weak-minded, easily-manipulated people who would fall for that sort of pressure.

"Maybe you should tell Howard that your cop friend is seriously interested in you," she says, putting her lighter back into the satchel she calls her handbag and which is likely to give my father a hernia if they should go out East to the outlets, where she makes him tote it around for her. "That is, if you ever hear from him again."

Mark comes in the front door with the posts he's made to separate our party from the rest of the parking lot. My mother comments that she forgot all about him, then says something to Bobbie about how it's just as well. Howard would never believe that this stud muffin could be interested in me, anyway.

I'm not sure if Mark hears, but he is certainly doing his best to convince my mother she's wrong.

"How are you feeling, Gorgeous?" he asks me, standing by the coffeepot and waiting for an answer before helping himself. We haven't talked about Drew's accusation, but it's sitting there in the room between us. "Your shoulder better?"

I say I'm great and he says I don't have to tell him that. He figured that out a long time ago.

Okay, maybe the accusation is only bothering me. It doesn't seem to be affecting him.

"A long time ago you weren't even born," my mother says and Bobbie has trouble keeping her coffee in her mouth.

"I'm old enough to know a good thing when I see it," Mark tells my mother. "And I'm looking at it right now."

My mother tells him to save it for when Howard is around. "If he ever shows up again."

Mark looks at me as if to ask if my mother is loony, then seems to remember that she is. He asks if she's helping with the bow-making and she tells him she's had enough art therapy to last two lifetimes and that the whole bat mitzvah is going to be…blah, blah, blah.

"And I'd have put my foot down about the whole thing and insisted we have it at The Plaza," my mother says, as if that were ever a realistic option from the standpoint of either availability or affordability. "But I thought Teddi had a good shot at Howard and these were his friends and, well, that's all down the tubes, it seems."

The kids and my father arrive at the same time and offer to help. I look at Alyssa, and Jesse, on my wavelength, offers to take Maggie for a walk and asks Alyssa to come along. He needs help keeping Samian, the cockapoo Lothario, at a respectable distance, or at least keep the two dogs from rolling in the daffodils. You can't help loving that kid.

He gives the male of the species a good name.

And speaking of the male of the species, my father sulks at the table. He stares at my mother, who develops a sudden interest in bow-making to avoid his gaze.

Dana peers over my mother's shoulder at the work she's barely doing and says, "You don't really have to do this, Grandma." She looks at me as if to ask *Isn't this bat mitzvah going to be awful enough?* I shoot back a look that says something between *you ungrateful wretch of a child* and *don't worry, she'll never even finish one*. She nods silently and quickly adds, "Not that you're not doing a great job."

"Look at these," Bobbie tells her, showing her the huge white bows with the lavender roses intertwined in their loops. "This is going to be so gorgeous."

Dana gives her a weak smile and the ubiquitous "whatever," then turns her attention to her grandfather, asking him what's wrong.

He insists, of course, that nothing is. Then he sighs such a heartfelt sigh that he might as well have told her he was going to have to give up broadband and go back to dial-up on AOL.

Or that my mother doesn't love him anymore.

I pick up David at the airport and get him, Issy and Cody—who I could just eat up, he's so delicious—into the car.

"I can't believe anyone flies anymore," David says as he settles into the passenger seat heavily. "Freakin' security. Hasn't anyone ever heard of privacy rights? Hands in my wife's luggage. They all but searched the baby's diaper for hidden explosives."

Issy tries to lighten David's mood. "Would have served them right if Cody'd given them a sample of his explosive diarrhea."

"Very funny." David does not want to be cheered up.

"So, bad flight, huh?" I say, as I fork over sixteen dollars for just over an hour's parking. *Stop at cash machine*, I put on my imaginary list.

"Bad mood," Issy tells me, as she settles Cody into Alyssa's old car seat and announces that he's already asleep. "David is dreading seeing your father," she says, to which David humphs loudly and says it's not Teddi's father he doesn't want to see, it's his own.

"The one I caught *shtupping* the housekeeper," he says, like I don't know where his animosity is coming from.

I tell David it's funny to hear him say *shtupping*. I'd have expected screwing, or the "f-word" or something less old world. "It makes me think that you're back thirty years," I say.

David doesn't say anything, but I hear Issy say something like, "Amen to that."

I can see this is going to be a fun visit. My mother will criticize everything Issy says and does, as much for herself as because Issy reminds her—being black, beautiful and from the Islands—of Angelina, the housekeeper with whom Dad had the affair. David will refuse to forgive either my father or Angelina, who actually raised David and me while my mother was in and out of South Winds Psychiatric Center. My father will be angry and upset.

Congratulations, Dana, on your big day!

"David," I say, knowing that I'm risking the very tenuous relationship we've forged over the last year or two, but thinking the thing just has to be said. "You know what happened between Angelina and Dad was hard on all of us. Mom went back to South Winds, Dad and I had to cut all ties with a woman we loved…"

David tells me he had no business loving another woman while he was married to our mother. Behind us, Issy lets out a breath of frustration.

"What?" he asks her. "If I had had an affair with Marguerite, you'd forgive me?" David asks her. I take it Marguerite was Cody's baby nurse, but now doesn't seem like the best time to clarify that.

"Would it be Cody's place to forgive you?" Issy asks him. "Or mine? 'Cause that man didn't cheat on *you*, David, he cheated on your mother—who, let me tell you, is not in danger of having sainthood conferred on her for this lifetime, honey, no matter how you paint that picture."

David opens the window, effectively closing the conversation because we can barely hear each other.

"Don't go doing that," she yells at him and slugs the back of his seat. I am amazed when he shuts the window. Oh, he pouts, but the window is closed. Is the conversation?

"I was older than Cody," he says finally. "I saw her on her knees in front of his naked body, I saw—"

"Through the eyes of a kid," I can't stop myself from saying. "You're grown now. You're older than Dad was when he and Angelina fell in love." It's the first time I've admitted that they loved each other. I've resented that Angelina can no longer be a part of my life, but until now I haven't ever been sad for my father and what he had to give up for my mother's sake. "They loved each other, David. I think that was what made it possible for you and me to survive. You have got to let this go."

David is silent. I have no idea if he is processing or if he is fuming. A horn honks and Cody lets out a startled cry.

"Okay," he says finally. He shifts in his seat to face Issy. "Would *you* forgive me? If you were my mother and—"

"I'm not your mother," she says. The air in the car is so tense it's like static electricity waiting to shock us the moment we touch something we shouldn't. "But no, I wouldn't."

David puts up his hands like he's won the argument and settles back in his seat. He stares out the window for a minute.

"That's okay, Issy-Honey," he says. "'Cause I'm not my dad."

CHAPTER 14

Design Tip of the Day
"The right decor can be transforming, turning the same room into a private library, a garden or a home theater. Floor covering can set the stage. For the examples above, think Oriental rug, sisal mat, commercial carpeting. Now think about the kind of room you are planning and imagine it with tile, with wood, with cement. Even within those categories there are so many choices: marble tiles, terra cotta, honeycomb."

—TipsFromTeddi.com

On the morning of Dana's bat mitzvah, I am standing in the parking lot at Madison on Park at 7:30 in the morning. I've left Bobbie in charge of the kids and the plan is for Mark to meet me here and for the two of us to get as much as possible set up before I have to get to temple for the service. Then Mark will continue working with Madison and Nick, and magically everything will be perfect when the service is over and all the guests arrive.

I am standing on outdoor carpeting under an immaculate white tent, twisting lavender satin streamers up the parking meter posts when the back door of Madison's opens and Howard and Nick come out. Howard is smiling from ear to ear.

Of course Drew's comment jumps to mind, but it's not something I can dwell on at the moment, now can I? Not with Howard apologizing so much for not showing up yesterday, Nick chiming in every now and then about how important Howard is, how he's busy, busy, busy.

"Work," Howard says, agreeing. He ruffles my hair affectionately, while I kneel down to tie off a streamer. "What can you do?"

I tell him that I called him at work. And that he wasn't there.

"Should have tried my BlackBerry," he says, stretching like my crouching is hurting his back. I don't bother answering.

Nick claps his hands and tells me how good everything looks. He says that he has ready all the food that could be prepared in advance.

"Let her taste the *arista al latte*," Howard says. "It's fabulous."

"You tasted it?" I ask, wondering how Howard could have been working all day yesterday and managed to sample Nick's cooking.

I watch the wheels turn in Howard's mind. He says he stopped in between lunch at next weekend's review and the office.

"For a bite," I say, and he almost says "yes" before realizing it.

"We were so busy yesterday," Nick tells me. "That review your friend wrote has been a godsend."

I say something about how Howard is *his* friend, as well, and all the while I'm twirling these ribbons around the meters and fastening the toppers.

"This party is going to be perfect," Howard says. "We're going to get a reputation for catering which the place should have had years ago. Maybe one day expand and take over the pizza joint, break down the wall—"

The "we're" doesn't escape me. I hate it when Drew is right about things I should know, and I resent Howard's keeping his interest a secret from me all the more for it.

"There's Mark," I say when I see his pickup pull into the lot. He waves and nearly runs over a woman hurrying out of the bagel shop at the end of the strip. I hear her shout an obscenity at him, and hear him give as good as he got. And I remind myself that if I want civility, I'm going to have to stay in my own house or move to someplace in Iowa.

Nick offers to help Mark get the posts out of the truck and Howard lays a hand on my arm to detain me a minute.

"I really am sorry about yesterday," he says soberly. "Something extremely important came up and I couldn't get out of it."

What can you say to something like that? "Uh-huh" seems to be the only thing I can manage as I try to pull away and help with the stanchions.

"So how's this for strange? Helene says the police talked to her about the murder you witnessed," he says. Now I'm all ears. "Don't you think it's weird that they talked to her?"

I make a non-committal noise.

"She's got this ridiculous idea into her head that the police somehow think I could be involved," he says, and his gaze keeps straying to Nick and Mark.

"I really should help them," I say, and start to move toward them, but again Howard reaches for my arm.

"You didn't tell them that you saw me at The Steak-Out that day, did you, Teddi? Or something like that?" he asks, and I feel my blood go cold. I tell him I told the police the truth—that I didn't see him there.

"*Were* you there?" I ask, thinking that this man has been alone with my children, he's celebrated Chanukah with my family, he's been part of our lives. The pole I am wrapping looks like I've tried to strangle it.

"No," he says, and blanches. "God, no. I mean, I was near there, but not there. And Nick, he was here, at the restaurant, preparing for the cook-off all day. Remember?"

I think that's what they call *leading the witness*, only there's no one around to object. Except me, of course.

"I checked with him, to be sure," Howard says. "Not that I thought he had anything to do with the murder or anything. Just to be sure he could account for his time, you know, if the police asked. I mean, if they were talking to Helene, who knows what they're thinking?"

I do, I think. *And you're not gonna like it.*

"Nick was busy preparing all day."

"Yeah, you said that," I say, but he seems so relieved that it's almost contagious.

"And then we all saw you that night, remember?" he asks, bringing to mind that old line from Shakespeare about protesting too much. I want to say, "Got it," but that would make it seem like we were scheming, wouldn't it?

"I remember," I say. "That was the night that Madison nearly chopped off her finger."

And speaking of the devil, out comes Madison from the back door, looking around admiringly. "Teddi! I love the plans you dropped off," she says, oozing friendliness. "Blood-red walls. How daring! And just think, if I cut myself again, it won't even show."

I say something like "Heaven forbid," but Dana's bat mitzvah is just hours away and I really am feeling the press of the clock so I'm really not up for this chitchat. Not to mention that Madison's warmth feels like something she turns on and off at will.

I move on to another post, wrap it quickly, pop on the topper and move to the next one.

"What a day that was," she goes on, following me around while pointing out to a couple of young men I assume are waiters where they should put out the tables. "In the morning we thought the biggest catastrophe of the day was not being able to find any tamarind paste. Thank goodness for Howard." She waves at him and Nick, then nods approvingly at where they are placing the stanchions.

"I really should—" I start to say, moving toward the last of the posts and checking my watch.

"And then, of course, Howard winding up right next door to where you were when that dreadful inspector got murdered..."

She's helping me spread the tablecloths (white so that they won't clash with my mother's ecru dress)and I'm surprised when the cloth floats down flat. I think I expect it to whirl around, like everything in my head. "Joe Greco?" I ask. Now he's *that dreadful inspector?* "I thought you knew him."

She says that of course, she did. The man was a scourge on the entire restaurant business. She says this while skillfully rolling napkins and placing them into the stemmed water glasses so that they look like candle tapers. "I've heard since he died that he was actually blackmailing people. And not just restaurateurs. Others who were sort of in the business, if you know what I mean."

I tell her I don't, but she isn't really listening to me. She's ordering the waiters to bring out the china and the flatware.

"God, we were waiting for Howard for hours to find that tamarind. I just knew they'd want us to do duck. It's so Long Island, don't you think?"

I look at my watch, and what I think is that I have about twelve minutes to get dressed before I have to head for shule.

I have already broken countless *Long Island Rules* with regard to dressing for my daughter's bat mitzvah. I have not gone to the salon and had my hair done in a way that makes it look like I didn't have it done (though, in my defense, it certainly does look like I didn't have it done). I didn't get my makeup done, either, but ditto on the look I've created. I don't think the rule about not showing up in jeans because you didn't have time to change is limited to Long Island, but it is one I refuse to break.

I tie on the last of the Maypole bows and watch as Mark and Howard put the last post in place. Things don't look half bad. Thank heavens it's not raining. The day is absolutely glorious.

Weatherwise, anyway.

Howard yells that he is taking off to change for the bat mitzvah, and I watch him head for his Mercedes while Mark heads for me.

"How are you holding up, Gorgeous?" he asks me, and I can see Madison assessing him and wondering about our relationship.

"I'm getting on top of things," I say with a half smile.

Mark looks me over. "I see a couple of things I'd like to get on top of," he says with a wink, no doubt enjoying the effect on Madison, who can stop wondering and just jump to the wrong conclusion.

Then he tells me it's time for me to hit the road and that he'll take it from here.

"My clothes are in the car," I tell Madison, and ask if I can change in her office. After she says, "of course,"

Mark offers to walk me to my car and carry my stuff back for me.

When we are out of hearing range I tell him that all his flirting is making me uncomfortable. I let him know that I realize he's just kidding around, but the rest of the world doesn't know he's not serious. And while I didn't really care what they thought when I believed we were both single, and everyone would know it was just banter if we were both married, the disparity bothers me.

He tells me he's only *technically* married and my estimation of him plummets to just a notch above Rio, and only there because he hasn't, to my knowledge, actually cheated yet.

I tell him that's like being "a little pregnant." You either are, or you aren't. Meanwhile he's fishing on the floor of my car for the strapless bra that has slipped off the hanger.

He asks if I don't think it might be a little more complicated than that since my cop friend wants to prosecute him for it.

I have to admit, while struggling to carry my clothes, makeup, curling iron and handbag, that Drew did call him a felon.

"Maracita is our housekeeper's daughter," he says. "Her mother's here illegally and so is she. She's a good kid and she was half a year from finishing Lawrence High School at the top of her class when they started talking deportation."

I tell him I think I saw the movie, but he shrugs like if I don't want to believe him, that's my choice.

"I was just the logical choice," he says. "We knew each other pretty well—well enough to convince INS if we had to."

I drop one of my good shoes in the remains of a puddle. Sir Gallant picks it up and wipes it on his T-shirt.

"Only now they're talking fraud and accomplice and jail time," he says.

"Were they talking about it before Drew met you that day at my house?" I want to know.

He nods, then laughs at my train of thought. Hey, it isn't beyond the realm of possibility, given his penchant for going after my friends. I wonder about that isolation thing that Bobbie accused him of as I walk right past Madison's office and stand in the restaurant looking around like I don't know what it is I'm supposed to do.

And I think that after the bat mitzvah is over, there are a couple of issues I'd like to talk to Ronnie Benjamin about—including my inability to concentrate on the matter at hand.

"Uh, you gonna dress in the window?" Mark asks, standing near the entrance to Madison's office, one of my high-heeled sandals dangling from his fingertip. "Not that anyone, especially me, would mind. Maybe I could sell tickets…"

Cheeks burning, I turn and hurry into the office, put down my clothes and grab my shoe from him, shutting the door in his face despite his offer to help me get out of things.

I check my watch again. I have minus two minutes to

be dressed and on the road, which means that I cannot look in that file cabinet and see if there are any legal papers just hanging around that corroborate Drew's claim. Really, I can't.

Of course, if I open the drawer and just look at the file folder labels while I get out of my T-shirt and jeans...

Ten minutes later I am down to my panties and the third drawer, running the risk of missing the beginning of the service and incurring the wrath of both my daughter and my mother.

And of course, there it is, two minutes later, in the bottom drawer as I am pulling up my panty hose. A neat, new folder with a handwritten label that says MOP/Rosen Agreement.

My fingernail goes right through my stocking because when I stick my nose into something, apparently the rest of me barges right with it.

I hurriedly put on the strapless bra I got at the specialty shop and which gives me cleavage Rio only dreamed about and then I slip on my lovely black-and-white dress. I decide I'll have to forgo stockings—which Bobbie had dictated already and I'd chosen to ignore—and pick up my makeup bag. I can hear my mother's voice in my head warning me to put a robe over my clothes before handling my makeup. And I imagine her finding a speck of makeup on my dress at the bat mitzvah and never hearing the end of it.

Hoping I won't get anything on it, I grab a white jacket from the hook and throw it over my clothes as I head for the ladies' room. In the mirror I look as haphazard as I feel. This was not the morning I'd envisioned when I was first planning Dana's big day. She and my mother and I were all going to be at the beauty parlor—opened specially for us by 8:00 a.m.—while Rio and the kids were home fielding calls from out-of-town guests.

What a difference a couple of years can make. I'd never have imagined that my brother, David, would be there, let alone with a woman and child in tow. Or, for that matter, that Rio would, too, and that the woman wouldn't be me.

I put on all the usual makeup the occasion calls for, concealer and base and blush and then, as I am leaning forward to use my eye pencil inside the rim of my eye just the way the girl at the Nars counter at Bloomingdale's showed me, I notice the logo on the cotton jacket I've got on.

Flatbush Produce.

Funny, but I have the sense I've seen their logo somewhere else.

I twist around so that I can see the back of the shirt. Sure enough, there it is.

A picture of fruits and vegetables on the side of a truck.

I've probably seen that truck a million times on the streets of Rockville Centre.

CHAPTER 15

Design Tip of the Day
"In decorating, as in life, some rules simply cannot
be broken. Here are three: scale, comfort/usability
and focus. No tiny, delicate rockers with a room full
of massive furniture, please. No Victorian settees in
the TV room, and no drawing the eye to something
you want to hide."

—TipsFromTeddi.com

I am late for my own daughter's bat mitzvah. I am sure
there is a circle in hell for mothers like me, but luckily
Jews don't really have hell, they have *gehenna*, which,
while a terrible place, isn't eternal torture. In fact, it's
more like purgatory and only lasts twelve months or less,
which is a lot shorter than I'm going to suffer for this particular transgression in this life, I'm sure.

My mother will see to that even after my daughter
takes her pound of flesh.

I have run from the parking lot in my bare feet and I
stop at the doors to the synagogue to put on my strappy
high-heeled Donald J. Pliner sandals, straighten my hair

and put on the stupid little hat my mother insisted I wear. There are little pebbles stuck to the soles of my feet, but I deserve worse for being late.

I deserve hot coals.

Beside the doors to the sanctuary are two bowls. One holds lavender acetate yarmulkes that have Dana's name and the date of her bat mitzvah inscribed in them. The other has genuine suede ones with a textured design that weaves together two Ms for Missy Moskowitz, the other bat mitzvah child being called to the bimah today.

Doesn't matter, I tell myself. *We don't care about Missy Moskowitz.* I can hear my mother now, asking just who "we" is, but I refuse to go there. I pull back my shoulders and smile at the usher who shakes his head at me and whispers that the ark is open.

I tell him I'm the mother of one of the bat mitzvah girls and that I need to get in there. Again he shakes his head. "Doors remain closed if the ark is open," he reminds me, though I know the rule well.

Only the thing is, I've never been really good at rules, so I nod my head sadly, walk toward the door to the outside, pull it open slowly, and then gasp.

"Oh, my God!" I yell, wondering if that counts as taking His name in vain, decide my excuse is good enough and besides, I'm already going to *gehenna* anyway...

The usher, clearly not buying my act, doesn't move.

"What are you writing there?" I scream out the door. "Stop that!"

I glimpse the usher. He is unwavering.

"This is my father's synagogue," I shout. "This will kill him!"

I glance back. The usher is shaking his head.

"Please?" I ask nicely. "My daughter will never forgive me. And worse, my mother—"

The usher studies my face. Then his jaw drops and the color drains from his face. "Aren't you June Bayer's kid?" he asks.

I nod sadly. I can see him considering the options. "Hell of a time to have to use the men's room," he says as if he's suddenly been stricken with the runs. He heads quickly down the hallway, calling over his shoulder, "Emergencies happen. Remember, no opening that door."

And then, with a look of pity, he slips into the men's room and I crack the door ever so slightly so that I can slide inside.

The holy ark, the *Aron Kodesh*, where the torah is housed, is indeed open and my father is carrying the torah back up the steps toward the rabbi who waits for it. This was to have been not only my job, but my honor. I was supposed to take the torah from the ark, carry it around the temple where the congregants could touch it with their prayer books while my family, including my bat mitzvah child, trailed behind me.

Everyone turns in their seats to stare at me, kind of like when the bride enters, only in an alternate universe. Dana glares at me with her I-knew-I-couldn't-count-on-you face. My mother doesn't even deign to look at me.

Missy, the child who is sharing Dana's special day and

whose mother had the foresight to book the temple's catering hall three years in advance, gives me one of those butter-wouldn't-melt-in-her-mouth Nelly Olsen smiles that says Mrs. Moskowitz was there on time and did the right thing. She surely did—she called "heads" and got to choose the redressing of the torah toward the end of the service, instead of divesting it of its silver breastplate and crowns, its mantle and belt.

I hurry up to the bimah to take over from my father under the scornful stare of Rabbi Ruben, whose eyes promise me fire and brimstone despite the six-pointed stars on his tallis.

The truth is I don't need him (or my mother or Dana) to convince me of my guilt. I feel awful enough about it. I stand with my head bowed while the rabbi undresses the torah, unable to meet his gaze. My heart—not to mention the torah—is heavy.

David, in the first pew with Issy and Cody, coughs until I look at him, then winks at me and gives me the thumbs-up sign. *You made it, you're good, you're golden.* My mother glares at him, but David pointedly ignores her. We are in this together, he and I. We are the two black sheep.

I watch Dana as the rabbi removes the silver finials that top the wooden poles on which the torah scroll is wound. My little girl looks nearly grown up. She has on lipstick and blush and looks radiant.

The rabbi takes the torah from me and carries it to the podium. He nods at me to take my seat and I descend the bimah and sit between my father, who squeezes my hand reassuringly, and Jesse, who looks at me like he wishes he, too, could have been late, or not come at all.

Drew comes in and sits in the last row of the temple. He looks devastatingly gorgeous, but he'd look even better if he were sitting next to me.

Howard, my mother's choice for the unoccupied side of my bed, is nowhere to be found. I know this because my head is on a swivel and I can't keep it facing forward no matter how hard I try and how beautiful and angelic Dana looks sitting up on that throne beside the one on which the cantor sits.

Rabbi Ruben does his thing in Hebrew, a language I understand very little of beyond the basic prayers thanking God for bread, for wine, for candles that burn for eight days, and proclaiming Him the *One and Only*.

In turn, the rabbi calls up members of our family to do the *aliyahs*, blessings that surround portions of the torah readings. I do one. David does one.

After the second or third blessing, Rio and Marion's baby begins to cry quietly. During my mother's blessing, she begins to wail like a siren warning doom.

The alarm continues until my mother stops reciting and everyone stares at Rio, waiting for him to do the right thing. "*Goyem*," he says with an embarrassed smile, as if it's only his not-quite-wife and child who aren't Jewish. As he hustles them toward the back of the sanctuary he adds, "What can you expect?"

I'm sure these are my mother's sentiments, exactly.

I stare at the *ner tamid,* the eternal light that hangs above the ark, and try not to laugh at the incongruity of it all.

I sober quickly as Dana starts her portion of the torah reading of today's service. The part of the torah which is read each week is determined by the calendar, but each bat mitzvah child can choose which part of the day's reading she wants to deliver. Dana's selection is from the end of Leviticus and deals with the rewards and consequences for obeying God's rules and laws.

How fitting that she should concern herself with the rules, since her mother can't seem to follow God's or anyone else's—and the consequences of breaking them—after I've just committed the *not while the ark is open* no-no.

All the same, she does a beautiful job and I can hear the congregation let out a collective sigh of appreciation that she has made it through all the Hebrew without a hitch.

Not that I was wishing anything less for Missy, but I might admit to a certain satisfaction when she repeats a line three times and has to start over. She gets an appreciative sigh, too, *that* she's done, rather than when.

Missy's mother and father go up together to hold the torah while Rabbi Ruben, with a sharp look in my direction as if to illustrate that "this is how it's done," re-adorns the torah and returns it to the ark while we all stand in respect.

Then Dana does her *haftorah* and immediately follows it with her *divar torah,* the speech she has written herself about the torah portion she has chosen and how it relates to her own life.

I have heard the speech a hundred times, but today, in this setting, with my father next to me and my brother down the pew and all our neighbors and friends listening, I am incredibly moved by it.

She uses her grandmother as an illustration of understanding the rules, though she fails to mention that it's our belief that my mother writes them, as well. She praises my father for actually following the rules, and for setting a good example of the religious life. She mentions her own father's tolerance for things he wasn't brought up with and has trouble understanding.

And then she adds a paragraph I've never heard, which is about me. "My mother," she says, "serves as a shining example of someone who strives to live a good life in the midst of people less true, less honest and less virtuous than she is, and she is never swayed."

I wait for the kicker, but there is none. She says she loves me, hopes to follow in my footsteps and someday fill my shoes. I look down at my $180 sandals that I didn't need and could have foregone for a Payless pair and my shoulders sag.

"But I hope," she says with a smile, "that I grow up to be more prompt."

"Amen to that," my mother says.

Design Tip of the Day
"They say *measure twice, cut once*. The same is true
for every detail—confirm, confirm, confirm. Take
nothing for granted. Or you can be sure that some
order, some arrangement, something crucial will
be fouled up."

—TipsfromTeddi.com

On the way to Madison on Park I can't help listing the
litany of everything that has already gone wrong. I
pretend that everything that can go wrong already has,
and that I have nothing to worry about.

Ha.

When I arrive at Madison on Park there are two police
cars and Nick is waving his arms wildly at several officers
who are rearranging our beautifully decorated faux catering hall. Apparently, they aren't *fauxed*, and "rearranging" might be putting it a little too gently. Dismantling
might be closer to the truth.

At any rate, no one seems to be trying to handcuff

poor little Nick. It would just be the icing on the cake to have the caterer arrested before the first course is served.

As I am sizing up the situation, and other guests are arriving, I see two officers gathering up my beautifully decorated stanchions. I run after them, as best I can in the four-inch high-heeled sandals I will never forgive Bobbie for talking me into, which barely allow me to teeter in place without falling over, never mind make tracks.

"What are you doing?" I ask when I finally make it to where they are. "We're having a party here."

"In a public parking lot?" one of them says. "I don't think so."

"My ex-husband got it okayed by the town." As soon as the words are out of my mouth I realize how ridiculous they are. Come on, it's Rio we're talking about. Whoever he schmeered is probably laughing her head off. In Aruba.

The cop just shakes his head.

"Okay," I say, as calmly as I can, because I see my father's car pulling into the lot and I know what my mother is already saying. "I have over a hundred people on their way here for my daughter's bat mitzvah party. There's a reason my ex-husband is my *ex*-husband. What can I do?"

The cops look at each other and shrug.

"Okay," I say again, and I point toward my father's Lexus. "My mother is in that car, along with my father and my three children, and if you can't help me, I'm going to have to lie down in front of it and let them run me over."

I can see one of the cops softening.

"What if I pay for four hours on all the meters?" I suggest. I don't dare do the math in my head because then I really might as well lie down in front of the Lexus right now and save my kids the debt.

"We don't collect meter money," the cop says, and he sounds like he really is sorry he can't help me out.

"You could just keep feeding the meters, I guess," the other cop says. "Nothing says the spaces have to be filled with cars."

I ask where I'm going to get all those quarters, and hear male laughter behind me. Drew is nearly doubled over when I turn around.

"I'll get them," Mark, appearing like my knight in shining armor, says, and he's off in a flash.

"No doubt to raid his piggy bank," Drew drawls, and he saunters over to shoot the breeze with the uniforms.

The band Rio hired is setting up, and while they are a tad on the older side, I'm grateful they've got instruments and seem to be tuning them. Well, I hope they are tuning them up and not playing them, or that proverbial last straw may have hit the pile. The way the day is going, I'm just wondering when the you-know-what will hit the fan.

People are streaming from the rest of the parking lot toward the party and I can hear the surprise in the air. It's not all bad, either. Some people are marveling at the ambience. At least, I think they are. It's hard to hear over the train whistle.

Rio is directing people into the restaurant for drinks, and it looks to me like Marion has already helped herself to a few.

"That's when class shows," my mother says to me. "How we hold our liquor." Then, as if she wants to lead by example, she asks my father to get her a double scotch. Neat.

David, a walking totem pole with his son, Cody, on his hip, his wife, Issy, on his arm and Lys on his shoulders, asks Mom if scotch is a good idea with all her medication.

"My granddaughter, the light of my life, is celebrating the most important day of her religious existence in a damn parking lot. I need all the anesthesia I can get." She pulls out a cigarette, catches sight of someone in the distance, and changes her mind.

"Where's the kids' bar?" some thirteen-year-old whose dress probably cost more than my engagement ring asks.

"You can get soda at the bar inside," I say, smiling sweetly as though this is what the girl actually means.

She thinks she hasn't made herself clear, and tries again. "No, the bar. You know, where they make the virgin daquiris and coladas and all that stuff. Where they have the mini pizzas and crap like that?"

I tell her that there is plenty of food inside I'm sure she'll like, and that they probably have some fruit punch at the bar. She looks at me like she pities me and the long afternoon I'm clearly facing.

"What an interesting theme," I overhear someone remark. "I wonder if there will be limos to eat the meal in, or maybe train cars."

"Why would there be tables then?" someone responds.

The answer comes quickly. "For the Viennese dessert table, I guess. She can't expect people to walk from the limos…"

"Was there a limo from where you parked?"

"They don't expect us to put money in the meters, do they?"

"The kids aren't going to just be here, are they? I mean, there'll be some arcade games and things, right?"

Wrong.

"Where's the digital pictures guy, Ms. Bayer? The one who puts your picture on a magazine cover?"

"When's the DJ coming with the CD burner so we can make our own CDs?"

It's going to be a long, long afternoon.

By now nearly all the guests have arrived, gotten drinks, and listened to the band play every song Frank Sinatra ever recorded including several he shouldn't have.

Mark and Bobbie and I have stuffed all the meters with quarters whose origin I haven't dared ask about. Especially with Drew eyeing my felon friend suspiciously. In fact, Drew is eyeing half my guests suspiciously along with a few people sitting in a black Lincoln at the far end of the lot.

"You were supposed to hire a DJ, not a band," I tell Rio as his glad-handing has him passing behind me. I see him put an envelope into his jacket pocket and put out my hand for it.

"I'm holding it for Dana," he says, patting his chest like the money is safe there.

"I'm getting ten bucks to do that, Dad," Jesse says. "Gotta earn my keep." Reluctantly, Rio forks the envelope over to him.

"Tell the emcee that it's time to have everyone take their seats and introduce us and then Dana," I tell Rio.

When he's gone, I thank Jesse and he pats my arm reassuringly. "Don't worry, Mom. I'm only charging you five."

I watch Rio talking to the bandleader and see the guy shake his head.

"What's the problem?" I ask when I reach them. Rio tells me that the emcee was arrested yesterday and the guitarist doesn't talk well. He doesn't sing well, or play well, either, but I don't think I need to tell them that.

I grab the microphone and clear my throat. Of course, I should have done that in the opposite order.

"Sorry. Could you all take your seats so we can welcome Dana Bayer-Gallo, the girl of the hour?"

I have seen stunned looks before, but never so many in one place. Then everyone goes back to talking and drinking and the kids are running around and beginning to stroll toward the bagel shop, lighting up cigarettes whose contents are questionable.

"No kidding, folks. Please. Take your seats and let's all welcome Dana with a great big hand."

If he weren't already in jail, I'd have the emcee for this band arrested for breach of contract. I might even *take out* a contract.

At any rate, Dana comes out from the back of the restaurant and people do applaud. Well, Mark applauds, Jesse applauds, my brother, David, puts two fingers in his mouth and whistles as he comes up to the mike and takes over.

He announces that my father will recite the *motzi* over the bread and my father, with tears in his eyes, says the prayer while Dana complains to me in staccato sentences about the band. I cut her off by telling her to take it up with her father, and wish her luck, because she certainly has my sympathy. Anyone under the age of sixty has yet to dance.

Bobbie comes up and whispers in my ear that it's time for the hora, and I ask her if she really thinks they'll know how.

"Every Italian band can play 'Hava Nagila,'" she assures me.

Turns out for the first time in recorded history, Bobbie Lyons is wrong.

My mother is fanning herself at the table, telling everyone within hearing range that she had nothing to do with the planning of this bat mitzvah and that I am simply an incorrigible daughter who always has to have her own way and see where it's gotten me?

The kids are asking when the real band is coming and where the dancers are. I tell them *they* are the dancers and they think I am kidding.

At least I have done the goody bags right, and they are all happy with their denim backpacks and the T-shirts that say they were at Dana's bat mitzvah, though I try to elicit a promise from each one that they won't wear them to school on Monday and make kids who weren't lucky enough to be invited feel bad.

Some kid has the nerve to say that the kids who weren't invited were the lucky ones. "They should get 'I didn't have to go to Dana's crappy bat mitzvah' shirts," I hear him say to one of his friends.

"Okay," I hear David saying. "It's been a long time since I played anything but reggae, but I'll give it a shot." He takes the guitar from the crooner and plays the first few bars of "Hava Nagila." Issy hands me Cody and shoves the drummer out of the way. Where she learned the hora is anyone's guess, but she plays a mean enough beat for everyone to start singing along and for the sound of our feet to drown out the music.

The kids get Dana to sit in a chair and the bigger boys lift it into the air. A minute later I'm up there, too, and for the length of the song I don't care that this isn't the bat mitzvah of my dreams or of Dana's, and that some parts of my life, well, aren't the best. This part, this moment, will be treasured.

I'm sorry when they lower my chair to reality.

Waiters come out bearing the first course, and I have to admit it is gorgeous. No wonder Howard was raving about the *arista al latte*. And people are oohing and aahing and saying it's the best they've ever had. The best what, they're not sure. I'm thinking I should have asked, because, if I had to guess, I'd say it could oink a short time ago. That would make it not kosher, and, like lying is worse in court, non-kosher is worse at a bat mitzvah.

Madison's timing is perfect. She comes outside looking for me and I excuse myself from a tangle of well-wishers just as they begin to ask about the wonderful concoction they are eating.

"Have you seen Howard?" she asks me. "The cake hasn't shown up yet and I thought maybe he could go pick it up."

"I assumed he was in the kitchen," I say, trying to keep any innuendo out of my voice, especially because I don't know what I'm accusing anyone of. I just know that I am pissed at Howard, who didn't even show up at the temple, and who certainly isn't helping me run this thing. And Madison isn't all that much higher on my *sucky and suspicious* list.

She tells me she hasn't seen him since yesterday. I don't bother reminding her that we were all here this morning in nearly the same exact spot, because I think that Madison has a little problem with facts and only notices them when it suits her, if ever.

She says she supposes she'll have to go get the cake, unless I want to. I remind her that this is actually my affair and that people might notice if I'm gone. And then I look at my watch and signal to Jesse and two of his friends that they have to feed the meters again while the band strikes up "My Way," for the third time and Madison and I stare in disbelief as the leader starts to sing it yet again.

And then, as we watch, an amazing thing happens. One by one, the members of the band are approached, whispered to, and replaced by first a keyboard player who can really play, then a guitarist who clearly knows that music has moved on since 1954. A drummer who rocks the lot takes over for the one who is half-dead, and a lead singer who makes Mick Jagger look like he's on Valium grabs the microphone.

"I'm going for the cake," Madison says, but I hardly hear her over the band and the rush of kids heading for the dance floor to freak dance to some guy who sounds so much like Ludacris that I have to wonder if he's the real deal.

Dana waves to me from the dance floor. She's dancing with a group of kids, which includes Bobbie's girls and Avery, *the Hottie*—who just a few minutes ago I saw hanging on the fringe of the lot like he was waiting for a ride out of here.

Alyssa and two other little girls are shaking booty I didn't know they had.

Jess and the guys are in double time between the meters so that they can get to the dance floor. And maybe I'm crazy, but all the boys' pants seem to be getting longer and I'm seeing a heck of a lot of boxer bands.

I find Rio trying to quiet Elisa, who is clearly freaked out by the music. I ask where Marion is by yelling directly into my ex-husband's ear, and he gestures with his chin at the dance floor where his teenybopper girlfriend/nursing-mother-of-his-child is making milk shakes, if you get my drift.

"You get this band?" I shout.

I get a dirty look for my answer. Call me petty. Call me vindictive. Call me anything you like, but I'm still going to revel in this moment when Rio's band looks like the graveyard shift compared to these guys. Never mind the shift—they just look like the graveyard.

Rio looks beyond me and his face goes white.

"Like the band?" a voice asks.

I turn, and there, along with his entourage, is Carmine D'Guisseppe. I stammer my hello.

"I liked Frank Sinatra," he says like he means the actual guy and not just the sound. Somehow I can hear him even though he isn't shouting. It's like the band lowered their volume to accommodate him. "But he's already dead. Your guy didn't have to kill him again."

"You're responsible for this band?" I ask, and Bobbie is suddenly glued to my side, nudging me.

"He was at the funeral," she whispers to me, pointing at the man at Carmine's side. *And at the train station afterward*, I'm thinking, *if I'm not mistaken.*

"I hope you don't mind," he says. "I was passing by, and being a music lover…"

I tell him that the kids are very happy.

"You don't think they'll mind if I request a slow song or two, do you?" he asks. Before I can answer, his cronies all assure him that no one will mind, and one disappears into the crowd.

A minute later a Beyoncé look-alike is singing "Smoke Gets In Your Eyes," and the kids have paired up pretty tightly, making some room for the grownups on the dance floor.

"Would you—" he starts to ask, and holds his hand out to me. Before I can take it, before I can even decide if I want to take it, another hand is holding my own.

"You don't mind, do you?" Drew Scoones ask Carmine. He waits for Carmine's nod, demanding it with a look, then nods and whisks me toward the dance floor.

"You know," he says to me, holding me in a death grip, "word around the precinct is that you're crazy. But I never thought you were this crazy."

I tell Drew to let me go.

"Not on your life, sweetheart." He pulls me closer against him, if that's even possible. I hate that he's so good on his feet and that I'm barely able to keep up.

"I'm not ready for this," he says and his hold is hard, like the line of his jaw. His words are clipped, staccato. "I'm not looking for this. I don't want this."

"Am I *this?*" I ask, smiling at my guests like I'm just shooting the breeze with the handsome man who is cracking my ribs.

"Can you be extricated from this?" he asks me in return, gesturing at the party I've managed to pull off— okay, with help—for my daughter.

"I don't want to be," I say quietly, waving at Aunt Essie, who hasn't spoken to my mother in fifty years.

"It can't work," he says. But pressed so tightly to him there's no hiding the fact that his body thinks otherwise.

"So let me go," I say as he whirls me around.

Mark shows up and tries to break in. All he manages to break is the mood.

"So, tell me," Drew says. "You and Carmine D'Guisseppe are good friends?" His upper body is stiff as a board. His lower half is doing just what the music dictates, and doing it with style.

I tell Drew that I didn't invite Carmine. He just showed up. And that I only met him once, we exchanged cards, the police knew about it, and that I'm having trouble breathing. He releases his death grip on me and I feel my strapless bra unhook. I look down and we can both see it inching up above the bodice of my dress.

"Can anything else go wrong?" I ask while Drew chortles. There are few things more annoying than the noise a man can make when a woman has a feminine issue he will never have to face.

"Your mother could be dancing with the head of a crime family," he offers, holding me close to him and swinging me around so that I can see for myself that my mother is in Carmine D'Guisseppe's arms.

And apparently enjoying it.

CHAPTER 17

Design Tip of the Day

"Sometimes it's who you know—or, more precisely, who your decorator knows—that makes all the difference. The same drapes can hang perfectly, *or not*, depending on who you hire to do the hanging."

—TipsFromTeddi.com

Two trucks barrel into the parking lot, and the sides roll up to reveal a mini amusement park. The kids go wild, running from booth to booth, playing games, stuffing Build-a-Bears. They're collecting coupons and turning them in at a prize booth that has materialized from nowhere.

Drew disappears, and I don't think he's playing games or collecting any prizes.

I find my father, sitting by himself. His back is turned toward the dance floor, where my mother and Carmine are cutting quite a rug. My mother's face glows like...dare I say it? Like a woman in love. Or like a woman who has just gotten some—loving, that is. Carmine throws his head back and laughs, and my mother dips her chin demurely, something I don't recall ever seeing her do.

I sit down beside my father and ask how he's doing, what he thinks of my decorations, what a nice day it is, and in the same tone, why my mother is dancing with a mafia don and why the man has saved this party for Dana.

My father says I should ask my mother, and I point out that at the moment she's busy. My father pushes back his chair and says something about enough being enough.

"You'd never have let *me* do this," he says, gesturing with his hands at the pandemonium that's passing for Dana's bat mitzvah. "But that man, that man can do whatever the hell he pleases and everyone licks his—"

"Boots," I fill in, because my father curses so rarely that I find it scary.

"—when he's done." He sits back down. "Joke's on him," he adds.

I confess that I don't know what my father means.

"You wanna do me a favor?" he asks, and if spite was something you could smell, my father would reek. "Just go tell him how old you are, Teddi. Would you do that?"

"Why? He doesn't know how old Mom is? Is that it? Like she's older than he thinks?" I can't believe it could matter. Size? Yes. Age? No.

"Do I ask you for that much, Teddi," my father asks, "that you even have to think about this favor?"

I tell him that of course I'll do it, I just don't understand.

He tells me I don't have to. "Carmine will," he says, and his eyes narrow not at Carmine, but at my mother.

As I'm coming to my feet, Madison comes over to the table looking like she had to fight for the cake. And like she lost.

She tells me she had an accident on the way back, but that she's fine. "A near accident, really," she says. Same old Madison.

She asks if Howard's shown up and I tell her that I still haven't seen him. If I am sounding snippy about it, it's because he promised he'd help, and he's just another in a long line of men who have disappointed me.

She wants Howard to see the cake, she says, "since he arranged for it."

This is news to me, but I'm so hyper from this party business that she could tell me that Howard arranged for a rabbi to come perform the conversion and circumcision Rio promised my father he'd get when we married, and I'd believe it.

"You're sure you haven't seen him?" she asks.

I have to admit I haven't. My dad hasn't, either. Neither has Nick when I ask him, or any of the waitstaff. I try him on his BlackBerry and have to leave a message. I look for Drew, and spot him at the edge of the cordoned-off area, cell phone pressed to his face. From his expression something is rotten in the state of Denmark, or at least in Rockville Centre.

I see him search the crowd until he locates me, closing his phone and making a beeline for me that is so purposeful it's like Moses parting the sea—the crowd opens for him and lets him through.

"I don't want to ruin your party," he says without preamble, and I figure that is exactly what he is about to do.

"So let it wait," I say. "Dance with me."

"You won't want to look back and think you were dancing," he says.

I don't have to ask how bad it is. I can see it in his face.

My kids are here and safe. My parents are…well, my parents. I can see David and Issy and Cody, and Bobbie is drinking too much but she's okay.

"It's Rosen," he says, and the knot in my stomach drops like a stone, pulling my heart with it. "He's at Mercy Hospital."

"He had an accident?" I ask, thinking of him hurrying to get here, worried that I would be angry because he was late, imagining that as they put him on the stretcher he was telling them he had to get to this stupid party…

But Drew is shaking his head. "More like an 'on purpose,'" he says. "It seems your friend tried to commit suicide. He's unconscious and they don't know if—"

I don't really have to hear more. I need to find Dana and my father, tell them I'm leaving, and I need to go to the hospital. After that, I need to—well, we'll see after that.

Dana is with my mother when I find her. I tell her that Howard is in the hospital and I have to go to him.

"This is supposed to be *my* day," Dana tells me indignantly, as if the world doesn't revolve around her on a daily basis and as if today she hasn't been crowned queen of all she surveys. "It's never about me, is it?"

Before I can find my tongue, my mother offers sympathy. "My little Dana," she says. "I know just what you mean. It's never about me, either."

I stare at both of them, waiting for them to get it, but they don't.

I sputter halfway to the hospital, vacillating between excusing a hormonally challenged, keyed-up teenager and wanting to go back and drag her out of the party to lock her in her room until she grows into a lovelier person than my mother is.

Maybe it's just that I don't want to talk about Howard, or think about him. Of course, Drew knows this and lets me exhaust myself on Dana and my mother before giving me more details.

He senses when I'm ready and finally says, "Poison. Called 911 at the last minute. By the time they got to him, he'd lost consciousness."

"He poisoned himself? Today? Ridiculous," I say. "There is no way that Howard Rosen tried to kill himself on the day of my daughter's bat mitzvah." He was too involved in the planning, the execution of the whole thing.

"Tomorrow would have been okay?" Drew asks me.

Of course it wouldn't, and I tell him so. But the fact that it was Dana's big day just makes me all the more certain. Howard loves us, maybe not in the way my mother wants, but he is part of this family. He just wouldn't choose today if he was choosing at all.

"Uh-huh," he says, like I'm grasping at straws.

"Okay, why would Howard commit suicide?" I ask, then catch myself. "I mean, *try to?*"

Drew shoots me a look that implies I know. "How many reasons would you like?" he asks.

"What? Because he was gay?" I ask. "That's ridiculous."

Drew says that Howard went pretty far to hide it, using me as a cover, for one thing. "And that was bound to come out along with a whole lot of other facts your friend didn't want anyone to know."

I tell him to stop calling Howard *my friend*.

"Distancing yourself?" he asks with a quirky smile.

"Howard is my dear, good friend. I just don't like the way you say it. It's like when Rio says *your daughter*, like the bad parts belong to me and the good parts to him."

Drew tells me that my *dear, good friend* bought into Madison on Park to stop it from going under.

I tell him that I consider that noble. A friend needed help and he provided it.

"Sure. But he didn't just *lend* them the money, he took a third of the business. And Nick isn't just Howard's friend. He's his lover."

I tell him how ridiculous that is. Ridiculous seems to be the only word in my vocabulary on the way to the hospital. "Nick's wife is pregnant. Even if Howard is infatuated with Nick—"

"Nick's bi," Drew tells me. "AC/DC, coming and going, whatever you want to call it. He and Howard are a couple. From what I hear, Madison knows and ain't too thrilled. But since Howard is saving her restaurant, she's not in a position to complain too loudly. In fact, best guess, she's the one who put him up to the great review he wrote—*after* he bought into the place."

It's a bit much for me to take in, and the good news just keeps coming.

"Don't think *Newsday*'d be too pleased with that little maneuver."

Even if I believed everything Drew is saying, I tell him it still doesn't mean that Howard would try to take his own life.

"So Howard sinks his life savings into Madison on Park. He risks his job at the paper. Joe Greco finds this out and ups the bribe amount to cover blackmail."

I tell him that according to Madison Watts, Joe Greco was holding up everyone for money. "And if he was holding them up..."

Drew admits that the thought had occurred to him, what with their relationship, that Nick might have done it and Howard was simply protecting him, but then, as he puts it, "Something else turned up. You'll agree that we've already established that your friend Howard's got motive and opportunity, right?"

Rather than agree, I tell him that we are almost at the hospital.

"Now the gun shows up in the trash from behind the restaurants..."

"Don't tell me it's registered to Howard," I say, admitting to myself that on the surface things look bad.

"Helene. His sister. Seems she bought it after the fiasco at her store last year. You remember that, don't you? You in the hospital after playing the hero? Anyway, she claims she didn't even know it was missing."

"So, let's say, for the sake of argument, that Helene knew all this. Maybe she wanted to protect Howard, and so she—" I start.

Drew shakes his head. "In the store with a customer when Joe bought it."

I tell him that I still don't think that Howard did it, never mind that he then tried to poison himself afterward. "I thought poison was a woman's weapon," I say, and Drew just gives me a snide look because now we're both admitting that Howard is gay. "You're an idiot," I tell him, shaking my head.

Drew concedes that maybe he is, but that it's not looking like it so far.

"So your contention is that Howard felt the net was closing in on him," I say.

"And Madison's pregnancy was the last straw," Drew adds. "He knew any chance for a life with Nick was over now, after he'd put his entire savings into keeping the guy's business afloat, hid their relationship to keep Nick's marriage alive and finally killed for him. You gotta admit, we got some pretty strong motive going here."

I tell him I don't have to admit anything, but it's hard to refute his scenario with more than my gut.

"And what makes you think that it was a deliberate attempt and not just an accident?" I ask.

He tells me that Howard left a note, and I find that my breathing is shallow and my heart is pumping a little too fast.

"What about the poison?" I ask. "What did he supposedly take?"

Drew tells me it was some kind of mushroom. "Apparently he knew a lot about that stuff," he tells me as he pulls into the hospital lot. "You want me to call upstairs and see if he's—" he starts to ask.

I guess he only has to look at my face to know the answer.

Helene is outside Howard's hospital room when we arrive, and I'm immediately contrite for having suspected her. It took nerves of steel to shoot Joe Greco between the eyes. Helene has nerves of bean curd noodles. Uncooked, brittle bean curd noodles. The kind that snap and splinter into tiny pieces.

Actually, Howard's nerves aren't anything to write home about, either. I make a mental note to mention that to Drew, who I know will be quick to believe it.

Helene tells me that the nurse is checking Howard's tubes or something, and that she can't bear to watch. I pat her arm and head on in. Hey, I'm a mom, and a mom has to deal with input and output for years—without the benefit of tubes.

But it's harder than I think, as I look at Howard filling the bed, pale and wan, not moving so much as a muscle. No fluttering eyelids, no twitching fingers. He lies as still as if he were dead while the nurse goes about her business.

Next to the bed, machines blink and click and fluid drips through a tube into his left arm. A whoshing sound like mechanical breath goes in and out, in and out.

I find it hard to breathe myself, to swallow.

"Mushrooms?" I hear myself ask aloud. *Who kills himself with mushrooms on purpose?*

"Beg your pardon?" the nurse says. I've startled her by being in the room and, I suppose, by uttering nonsense.

I tell her I was just thinking aloud, then ask if it's all right if I talk to him. She tells me that studies prove that some people hear in comas, and I gasp, because until this moment I've been thinking of Howard as merely unconscious, like Jesse's five minutes in the netherworld that time he was hit in the head with a broken bat during a little league game. I remember the sick feeling easily, because I have it again, that shaking inside my chest, that fragile sense that if I breathe too deeply, move to fast, think too hard, the world will end.

Okay, that *my* world will end.

Coma. I don't like the word so I push it from my mind.

"It's me, Howard," I say, clearing my throat as I stroke his arm. "It's Teddi. I'm here."

The machines show no sign of response.

The hair on his arm is stiff, the muscle firm, and I'm reminded of how many times I've leaned on that arm, depended on that arm, counted on it. I think of Howard retrieving Dana's hamster from the bowels of the washing machine and putting him into the cage for me to surprise Dana with on Chanukah.

I remember him taking charge when Maggie flipped out over the hamster and managed to get tangled in the tablecloth and pull the lighted menorah along with it off the table and onto the carpet where it caught fire and set off the smoke detector. Howard never threw up his hands and said, "What do you want me to do about it?" He always held them out to me, palms up, and said, "What can I do? How can I help?"

Thinking of him in the past tense, about how he was and what he did makes me feel like he's already dead, and I can't bear that.

Drew comes up behind me. "Sorry for the timing, Honey, but I need to ask. Was Howard acting any differently the last few days?"

I am slow to answer, as though I'm actually considering the question. Instead, I glare at him and say that this isn't the time or the place. And when I see that he takes that to mean "yes," I adamantly tell him Howard was perfectly normal. Predictable. He was Howard.

"You're sure?" he says, like something doesn't jibe. "Because we're getting a different picture from other people who knew him."

"*Know* him," I correct. My gaze jumps to the monitors as if to reassure myself that my tense is right.

Drew tells me that Howard's sister says he was nervous and skitterish. Drew looks at me like if anyone ever described *him* that way, *he'd* commit suicide.

"And then there's Madison Watts," he says, as though that woman has never so much as *massaged* the truth.

"The woman who told you she was sleeping with Joe Greco when he was in prison?" I ask sarcastically.

Drew avoids my gaze.

"What?" I ask.

"Technically," he says, and now he's staring into my eyes like he wants to be sure I understand, that I'm getting it, "she didn't tell me that. *You* did."

I don't dare ask what he's implying, because if it's what I think it is, I will have to write Drew Scoones out of my life forever, and at the moment he's only out for the next decade or two. I just turn away and grasp Howard's hand. "I know you didn't try to commit suicide," I tell him, running my thumb across his knuckles. "And I will prove it, somehow."

From behind me, Drew puts his hands on my shoulders, but I slip beneath his grasp. "According to Madison, Howard told her he was contemplating suicide. She said he told her he'd done something 'awful, unforgivable, a sin,' and he couldn't live with it."

"And," I tell Howard—purposely ignoring Drew—"I don't think for one second that you killed Joe Greco, and I'm going to prove that, as well, to the entire idiotic, incompetent, wrong-headed, lazy Nassau County Police Department."

"Hey, there's no reason to impugn the entire department. Why not just call me a fuck-up and leave the rest of them out of it?"

"But you're not a fuck-up." I turn and face him, the shuddering in my chest going into high gear as I take deep, deep breaths—the better to breathe fire, I suppose. "You just have your head up your behind."

"Evidence is evidence," he says, like it's in the Constitution or something. "And I didn't say I was sure of anything. Investigations have stages. Phase One is the gathering stage. Phase Two is the sifting stage."

"Phase Three is the stage where you jump to the wrong conclusions. Oh, wait. That's back somewhere in Phase One, isn't it? Before you bother collecting any evidence to the contrary."

He asks if I have evidence to the contrary. I tell him I know that Madison Watts is the biggest liar on Long Island, and that only the government tells bigger lies.

I've gone a step too far. Like I used to do with Rio. My argument gets lost because I've gone after the raw nerve instead of the whole tooth.

"So the notes from Greco with amounts, meeting places, that sort of thing that we found in Howard's apartment? Those some government plot to make your friend look guilty? Or wait—maybe it was aliens...."

I tell him that's likelier than that Howard tried to poison himself with mushrooms. But even I have to admit it doesn't make for a good argument.

Mark comes in with Bobbie, reporting that the bat mitzvah is over, that my parents have taken the kids home with them, and that elves are doing all the cleanup.

"Your mother and Carmine D'Guisseppe," Bobbie starts. She stops when she realizes that this isn't the time or the place. "How is he?" she asks, gesturing with her chin toward the bed, but not looking at Howard or the machinery surrounding him.

I tell them that he is unconscious. I can't push the C word from my lips.

Bobbie says she can't believe that he would commit suicide, and adds, "especially not today."

"Exactly," I say, while Drew responds with a grunt, like all of us women think alike. I'd have thought, living on Long Island his whole life, he'd have a better sense of *The Rules*, which include not ruining someone else's big day with your problems unless you bring them to the party and share them with everyone else so the others can compare their troubles to yours.

Anyway, I tell her that the police actually believe that to kill himself, Howard supposedly ate poisoned mushrooms on purpose. She thinks I'm joking.

"What? You think the guy ate them by accident?" Drew asks. "A guy who has a certificate hanging on his wall that claims he's a member of the North American Mycological Association?"

Mark, Bobbie and I all look at him blankly while he smugly tells us that makes Howard a mushroom expert.

I bet him ten dollars that he had to look the word up, while Bobbie says, "Half the members of that society or association, or whatever it is, probably die eating some mushroom they think is safe. I bet there are statistics that—" Bobbie claims.

"How many of them leave suicide notes, do you think?" Drew asks, effectively shutting Bobbie up.

I tell Drew that I'd like to see the note and he tells me I will. "He e-mailed it to you," he says. "Could be the first Internet suicide note on record."

"You mean he e-mailed me a copy," I say. "But he wrote it in longhand, right?"

Drew hedges.

"You're taking seriously a note that absolutely anyone could have typed out and sent as evidence that a man tried to take his own life?" My voice cracks and I glance at Howard as if I'm afraid my shouting will wake him up.

As if that wouldn't be a wonderful thing.

Drew denies that he considered it evidence. "One more piece of the puzzle, is all," he says. And then he addresses Howard. "I don't know exactly how you managed to get her in your corner, Rosen, but you can rest easy knowing she's there. If there's anything to be found, Miss Marple here will find it for you."

Miss Marple? That's how he sees me? Not that Mariska person from *Law & Order: SVU?* Not Jennifer Garner from *Alias? Miss Freakin' Marple?*

Mark asks me how I think it went down, and Drew looks me over from head to toe like I'm hiding what I know on my person.

I give it my best shot. "I think someone wanted it to look like Howard committed suicide. I think they supplied the mushrooms. I think they wrote the note."

Mark asks why someone would want to kill Howard, and Drew crosses his arms over his chest like he'd like to hear my answer to that one himself.

"Because he saw something. He was just a couple of doors down from The Steak-Out when Joe Greco was murdered. He must have seen someone…" I say, then stop, because I don't know that Drew even knows Howard was near the murder.

"Claims he didn't see anyone," Drew says, as if to relieve me of having outed him.

"Of course, he might not know he saw someone," I say, keeping to myself the fact that it's possible he was protecting someone, and that that someone was getting scared that if push came to shove, and Howard's own neck was on the line…

Naturally Drew says, "Or he might have been protecting someone," like he was the first to think of it.

"Ha," I say, and start lining up my ducks. "Howard is a good man, but he's no hero. Do you honestly think he'd have the guts it takes to let himself be suspected if he knew who the real killer was?"

Drew says that Howard hadn't felt the screws tightening yet. Not really.

"They were tight enough for him to try to commit suicide, but not tight enough for him to give up the real killer?" I ask. "I think not."

Drew is non-committal, while Bobbie and Mark vociferously agree with me.

Drew tells me that my theory has more holes than Swiss cheese and I say his is a sieve. Bobbie says something about rocks and scissors and that a sieve beats cheese or some such thing. She puts up her hands in mock surrender when we all look at her like she's gone round the bend.

The nurse returns and says that we've got too many people in the room. Drew says he's got to go, anyway. "Off to *detect*," he says before I can, and gives the nurse his card, asking her to have the desk call if there is any change in Howard's condition.

I ask Mark to stay with Howard while I make a phone call, tell him I'll be just outside the hospital entrance and that I'll be back in a few minutes. He tells me to take my time and sits down in a chair by the foot of the bed.

Bobbie says she'll check out the gift shop. When I give her a look that says shopping is a totally inappropriate response to the situation, she tells me Howard would be the first to say the room was gloomy and needs sprucing up. "Do you want him to wake up and think no one sent him flowers or a hospital teddy or anything? That no one cares?"

I am forced to concede the point and we go down in the elevator together. I ask her to go home after the gift shop and walk Maggie May, and she says she will, though she'd clearly like to do something more constructive.

I know how she feels, because while I should be calling my parents to check on the kids, apologizing to Dana for running out and asking my mother how she knows Carmine—*if* she knows Carmine—that's not who I'm calling.

Ronnie Benjamin answers the phone herself, and I'm relieved that she is between patients. She's got twenty minutes. Sure we can talk.

"Tell me about pathological liars," I say.

"You aren't one," she tells me. This comes from all the times I've asked her if I'm paranoid, or if I'm beginning to show signs of Alzheimer's, or if I'm losing my mind.

"Not me," I say. I tell her about Howard being in the hospital and the police believing it's suicide because Madison Watts has told them that Howard said he'd done something he couldn't live with. "Every time that woman opens her mouth, lies slither out. I've caught her half a dozen times, and most of the time her lies seem to have no purpose at all."

Ronnie tells me that there is no clinical diagnosis for pathological lying, that its not in the DSM-IV, which I know is the psychiatrist's bible. But, she tells me, there are certainly chronic liars. People who tell falsehoods for gain, or for no apparent reason at all.

"So can it sometimes have a reason and sometimes not?" I ask. "A man's innocence, if not his life, may hang in the balance."

Ronnie says that she sees my life hasn't changed much. "Most of my patients suffer from boredom, you know."

I tell her I wouldn't mind a little of that, and she laughs.

"Unless your liar has MPD, Multiple Personality Disorder, and doesn't know she's lying, then she can have a motive or not. Sometimes it's a habit, sometimes a game, as in, *how big a fib can I tell and still get away with it?*"

I tell her I thought all of those sorts of people were in

Washington and she laughs. "So then she could lie to protect herself," I say.

"Or someone else," Ronnie agrees. "Does that help?"

I tell her it does. I only wish I could figure out who is protecting whom.

CHAPTER 18

Design Tip of the Day
"A few notes about hallways: A long hallway, done in tile or wood, requires a runner to soften the sound of footfalls. Too many doors can remind one of a French farce or a nightmare, and while you can't always remove doors, you can differentiate them enough from one another. Hallways are great places for collections or displays, adding interest to a functional space."

—TipsFromTeddi.com

It occurs to me, as I am walking back down the hall to Howard's room, that no matter who is protecting whom—whether it's Madison or Howard protecting Nick, or some other mutation of that—at the moment, no one is protecting Howard. And if, as I suspect, someone tried to make it look like Howard committed suicide, that same someone will want to finish the job.

And what better time than while Howard's still in a coma and can't defend himself?

So, with that thought in mind, I'm running down the

hall to Howard's room, and I'm so relieved to see big, strong, healthy Mark still sitting in the chair where I left him, and Howard's machinery still buzzing and clicking and blinking, that I break out in tears. Mark is out of his chair in a heartbeat, holding me awkwardly and telling me that everything is going to be okay.

That's the great thing about being young. Life hasn't taught you that everything doesn't necessarily turn out okay. That sometimes life plays dirty tricks on you.

But experience also teaches you that you can sometimes play just as dirty and not let life beat you.

And I am not about to let life beat any friend of mine.

I explain my plan to Mark. And I tell him that I am afraid to leave Howard alone and vulnerable. While I talk, I rifle through the drawers in the bedside stand, looking for the key to Howard's condo. I ignore Mark's question about what I'm looking for and continue laying out my strategy.

"So I'm afraid that the killer could come here to finish the job," I say as I wrap my fingers around Howard's keys. Mark doesn't bite, so I add, "And if he does, and finds me here, protecting Howard—"

I pause to let Mark jump in and play the hero, and he doesn't fail me. He offers to stay, but he clearly thinks it's along with me, not instead of me.

I don't have time to break it to him gently. I just hold out my hand for his keys and say, "I'll need to borrow your truck."

While he fishes in his pockets, I gather up my handbag

and find the shoes I abandoned as soon as I walked in the door. As he's handing over his keys, it all clicks for him and he realizes that my plan is to go slay dragons on my own.

"What about Bobbie staying with him?" Mark asks, not even looking at poor Howard, lying defenseless in the bed beside him. "She ought to be useful for something," he adds, letting his true colors show.

I explain that Bobbie is vital to both my business and to me, though I don't explain how, because, frankly, some days, when she goes off in search of the perfect belt or the nearest Starbucks, I have to wonder myself.

And then, of course, I remember that she is the one, the *only one*, who said I could start this business, that I had the smarts and the talent to make it a success. And she's the one, again, *the only one*, who cheers my successes and manages to mitigate my failures.

I tell Mark how Bobbie is the cheerleader at the front of the *Teddi Bayer Parade*. And that somehow, because she's Bobbie, while she's out there in front with the baton, she's also got my back.

"How many people can you say that about in *your* life?" I ask Mark, who stands mute, then puts his hands up in mock surrender. "I thought so," I say as he mumbles his apology.

I keep on praising Bobbie as I slip on the damn shoes she made me buy, fight with the dress she insisted was perfect if I just held my breath for a few hours, and grab up the purse she loaned me, which holds a lipstick, a tampon, a credit card wrapped in a twenty dollar bill and the single key to my car. "Don't forget how she came with me to Joe Greco's funeral," I say, heading for the doorway and leaving Mark no choice but to stay and watch over Howard.

I'm down the hall before he has the chance to think about calling someone else, like maybe Drew or the police. Not that I think they'd guard Howard without my convincing them he's actually the killer and could wake up from his coma and make a quick escape.

I find Mark's truck in the parking lot, haul myself up into the driver's seat and hope his gears work like my old Corvette's. I lurch back, narrowly missing an old woman with a walker, shift into First and lurch my way out of the parking lot.

All the way over to Howard's apartment I run scenarios in my head. Howard really did write an e-mail suicide note to me and then killed himself by ingesting poisonous mushrooms. *Oh, puhleeease*, I think, as I manage an overly wide turn onto Jericho Turnpike and head toward his condo.

Okay, I switch the scene and try imagining that Howard was forced by one of Joe Greco's brawny pallbearers to eat the mushrooms. I see the man laughing as Howard forced down each one, Howard commenting on their texture and lamenting the fact that something that tastes so good will soon prove fatal. In the Lexus next to me I see a woman on her cell phone, and I modify the scene so that Howard's would-be murderer isn't laughing at all—he's on the cell phone with Ma Greco, reporting that Howard is done for.

Uh…not.

What if Howard ate the mushrooms by accident?

Okay, that seems the most plausible, and I go with that as I run a Stop sign and notice the cop too late.

I pull over when he toots his siren and flashes his lights. He saunters slowly toward the truck and asks me for my license and registration.

You remember that Bobbie's bag held my lipstick, a credit card, a tampon, etc.? You remember that nowhere in that list was a license, or a registration? Not to mention that this isn't even my truck.

I explain my situation to the cop, who looks young and short from my vantage point in the truck. I refuse to use Drew's influence, so I tell him to just write me up, give me the tickets, do whatever he has to do, but add that this is truly a matter of life and death, and that I have to get where I'm going.

"It always is, ma'am," he says. "You wanna step out of the vehicle, please?"

"No, I don't want to step out of the *vehicle*," I say, catch the look on his face and add, "but I will."

Mark's truck doesn't have much of a running board, and I miss it on the way down and nearly fall into the officer's arms. He's a lot taller when we are both on equal footing, and while he isn't drop-dead handsome, he is kinda cute in a one-too-many-doughnuts sort of way.

"Long way down," I say as I straighten my dress and try to discreetly put my boobs back where they belong.

He says something into the little gizmo on his shoulder and tells me that he's running my license plate. "You see that Stop sign back there?" he asks while he waits for headquarters to verify that I'm a child molester on the lam and he can arrest me.

"Actually, I didn't," I tell him. "You see, my boyfriend is in the hospital. Well, actually, he's not my boyfriend. He's gay. I know it, and my real boyfriend knows it, only my real boyfriend doesn't know that he's my real boy-friend. And he, that is, my *real* boyfriend, thinks that the man in the hospital killed someone, and then tried to kill himself, but I don't, and so I left my friend—he's not a boyfriend, he just talks like he is—"

The cop smells my breath. "You have anything to drink today, ma'am?" he asks, and I see his mind working as he takes in my dress and his gaze runs down my body to my bare feet.

"Daughter's bat mitzvah," I say, trying to explain why I look like I went out last night and never made it home. "And bad shoe choice. I mean, they looked good but—"

He interrupts me to ask again if I've been drinking.

I tell him that I probably had some champagne. And wine, but that it was hours ago and I'm sure I'm not drunk. That, actually, I'm always like this. And I remind him that I really, really have to go, which sounds like I need a restroom, which, it occurs to me, I do, which apparently is just too damn bad.

"Do you have any ID, ma'am?"

I tell him that I have a credit card with my name on it, but that it's up in the truck.

"Which isn't yours," the cop says.

I tell him that the truck belongs to Mark Bishop. Only he shakes his head. I say it could well be owned by Mark's company, that he's a contractor, and as I'm talking, he keeps shaking his head.

"Oh, my God. Are you telling me that I stole this truck instead of taking Mark's? That this isn't his truck? That can't be. The key worked, and I've seen this truck a mil—"

He tells me the car is owned by a Maracita Valles.

"That's Mark's wife, I think," I say. I don't dare go into that whole mess.

"The boyfriend?" the cop asks, and I can see he clearly doesn't believe me. And he doesn't like me much, either.

"The one who talks like he's my boyfriend," I mumble.

The cop scowls at me. He's not nearly as attractive when he scowls, but I don't think this is the time to tell him that.

"Actually, I don't have a boyfriend," I say with a sigh, shaking my head.

"Or a license," he says. "Or a truck."

There's really not much I can say, and we stare at each other for a minute before the cop says he's sorry, but he'll have to take me in.

"I'm telling you, this is a matter of life and death. Call Detective Scoones and he'll vouch for me. Tell him—"

"Lady," the cop starts and I know that I'm in trouble now that I'm not *ma'am* anymore.

I tell him that I'm calling Drew and turn to hoist myself into the truck in the hopes that maybe Mark's cell phone is there. Before I can get a foot up on the rail, my arm is being bent behind my back.

"Hey!" I say, twisting my head to see him pulling out his cuffs and clapping one end on my wrist. "Stop it!"

In an instant, a familiar long black Lincoln pulls up, screeches to a halt, and I watch as two of Carmine's men in spiffy jogging suits get out and look at me and the cop. The older one, who reminds me of a penguin and always has a twinkle in his eye, winks at me, then proceeds to pull out a pretty convincing gun.

"Oh, God. There's a man with a gun behind you," I say with a gasp. The cop gives me a look that says he's not falling for it. "I'm serious," I say, and, as if to prove me true, a shot rings out.

Doughnut Cop pushes me to the ground, turns and sees the car. He crouches on his haunches and orders me to stay down while he shouts into his shoulder walkie-talkie. Slowly and smoothly the Lincoln begins to inch forward—despite the fact that no one appears to be in the driver's seat. I don't see Carmine's men anywhere.

The cop, still crouched, takes cover behind his own car, then crawls into it and slinks down, pursuing the driverless Lincoln.

"Psst," I hear from the other side of Mark's truck. From my vantage point on the ground, I can see a pair of Velcro-closure sneakers, the cinched bottoms of jogging pants, and a meaty hand waving frantically at me. I crawl under the car and the same hand yanks me to my feet on the other side. "You okay?" Carmine's penguin asks me, his brows furrowed.

I nod.

"Good. Then get the hell outta here," he says, opening Mark's passenger side door. "We'll keep your little *boy in blue* busy.

"Go ahead," he says when I hesitate.

I don't think, I don't consider, I just get in the truck, start the engine and take off. Later I'll explain the whole thing to Drew.

Or, maybe not.

You know how sometimes you pull up to a place and you get that spooky feeling that something just isn't right? That the street is too quiet? That the sun is too strong?

Well, when I pull up to Howard's condo, none of that is the case. It's a nice community of single-floor units and duplexes, with one, two or three bedrooms, and there are two mothers in jogging suits sitting with those baby carriages you can run with at a bench near the corner, a couple of kids on hot wheels, and a maintenance man with a tool box heading into one of the duplex units.

There are also no parking spaces. I have to troll around the entire complex and finally I leave the truck near the duck pond after which the complex is named.

I consider trying to walk in my bat mitzvah shoes and decide it's hopeless. Now that it's nearly evening, I'm cold in my strapless dress. This day wasn't supposed to last this long. And it's not over yet.

I grab one of Mark's work shirts out of the back of the truck and throw it over my shoulders. It comes down to my knees. I try to get a glimpse of myself in the side-view mirror, am appalled by what I see and head down the block to Howard's unit, anyway, because loyalty comes before beauty—and I bet that isn't in the *Secret Handbook of Long Island Rules*.

I try to look inconspicuous as I go up to Howard's door. Of course, this isn't easy since my dress is utterly ruined from crawling under Mark's truck. And while the shirt I took out of the back is hiding the worst of it, it's not exactly what you'd call a "look." Then there's my bare feet, and my hair coming down in various clumps around my face, and the scabs on my elbow.

Oh, and did I mention the handcuffs hanging from my left wrist?

And, working against the blend-into-the-scene effort I'm making, I find yellow police tape crisscrossing Howard's door, *Do Not Cross* warnings printed all over it.

One of the mothers watches me suspiciously and summons the children closer. I can't blame her. If they were my kids, I'd hustle them right into the house. I smile, wave, and make a halfhearted attempt to straighten my hair. They simply stare in return, so I do what I've come to do.

I slide Howard's key into his lock, turn it, slip under

the tape and let myself in. Howard's condo complex consists of single and two-story units, each with its own door to the outside. Since Howard's unit is on the second floor, once I'm inside I have to climb the staircase. As I do, I realize that my knees hurt. Great. They're bleeding from my trip to the ground courtesy of the Nassau County policeman (who was, in all honesty, trying to save my life when Carmine's men started shooting).

I'm praying that Howard's house doesn't have a mirror in it. I'm afraid that if I see myself in it, there will be a second suicide attempt here.

No, no, no. I'm not buying into that. Howard didn't try to kill himself and I intend to find the proof right here. Limping up the stairs, I go over the layout of Howard's apartment in my mind. I know it well, not because he's brought me here to see his etchings, but because I gave him some decorating advice. (Hey, I thought once we were here, in his bedroom, that maybe...but that was before I knew which way the wind was blowing.)

We did this wonderful armoire in the bedroom which, when opened, turns half the room into an office. Since he supposedly wrote me a suicide e-mail, that seems like the best place to start.

The apartment is surprisingly neat, considering what happened here. I mean, the poison must have caused a seizure, or at least pain, yet nothing seems out of place. I suppose that the police must have taken the plate and fork and all for the lab, but still...

A noise tells me I'm not alone. I stand perfectly still

and try to figure out exactly what it is I'm hearing. Is it a bird outside, pecking near the window? Or is it the sound of someone hitting computer keys? I tiptoe toward Howard's bedroom in my bare feet, imagining how loud I'd have been in my strappy sandals, and I angle myself so that I can look in without being seen.

At the computer, his back hunched, his hands busy, I find Nick Watts, scrambling through what looks like e-mails. He glances up, and I realize that I am seeing him in a mirror.

And he is seeing me.

Beside the keyboard is one of Howard's knives. I see it and Nick sees that I see it, and he reaches for it.

"Teddi," he says slowly. "I can explain—"

And I'd really like to hear that explanation—only I'd like Nick to be behind bars while he's giving it. So I turn on my (God bless them!) bare feet and run to the stairs, all but flying down them. I fling open the door, break the police seal as I scurry out, and all the while I'm hearing Nick's heavy footfalls behind me and hearing him calling my name.

I take off in the direction of Mark's truck, but get swept off my feet and hurled into—you guessed it—a black Lincoln, to the astonishment of the mothers still seated at the corner, who, it seems to me, should have had the good sense to gather up their kids and head for the hills by now.

I am all but butt-over-boobs in the back of the sedan, and I right myself as best I can in a car going eighty miles an hour down the narrow streets of a residential development that's got kids riding bicycles around on the roads.

A gentle hand steadies me, and Carmine asks me if I am all right.

"What do you want with me?" I ask. Carmine grimaces, and I think I've reached the end of the line. "Are you going to kill me?"

He takes a swig of Mylanta, dabs his lips and asks why he should kill me.

"Isn't that what you do?"

Instead of answering, he takes a second swig. He still has on his bat mitzvah suit; the boutonniere in his lapel is only now beginning to wilt. I, on the other hand, look as if I've been through a natural disaster. Film at eleven.

"I don't know," I say, the steam pretty much running out of me. "You keep following me, and now you kidnap me and—"

He lets out a big, sad sigh and tucks his silk hanky back into his breast pocket. "Have I hurt you? Have my associates hurt you?"

He waits while I look down at my bloody knees, my ripped dress, the handcuffs on my wrist. Only the truth is that Carmine's men didn't do that to me, the police did.

I have to admit that Carmine's been more my guardian angel than the devil he's supposed to be. He beams.

"That's what I am," he says, thumping his chest. "Your guardian angel."

"But why?" I ask as we circle the development and I

see that two men in jogging suits are standing in front of Howard's place. Between them is Nick Watts.

"I think that man tried to kill my friend Howard," I tell Carmine. "I found him upstairs with a knife and we need to call the police because if we don't, he's going to try to finish off Howard and—"

Carmine asks me what relation Howard Rosen is to me. "I think," he says, "that the man is light in his loafers. You won't get what you need from this man."

I tell him that Howard is just my friend. My very good friend, and that I have to tell Drew—

"Now Scoones, he's all right," Carmine says, like I want his opinion on the men in my life, of which he seems to have become one.

"I have to tell Drew about Nick Watts—" I start, but he waves away the problem with his hand.

"Taken care of."

I find it hard to swallow and it takes me a minute to ask exactly what he means by that.

"He's not going nowhere," he says, busying himself with resettling on the leather bench seat, pouring me a drink of Perrier, holding it out to me. "Go ahead. I didn't poison it."

I take it and gratefully have a sip. I look out the window at Nick. "You aren't going to whack—"

The man in the seat beside me looks mortally wounded. "I told you. Don't worry about Nicky Watts," he says.

I start to ask what they have in mind, but he shakes his head. "Don't worry. It'll give you wrinkles."

"Wrinkles are the least of my worries," I say. "At least today. Tomorrow, I might worry about them again. We have to call Drew. Can I use your phone?"

Carmine tells me that my boyfriend will get Nick Watts in good time, and until then he's in good hands.

"I don't understand your interest in any of this," I say. "I know that Joe Greco was somehow connected to the mob, but I can't put all the pieces together."

"Joe was nothing," Carmine tells me. "A gnat. Small potatoes. What he produced isn't missed. We might not have given him protection, but the harm that befell him was not at our hands. I hope you will believe this."

Believe it? I can hardly understand it.

"But you—you are someone I can't let anyone mess with." He reaches out and runs the back of his hand down my cheek.

This I'm afraid I understand. "You're creeping me out," I say before I can censor myself. "I mean," I say, backpedaling as fast as I can, "you're a little...and I'm...I mean, we..."

Carmine shudders and then gives a slight shake of his head. *It's not like that*, his gesture says, and I let out the breath I am holding.

He tells me I seem to have a penchant for putting myself in danger—okay, what he actually asks is if I have a death wish—and he wags a finger at me. "So why is it you're all the time playing Supergirl?" he asks.

It's a good question. "I don't mean to," I tell him. "I should know better. I'm old enough to know better."

He agrees, which hurts a little.

"It's not like I go looking for trouble," I explain. "It just finds me."

"Maybe you should practice ducking," Carmine says. "I'm getting too old to play the knight in shining armor routine. And like you said, you're too old—"

I tell him that I said I was old *enough*, not *too* old, and he laughs.

"You look very young for your age. Like your mother. In fact, you don't look a day over forty," he tells me, patting my knee, which smarts almost as much as his comment.

"Well, that's good," I tell him, "since I'm not."

His jaw slackens just a little, and he exchanges a look with his driver, who stares at him in the rearview mirror.

"What?" I ask. "You want to see my driver's license?"

Carmine asks how old I am. I tell him that I'm thirty-nine. "For the first time," I add.

He asks if I'm sure I'm not forty-six. I look down at myself, quite the worse for wear, and tell him that I'm sure. I have a brother who is forty-six, and I'd know if we were twins.

"The guy at the bat mitzvah?" he asks. "David? He's forty-six?"

I admit that David looks great. Hey, he lives a couple thousand miles from our mother, so why shouldn't he?

"Son of a gun," Carmine says, and slaps his knee. "Your mother is a pisser, there's no denying it."

There's something we're dancing around here, and I decide that it's time to set it to music.

"By any chance, did you know my mother back in the day?" I ask, holding my breath as I wait for the answer.

"What day would that be?" he asks, avoiding my question.

If I ask, and if he answers, it could change reality as I know it. Do I really want to know? Now?

The problem with me is that I can't stop myself from crossing that line, whether it's police tape or emotional boundaries. So I step up to the edge of the cliff and jump.

"Did you know her, say, forty-seven years ago?" I ask.

Carmine considers the question. I think he is weighing his options. Finally he says that he knew her, briefly, once upon a time. He gets a faraway look in his eyes, and I could swear that they get watery. "It was a long time ago. I lost track of just how long. A long time ago and a coupla worlds apart," he says.

I had to ask. I just had to.

"You're lying," I say, but I know he isn't. I saw the way my mother looked at him. I saw the way my father looked at him, like he knows, like he's always known.

Carmine doesn't say anything. He looks at me with affection, but I can't tell if it's love or pity.

"Boss?" the driver says, and he gestures out the window where Nick is being "helped" into a black Escalade.

"What are you going to do with him?" I ask, and Carmine says he'll babysit him, *if I know what he means.* I make him spell out the fact that he won't hurt him, but that I don't have to worry about Nick hurting Howard.

I tell him that I should call Drew. He snaps his fingers

and his driver passes me back a phone. As I take the phone, I notice his driver only has two fingers and a thumb on his right hand. I don't mean to, but I gasp nonetheless.

Carmine smiles at me and before I can dial, he says, "Yeah, you should call him. And when you do, be sure to tell him how you ignored the police tape, busted into your friend's place and nearly got yourself killed. Don't forget about how you ran away from the cop, how you got a nice little bracelet there you ought to return… Of course, he ain't gonna like it."

He stares at me hard, then acts like he's just come up with a better plan.

"Or, second scenario—I could turn Watts over to the cops, tell 'em I was just a good citizen, out doing my duty, earn a couple brownie points along the way…"

I look at the phone in my hand and figure his plan is better than mine. I ask if instead I can call Bobbie, who's bound to be worried about me, and ask her to pick up my kids from my parents' place and bring them back home.

Carmine offers to get them himself. I think about the way my mother looked at him when they were dancing and decline.

"My mother and father—" I start to say, but he interrupts me.

"She told me," he says, and he looks sad as he picks at a spot on his trousers.

"That she owes him?" I ask.

"That she loves him," he answers.

* * *

"You're sure you'll be all right?" Carmine asks as he drops me at my car behind Madison on Park.

I tell him I will, eventually. I've a lot to sort out and now isn't the time because I want to hurry back to Howard at the hospital. He offers again to drive me there, have someone take me there, whatever I want, but I tell him I just want to stop into the restaurant and see if Madison is there. I figure I'd better tell her about Nick before the police show up on her doorstep.

"You're sure Nick can't get to her?" I ask Carmine. "She's pregnant, you know."

"Nick's not gonna be bothering anyone," Carmine says. He looks at me and smiles. "And no, he ain't gonna be *swimmin' with the fishes.*"

"You aren't really in the mafia, are you?" I ask him.

"Go straight home, Teddi," he tells me. It's the first time he's called me by my name, and I can see it takes him by surprise as much as it does me. "Friends?" he asks.

"The jury's still out," I say.

"Jesus! What's a guy gotta do?" he asks. "Didn't I save your neck half a dozen times already?"

"What's half a dozen times between friends?" I ask as I get out of the car and realize I no longer have my purse, that I must have left it in Mark's truck or in Howard's apartment. That means I don't have a key, either.

"No problem," Carmine says. "Vito here can get you started."

I figure Vito probably started out hot-wiring cars, and

I tell them I'll just run in to the restaurant and be out in a minute. Carmine waves me off and sits back in the limo.

The restaurant is dark, empty. At first I'm startled, but of course, Nick isn't here to do the cooking, so Madison must not have been able to open. It all makes sense. I call out to her, but there is no answer.

"Anyone here?" I shout, figuring that she'd never have left the back door unlocked. "Madison?"

I hear a groan from the office and head for it, my fashion statement "bracelet" clanking as I go. What if Nick was here first, before he went to Howard's, and Madison confronted him and he...

He what? Madison is carrying his child. Not to mention that Nick just doesn't fit my idea of a murderer.

I hear another groan, this one louder and more anguished than the first.

"I'm coming," I call, and I push open the office door, expecting to find Madison on the floor, writhing in pain, losing her baby.

Instead, she is sitting in Nick's chair, a gun in her good hand. Her hair is pulled back severely, like she means business, though several strands have pulled free and hang limply around her face. Her makeup is melting off, dark smudges beneath her eyes making them sink into her face. Her blouse is torn slightly at the shoulder and for the first time I can see signs of her pregnancy, the fullness of her breasts, the slight rounding of her belly as she pushes back the chair.

She stares at me as though she is trying to place me, to fit me into her plan. And then her eyes narrow and her lip curls. Satisfied with some plan only she knows, she gestures me in with a look more frightening than the gun in her hand.

Across from her is the source of the groans—a young waitress in a short skirt, trussed like a turkey. She is tied to the chair and her mouth is gagged with cheesecloth. And she can't be more than a few years older than Dana.

"She accepted delivery of the cake," Madison says, gesturing at the girl with her gun.

I don't understand the significance, and she can see it in my face. She seems content to wait while I puzzle it out. "But the cake wasn't—" I start to say, remembering her saying she had to leave to get it. She needed the excuse to go somewhere....

"You went to Howard's?" I ask.

Madison refuses to help me. She merely shrugs. *Figure it out yourself.*

"You know, in the movies, at this point the bad guy always tells the good guy how he did it," I tell Madison, who smiles at me as she shakes her head slowly back and forth to indicate this is not a movie. I glance at the waitress, whose huge eyes follow my movements as I take first one step, and then another, closer to the desk.

"You always did have a good sense of humor," Madison says, arching her back as though it hurts her. "At least that's what poor Howard used to say."

"Don't you want to brag about how clever you were?" I ask.

She doesn't answer for a moment, and I suppose she is running the scenario through her head. "When they do that, your bad guys, somehow it always buys the good guy time. And then they don't wind up dead, do they?"

"Actually," I say, "that's the best part."

Not surprisingly, she disagrees.

"So the way I work it out," I say, figuring that if she isn't going to buy me some of that time, I'll have to do it myself. The office is hot, and sweat is trickling down between my breasts. It's hard to take in enough air, let alone think. I gulp some and continue. "You went to Howard's to cover up what Nick did, right? I mean, to protect him from being found out. Is that it?"

The little waitress shakes her head vehemently, and Madison gets up and comes around the desk. She holds the gun to the girl's temple. "You want to be tomorrow's special? *Kristine à l'orange?* That way there's no body. No evidence. They'll write you off as just a runaway and no one will be the wiser."

"Okay, stop scaring her," I say bravely. "Jeez, it's hot in here. Aren't you hot, Madison?"

She looks surprised, like she hasn't noticed the heat, or maybe it's that I'm not pooping in my pants. Little does she know how close I am.

"I mean, with the baby and all. You must be boiling." I slip off Mark's giant shirt and fan myself with my hand while I glance around the room like I'm looking for something better to use.

And there, hanging on the coat rack, is the produce jacket I wore when I was putting on my makeup. Only now that I think about it, it wasn't big on me, like Mark's shirt is. I can feel my jaw drop with the realization.

"You were there. That day at The Steak-Out. You were the produce delivery guy." Why didn't I tell Drew about the damn jacket this afternoon? I had the thing on. How could I not have noticed?

"So you did see me," Madison says. She is playing with the girl's hair, stroking it, lifting locks of it and dropping them like she is getting ready to prepare Kristine for the oven. The child strains to pull her head away, and Madison yanks on her hair to let her know who is boss. "And Howard saw our car. Idiot thought it was Nick. Almost went to pieces thinking his precious Nick could kill someone. He imagined himself Nick's great love, and he didn't know how preposterous the idea of Nick as murderer is."

"Are you saying Howard saw you?" I can't believe he would go to jail for Madison. She shrugs, more interested in terrorizing Kristine than in answering me. Her look says maybe Howard did, and then again, maybe he didn't.

Like me, he probably didn't even know he saw her. So she was there, and she killed Joe Greco.

"Did you really ever have an affair with him?" I ask and she looks at me like I have to be kidding. "I never could picture the two of you in bed together," I admit.

"I couldn't picture Howard with you, either," she says, like he'd be stooping to some lower level.

"I'll let that pass," I tell her, since she's got the gun. "So your finger—you didn't, by any chance, cut it on purpose because you thought there might be fingerprints if the gun was found, did you?"

Madison asks why she would do that when Howard was the shooter. I can see she's losing patience with me, and I'm thinking, hoping, praying, that Vito and Carmine are, too, and that any minute now they'll burst in looking for me. "Howard, the bane of my existence, shot Joe Greco because he was bleeding all of us dry. He did it to protect the restaurant from going under, I guess. And then he couldn't live with it and he killed himself."

"Yeah, only he's not dead," I tell her, and I can see she's surprised. She tells me I'm lying. I point to the phone. "Call the hospital. They'll tell you he's in a coma."

She says that's as good as dead, and she starts rolling up her sleeves like she's getting ready to do us in and get it over with.

"One thing I need to know. How'd you get him to eat the mushrooms?" I ask, stalling for time, figuring that any minute Carmine will send Vito in for me.

She can't resist telling me. "Easy. I told him Nick prepared them special and wanted him to test out whether they were good enough to serve at your precious party." I pick up a folder and fan us both with it. Maybe if I keep her cool… "Then, when he was writhing on the floor, I told him they were poisoned, that Nick knew it and wanted him dead."

"Only he didn't," I say, and now I'm getting frantic because she's tying on an apron, pinning up her hair like she really is going to make Kristine tomorrow's special. "Or did he?"

"Nick doesn't know what he wants. I have to tell him." She takes a minute to sit on the edge of the desk, stretches her head back and rolls it in a small circle.

"Tired?" I ask. "I remember being pregnant. I could fall asleep anywhere, anytime."

Madison says she can't afford to be tired. She has a lot of cooking to do. *"Kristine en croute, Teddi à la king."*

"You're going to claim I'm a runaway, too?" I ask dubiously. "They might buy it for Kristine, a kid, but me? The mother of three? Friends with a detective? You think they'll just write me off, as well?"

I can see the wheels turning in Madison's brain and I've got to derail them, and I've got to do it now or Kristine, who is crying silently, isn't going to ever get to grow up.

"You're going to have to do better than that," I say, wondering where the hell Vito is and how much longer I can stall.

Finally, like a message from heaven, we hear knocking. "Door locked automatically when you shut it," Madison tells me when I breath a sigh of relief. "So I'm afraid that no one is going to be able to come rescue you."

"It won't stop them for long," I say. "Not long enough to dispose of two bodies, anyway."

Madison agrees. She orders me to untie Kristine's legs. "We're all going to take a little walk to the back door," Madison says. "And you're going to tell whoever it is to go away."

"They aren't going to just go away," I tell Madison. "They're the mafia. They don't just fold their tents and give up."

"They'd better," she says with stony resolve. "Or they'll find the two of you dead."

Kristine wobbles, and I help her keep her footing. My handcuffs get caught on her bindings and while I disentangle them, I whisper to her that everything will be okay. Behind us, Madison laughs.

"Tell them to go away," she orders me when we get near the back door. "And make it good, or Kristine is dead. And I know you wouldn't want that on your conscience."

I stand near the door and shout out that I'm going to stay awhile to comfort Madison and they can just leave.

"The boss won't like that," Vito says.

"Your boss isn't the boss of me," I say, sounding like one of my kids.

"You'd better open the door," Vito says. Madison puts the gun against Kristine's head and cocks the trigger.

"It's got some sort of automatic lock," I say as fast as I can. "And Madison isn't feeling well, so I'm just going to stay in her office with her while you guys go get my children and bring them home. If they don't have their key, try the *front windows*. I might have forgotten to lock them."

Vito repeats that Carmine isn't going to like it, and I say he should tell Carmine that *breaks* my heart.

And then Madison shoves me back toward the office while I pray that Carmine decodes my message.

"Well, have you figured out how to get rid of me?" I ask Madison when we're back in her office. "Another suicide attempt would seem too coincidental. I know! You could claim that Kristine and I were lovers and we ran away together... No, I don't think Drew would buy that, though he might like fantasizing about it.

"Isn't it funny how men like to fantasize about two women together, but women don't like to imagine—"

Madison tells me to shut up.

"Must have made you crazy," I say. "Thinking when you were with Nick that he'd rather be with Howard. I mean, another woman—"

Madison raises the gun to strike me with it, but I put up my hands to protect myself.

"Wait. Bruises on the body. Better figure out how I died, first. Of course, Carmine D'Guisseppe knows I'm here, so this is really going to be tricky..."

I can see the panic rising in Madison's eyes, which doesn't compare to the panic I hope I'm hiding. I wish I knew where I was going with this bid to make her mad. All I know is that I'm desperate, and a rattled Madison is better than a clear-thinking one.

"Okay, I've got it," I say. "Kristine came in to rob us, since she'd need money to run away, right? So the safe is open, I'm dead by Kristine's hand, you've got a knock on the head—not too bad, because we don't want to injure the baby—and she's gone.

"Of course, there isn't a lot of time. You'd better open the safe first."

Madison considers for a second, tries to see the flaw in the plan, and then turns to open the safe. Which gives me just enough time to grab the adding machine and smash it down on her head. I don't wait to see if it's knocked her out. I scramble to tackle her, putting all my weight behind it and kicking the gun away as I do.

Kristine is doing her best to scream through her gag, and while I don't even hear the glass breaking out front, I couldn't be happier to see Drew and two uniformed policemen, guns drawn, in the doorway. Vito and Carmine, out of breath and clearly shaken, are right behind them.

I look up at Drew from my seat straddling Madison. "What the hell took you so long?"

CHAPTER 19

Design Tip of the Day
"One of the nicest features any home can have is a
quiet area, an oasis of calm. Someplace where you
can recover from the events of the day. These
should preferably be underfurnished, carpeted,
monotoned and feature a fountain, soft music and
dim lights."

—TipsFromTeddi.com

I didn't believe your mother when she called," Drew
says as he drives me to the hospital to see Howard.

While he fiddles with the heat, I ask just what my
mother said.

"That you'd never leave the kids with her for dinner
without instructions. You cold?" he asks.

I nod. Actually, I'm shivering, but I don't know if it's
the temperature or what I've just been through. "She
called the police because she didn't know what to feed my
kids?"

He looks at me with pity and explains that she didn't
call *the police*, she called *him*, looking for me. Then she

called back half an hour later claiming that Mark said I was going to Howard's place. "So I ran over there and was handed Nick Watts on a platter," he says, looking at me like he'd like to know just how I managed to make that happen.

I wait for him to continue.

He tells me how he had to take Nick in and book him, and that my mother called twice after that to say that I still hadn't shown up, it was already dark, and wasn't he worried?

"Were you?" I ask, turning up the heat in the car.

"Well, I gathered that you were with Carmine D'Guisseppe—"

He continues talking for a while until I can't help laughing.

"What?" he asks.

I can't hide my amusement and don't even try. "Having anything to do with my mother turns even you into a babbler, doesn't it?" He *humphs*, throws the car into Park, pulls a jacket from the backseat for me and wraps it over my shoulders as he ushers me into the hospital.

"You," my mother shouts at Drew as we enter Howard's room to find her and my father there, along with a nurse seeing to Howard. "I don't know why I should even be talking to you."

"To punish him," my father says under his breath, but my mother just shoots him a dirty look of dismissal.

"Thanks for sending him, Mom," I say, keeping to myself the fact that I really didn't need him to come rescuing me. I ask the nurse how Howard is doing and she nods as though maybe, just maybe, he'll pull through.

"This is your best chance, *Police Boy*," my mother tells Drew. "We sent the carpenter home and when the competition there wakes up, it'll be too late."

I ask if there's been any change, any reason my mother has said *when* and not *if*, but my father shakes his head. "He'll be all right, though," he tells me. I think he'd like to say that he's a Bayer, but he knows he'll never be related.

"So you found her all right," my father says to Drew, unaware that my life was in danger. "I was beginning to get worried, what with it being so late."

"Yeah, I found her," Drew says, pulling out his keys and grabbing my wrist to take off my cuffs. My mother stares at my wrist, Drew enjoying the shock. "Gave us the slip, but we've got her back."

"Did you arrange—" I start to ask, but Drew cuts me off.

"Rosen's watch was broken when he went into seizures," Drew says. I notice he has only unlocked one of the cuffs. "I went back to his place to compare the time the e-mail was sent with the time on his watch."

"And?" my father asks, thought the rest of us have put it all together.

"And I found Teddi's handbag. Now, knowing a woman and her handbag are rarely parted, I got to worrying…"

"What about the six times I called you?" my mother asks. "That didn't set off bells and whistles?"

I can see Drew looking around the room while he's holding the open cuff. "You wouldn't dare," I say.

He looks down at Howard, paler every minute, and says something like *not here, not now,* and he winks at me.

Before the glow can reach my toes, it's ruined by my ex-husband, Mario Gallo, who comes into the room all bluster and show.

"I thought I'd find you here," he says, but when Drew asks him why the hell he would, he admits that Dana told him where I was. "I need to talk to you. Privately," he adds.

"She's not giving you a cent," my father says as I accompany Rio out of the room and wish that Drew had handcuffed me somewhere so that I wouldn't have to.

"I heard you and Carmine D'Guisseppe are like having an affair or something," Rio says. One look at my face and he adds that he knows that's not true. That it's stupid, idiotic. "Still…"

"What do you want?" I ask him, my patience wearing thin. I am tired, cold, worried about Howard, confused about Carmine and about Drew.

Rio does that quick shrug of his shoulder that once upon a time I found sexy and now see as just a tick. Over his shoulder Carmine D'Guisseppe and two of his associates are coming down the hall.

"You want to repeat that?" I ask, turning Rio around so he can see Carmine. Rio crosses himself quickly. He's a very religious man. He believes most strongly in the Eleventh Commandment: Thou Shalt Not Get Caught.

The blood drains from Rio's face as Carmine kisses me lightly on the cheek.

"This is my ex-husband," I tell Carmine. "He needs an honest job so that he can support his new family. He needs not to be involved in anything that could send the father of my children to prison, and he's watched carefully by your friend and mine, Detective Scoones.

"Can you help him?"

Carmine asks if Rio can do anything. I ask if screwing up my life counts. Carmine says he'll take care of it, and hands Rio a card. "Tomorrow morning, you report there." He lifts Rio's chin with his finger and then feigns a punch to his nose. "You keep your nose clean and you'll be okay."

Rio doesn't say a word. I prompt him to tell Carmine he's grateful.

"Is he, you know, brain-damaged?" Carmine asks.

I tell Carmine that Rio is afraid of him.

"Good," Carmine says.

And then, just when it feels like maybe my life will turn out okay, I hear my mother gasp, the nurse kick everyone out, and a yell for *Code Blue*.

CHAPTER 20

Design Tip of the Day
"Nothing sets a mood like flowers. They mark the big events in our lives—weddings, births, anniversaries, and yes, even funerals. Their ephemeral quality reminds us today is important and demands that we take note."

—TipsFromTeddi.com

A week later Howard is nearly recovered and we are all gathered in his hospital room, annoying the nurses by all but throwing a party. Howard, an ascot around his neck, is sitting up in his bed directing everyone about. Helene has brought his iPod with his Bose docking station and the Bill Evans Trio is serenading us with wonderful jazz.

At least, those people who appreciate jazz over country music think so. Those of us with tin ears, well...

Helene pulls me aside, telling me that several of her customers are postponing their orders and that she has a sneaking suspicion that Carmine is somehow behind their sudden desire to put off their purchases. Do I know what that is about?

"How would I know?" I ask. Looks like, *fortuitously*, I'm going to be free to decorate Carmine D'Guisseppe's place after all.

Howard wants to be brought up to date on how I figured out that Madison was actually the killer, and I go over the whole business again, making sure that it's clear that I absolutely didn't need to be rescued and that if I'd had to wait for the police or "other help," I'd have been victim number three.

"Hey," Carmine says with misplaced pride. "The woman just doesn't need as much protecting as I thought." I think he still thinks we've pulled a fast one on him, and that I'm really forty-six and possibly his.

"Yeah, well, she still needs protection from herself and her *act-first-and-think-second* instincts," Drew says.

I agree with him, shooting him a knowing look that cuts him to the quick, since what I mean—and he knows it—is that I should have thought before I slept with him.

He takes out a pair of handcuffs and fiddles with them. I suppose he thinks no one else in the room gets his message, but Bobbie and my father both blush, my mother guffaws, and Carmine tells him to put the damn things away.

Everyone seems happy except poor Howard, who doesn't brighten until Nick comes into the room bearing a potted hydrangea plant. He's wearing a dapper little outfit, plaid pants and a bright pink shirt, but he is washed out and his hair is grayer than I remember. Maybe it's just that he doesn't have his chef's hat on.

"I'm sorry," I start to say, "about Howard's condo and thinking—"

Nick waves my apology away. "If I'd found you there, I'd probably have thought the same thing."

"It's over, then?" Howard asks him, gesturing for Nick to put the plant on the dresser.

Nick nods, while both Drew and I say that we told him it was, didn't we?

"I spoke to the D.A.," Nick says, and he plays with the leaves on the hydrangea, picks off a few dead blossoms and turns the plant this way and that. Finally he looks expectantly at Howard. "She says I should get sole custody of the baby."

"That's good," Howard says, and suddenly he's brushing nonexistent specks off his pristine blanket.

"Well, that kid's gonna need two parents," Bobbie says, and thrums her acrylic nails against the bed rail.

No one says anything.

Finally, because for heaven's sake, we all know, don't we? I say, "You know you two can count on me. You guys are going to need a lot of help raising that child, and God knows I've got plenty of experience."

Howard looks lovingly at me for the first time ever. I take his hand in mine and he squeezes hard.

"Count me in," Bobbie adds. And now everyone is beaming from ear to ear. "In case it's twins."

"And me," says my mother. "Of course, that's strictly for advice. I don't do diapers."

Everyone is looking at Drew, who seems to find his loafers fascinating. Finally, looking like "he don't know nothin' about birthin' babies," he agrees that somebody's going to have to teach the kid how to fight.

"I could—" Carmine starts to say, and I shake my head just a little, just privately, between him and me. "But I got places to go," he says.

My father takes my mother's hand and she smiles up into his face. "My June," he says softly, running one hand down her cheek lovingly.

"Your entire calendar," my mother corrects, and my father's eyes well up with tears.

"My entire life," he says.

David watches them, and has to be nudged by Issy and reminded that they have a plane to catch. David is aware of what might be, but he and my father have elected not to be tested, both satisfied finally to be father and son.

"Where are you planning to go?" Helene asks Carmine. She looks like she'd like to accompany him, but it's clear he hasn't eyes for anyone but the Queen of Ecru.

"Someplace warm," he says. "With a beach, and clear water...."

My father swallows hard. It has taken years for David to come back to the fold, and to lose him now might be more than my father can bear. He stares at Carmine, helpless to stop him from pursuing David to the ends of the earth, or at least the Bahamas.

But Carmine stretches, and bends the blinds to look out the window. "I'm thinking about moving to Hawaii." He turns and looks at my father. "Whaddya think?"

"I like it," my father says as the nurse comes in, unplugs the music and tells us all it's time to go home.

Design Tip of the Day
"Better than five-hundred-count sheets, better than down duvets, there's nothing that beats a warm body in the bed beside you."

—TipsFromTeddi.com

"You didn't really post that, did you?" Drew asks me as he looks over my naked shoulder at the laptop on my bed.

I turn so that I can feel his skin against mine and tell him, "Damn right I did."

"You've been pretty gutsy since Howard recovered," he says.

I tell him that business is good, my parents are acting like newlyweds, David and Issy are expecting another baby, and that my life is good. I leave out his part in it, though I have to admit that without nights like last night I wouldn't be stretching and reveling in the moment, now would I?

"Teddi, I—" he starts, but is interrupted by his cell phone vibrating across my nightstand and crashing to the floor. I know better than to tell him not to take the call, but I don't make it easy. He has to scramble over me to reach down for it, and I enjoy every minute of his struggle.

"Scoones," he says into the phone. "Yeah, I'm here, and I suggest it's the last time you ask that, Nelson," he says, covering my nakedness like Hal can see through the phone.

Or like the party is over.

"When?" he asks. "With a *what?* Isn't that what they use in the meat district? What the hell…?"

He's searching for his clothes while he talks, trying to keep the phone between his ear and his shoulder while he dresses. I get up, too, and start slipping into clothes. He shakes his head at me.

"You're not coming," he mouths.

I ignore him, slipping into my jeans and pulling a T-shirt over my head.

He is getting more details. "She was wearing what? That's it? Nothing else?"

I slip on my loafers. He mouths "no" at me while writing down the address.

"Okay," he tells his partner. "I'm on the way. Alone," he adds for my benefit.

He's loading his pockets with his wallet, his badge.

"I'd just wait in the car," I tell him. "You know I'm good at this detecting business, and I—"

He grabs me, knocks me to the bed and kisses me hard, a hands-over-head, toe-curling, knee-sagging, consciousness-blowing kiss.

"Sorry, honey," he says as he gets up. "I'll be back, I promise."

I go to get up and find one wrist handcuffed to the bedpost.

"Hey!" I shout. "Drew! It's not funny."

"Key's on the kitchen counter," he yells back from down the hall.

But he isn't really going to just leave me here, half-dressed, attached to my bed, right?

The front door slams and I hear him start his car.

I should be furious. I should be embarrassed. I should not be thinking *meat district? Not wearing anything else…*

But, of course, I am…while I'm reaching for that bobbie pin on my nightstand so that I can get myself out of this mess. And then see if, from the impression on the note pad, I can find out where it is I need to go….

* * * * *

Every life has more than one chapter and
NEXT offers another great lineup
of titles in the coming months.
For a sneak preview of
BLINK OF AN EYE
by Rexanne Becnel, coming to NEXT in February,
please turn the page.

What should I do? I gripped the driver's side headrest.

Go drown yourself. That's the plan, isn't it? So go do it. In three feet of water?

Except that those three feet looked like they would soon be four. Or more. "Just wait," I muttered. "Just wait a little longer."

Within fifteen minutes the water was over the seat cushion and rising, almost as deep inside the car as outside. I shivered as my capris soaked up the chilly water. Was I going to drown in a Toyota with the doors locked and the windows up? Or would I get out of the car and head toward the lake and deeper water? Assuming I didn't drown before I got there.

That's when a dog slammed into my front windshield. Somehow it righted itself, scrambling around for footing on the wet hood. Then it stood there, spraddle-legged and terrified, staring me straight in the face.

I heard one yelp—or maybe I saw it. Either way, when the next wave sent the animal sprawling, sliding off my car, I didn't stop to think. I shoved the door open, lunged through the opening and into the water, and somehow caught the animal by the tail.

I managed to get ahold of the dog's collar just in time. The next thing I knew, we were both underwater.

It wasn't rainwater, but salty, brackish water. Don't ask me why I noticed that. But as I came up sputtering, with Fido still in my grasp, I knew that the worst had happened to New Orleans. Hurricane Katrina had caused one of the levees to break.

Between the tearing winds, the punishing waves and the debris missiles from the hurricane that followed, I could easily have just let go. Given in. Given up.

But I couldn't.

It was because of the dog.

He was a medium-size mutt, black and white, totally nondescript like a million others. Mainly, though, he was petrified with fear. He'd decided I was his salvation and kept trying to climb into my arms because the water was too deep for him to stand in.

Unfortunately, between the wind and the waves, it was too tough for *me* to stand in. Tree branches, lawn furniture, street signs, garbage—it was like being inside a giant washing machine set on spin.

One thing I knew: avoid the cars. Because if one of them pinned me to a tree, I was a goner.

I know, I know. Five minutes ago I'd wanted to be a goner. And I still did. But I needed to save this dog first.

I could barely keep my eyes open; that's how harshly the winds whipped around me. Like a drowning blind woman, I flailed around looking for something solid to cling to. Then I slammed into a fence. And the gate led to a house. Somehow I dragged myself up the steps. The minute Fido's feet hit something solid, he was out of my arms. Right behind him, I crawled up the long flight of steps, out of the water and onto a porch. There I curled into a ball in a corner against the house. Fido, wet and stinky, wormed his way into my arms and that's how the two of use spent the next few hours. He shivered and whimpered uncontrollably. I shivered and alternatively cried and cursed.

You'd think someone who wanted to be dead wouldn't be afraid of anything. That she would stand up to the storm, beating her chest and screaming, "Come and get me, Katrina! Come and get me!"

But it was terrifying. It seemed like hours went by with no change.

Fido finally stopped shivering, but he kept his anxious brown eyes on me, as if I might disappear if he looked away. Who did he belong to? And why on earth had they left him behind?

He wore a collar with a tag that identified him as Lucky.

Lucky. Yeah, right! Lucky to be huddled on somebody's porch with a crazy woman while the whole damned city returned to the sea.

She had nothing to lose…

With a hurricane bearing down on New Orleans, the failed nurse-turned-waitress viewed it as an opportunity—to escape her tattered life. It was time to rebuild—her life, her city— on a foundation of hope.

Blink of an Eye

USA TODAY bestselling author
Rexanne Becnel

HARLEQUIN
Next

Available February 2007
TheNextNovel.com

HN77

It's never too late to take that flying leap

Two friends set off for the Tuscan countryside to heal wounds of the past. Through the strength of their friendship, both women discover they can face the future and embrace its limitless possibilities....

Late Bloomers

by

Peggy Webb

This February...

Catch NASCAR Superstar **Carl Edwards** *in*

SPEED DATING!

Kendall assesses risk for a living—
so she's the last person you'd
expect to see on the arm of a
race-car driver who thrives on the
unpredictable. But when a bizarre
turn of events—and NASCAR
hotshot Dylan Hargreave—inspire
her to trade in her ever-so-structured
existence for "life in the fast lane"
she starts to feel she might be
on to something!

Collect all 4 debut novels in the Harlequin NASCAR series.

SPEED DATING
by *USA TODAY* bestselling author
Nancy Warren

THUNDERSTRUCK
by Roxanne St. Claire

HEARTS UNDER CAUTION
by Gina Wilkins

DANGER ZONE
by Debra Webb

On sale
February
2007

NASCARFEB

HARLEQUIN *Romance*

What a month!

In February watch for

Rancher and Protector

Part of the Western Weddings miniseries

BY JUDY CHRISTENBERRY

The Boss's Pregnancy Proposal

BY RAYE MORGAN

Also in February, expect
MORE of what you love
as the Harlequin Romance line
increases to six titles per month.

REQUEST YOUR FREE BOOKS!

2 FREE NOVELS PLUS 2 FREE GIFTS!

There's the life you planned. And there's what comes next.

NEXT07